One Mad Year

An Aussie Bloke's Tale

Mike Lathouras

NATIONAL
LIBRARY
OF AUSTRALIA

A catalogue record for this
book is available from the
National Library of Australia

Publisher:
Inspiring Publishers
P.O. Box 159, Calwell, ACT Australia 2905
Email: inspiringpublisher.com
http://www.inspiringpublishers.com

National Library of Australia Cataloguing-in-Publication entry

Author: Mike Lathouras

Title: **One Mad Year**

ISBN: 978-1-923087-81-1 (Print)
ISBN: 978-1-923087-80-4 (ePub2)
ISBN: 978-1-923087-79-8 (PDF eBook)

Due Punithment

It was one of those weeks that took a lot of effort to get through. Steve Smith was glad it was over. Kicking off the working year seemed tougher than usual. His two-week Christmas vacation had done zilch to rejuvenate him, and his "honey-do" list at home remained as formidable as ever. In this very moment, though, he felt a regal sense of ownership over his immediate surroundings. His spanking new five-burner barbecue was ablaze on his back veranda, heralding a grand cook-up for his girls. Smith took a hearty swig of his beer—the cold, bitter beverage was the perfect final note to this symphony of the senses. His gaze momentarily strayed to the Allen's place next door.

"Ah, bloody hell, not again," he murmured to himself, his eyes lingering on the couple canoodling beside their pool. He rescued a rogue sausage teetering at the edge of the barbecue and cast another glance their way, just in time to see Stacey's towel plummet, exposing her back down to her knees. This time, he fumbled with his volume. "Holy shit!" He dove behind the barbecue lid, praying they hadn't overheard his outburst.

"Mum! Dad's thwearing again!"

His four year old daughter was already sprinting through the kitchen, sounding the alarm as though the house was ablaze. "Dammit! Where did she spring from?" He tried to head her off while stealing another look next door, but Stacey had covered herself and they were on their way inside.

"I did not!" His defence was as hopeful as a cricket team facing a daunting score with just one wicket left.

Smith pivoted back, slammed the barbecue lid down, then dashed through the kitchen to start the damage control. He arrived just in time to hear his youngest girl presenting her case as if she were a seasoned lawyer in a courtroom drama. He opened his mouth to mount his defence. It was a moot point; the judge, jury, and executioner had already assembled.

"Did he now?" Rebecca Smith, fresh from the shower, stood with her hands on her hips. Her long brown hair was still wet; a testament to her hurried response to the latest home-front crisis. Its dampness had seeped into her top, outlining her breasts—a detail Smith noted with a raised eyebrow, only to be briskly dismissed by their owner. "And what did we agree would happen to Daddy if he swore?"

"I never agreed to that." He swiped some steak fat off the back of his hand with a tea towel, looking up in time to see his wife's head shake in silent rebuke.

With a face twisted into a melodramatic scowl, Sally turned slowly from her mother until she was pointing right at him. It was like a scene lifted from a horror flick. With a gap-toothed grin spreading across her face, she exclaimed with malicious delight, "I pick your punithmint!"

"I said I never agreed to that."

"You did, but that's not the point." Bec pointed an admonishing finger at her accusatory daughter, struggling to suppress a grin. "Sally heard you. Right, Sally?"

Sally drew a slow, deep breath to prolong the drama when her six-year-old sister's voice chimed in from the lounge room. "I heard Dad, too. He said shit!"

Both parents reacted instinctively from their respective corners.

"You stay out of it!"

"Julie!"

As Sally's spotlight moment in the "prosecution" drama was abruptly hijacked, she darted toward her dad, delivering an unexpectedly fierce blow to his groin. Her clear lack of intent to debilitate was a far cry from the power and precision of her strike. Caught off guard, Smith keeled over with a groan, narrowly avoiding a repeat performance of his swearing crime. A peal of laughter from his wife startled the children into looking her way.

Crumpling to his knees with a guttural groan, Smith sprawled out on the kitchen floor.

Bec managed to chide Sally half-heartedly for her sudden assault, her reprimand garbled by stifled laughter. Seizing the moment of unaccustomed access to her usually towering dad, Sally started to kick his backside with gusto, perhaps realising her sentencing hearing was rapidly becoming moot and oblivious to the pain she had inflicted. Bec's slippered feet momentarily appeared within his line of sight before strutting off, replaced by Julie's bare feet, which soon scampered away after the others. Even the dog, formerly lying in strategic wait beside the barbecue for a fallen sausage, nonchalantly sauntered past, casting Smith a brief, indifferent glance before tailing the girls into the lounge room.

"Bloody traitor!" Smith grumbled, immediately realising he'd transgressed again, albeit this time out of earshot. He let out a lengthy sigh, savouring the coolness of the kitchen floor for a few more seconds as he waited for the throbbing in his groin to subside.

Bec, leaning into the hallway, tossed him a token shot of sympathy. "Get up before you burn dinner. And watch your mouth next time!"

He hauled himself onto his knees, his nether regions still smarting. Sally really did a number on him. Hobbling to the barbecue, he noted with dismay that their dinner was now sending up wisps of smoke.

His gaze drifted next door, curiosity piqued about Jim Allen's current engagement with Stacey after their poolside cuddle. "I bet he isn't sprawled on the kitchen floor nursing his crown jewels," he muttered to himself.

A Relaxing Weekend

Saturday morning started with a 7 a.m. raid by the girls on their parents in bed. They had woken early and played cooperatively for at least an hour until things broke down and ownership of this Barbie or that toy horse was asserted. A run for Mum to take sides was then on. Sally jumped up onto the bed, then onto her dad's back and Julie went for her mum, who was typically more concerned with "who-started-what." Smith turned over with a groan to protect his previously pulverised gonads and pulled the pillow over his head, which seemed to invite Sally to bounce her backside on it.

"Bugger off…!" his protest into the mattress was muffled and half-hearted.

Sally's pillow-assisted bum thumping escalated in intensity, causing Julie to regret her less action-packed approach. She switched tactics and lunged for his neck, causing him to jerk his head aside to protect his nose from potential damage. Defending himself, he fashioned his hand into a claw, snapping it near their heads. The girls shrieked with delight and feigned outrage at the playful threat. They adored "the craw" game, much to Bec's chagrin, who always complained it was invoked too close to bedtime. Seizing the initiative, Julie clutched his hand and pulled it towards her chest with all her might, over-extending his shoulder. In a panicked reflex, Smith twisted his body to follow his contorted arm, sparking pandemonium.

Sally was the first to topple, landing face-first on the carpet beside the bed. In a frantic attempt to brace her fall, she snagged a handful of Julie's hair, promptly dragging her sister along for the chaotic tumble. Julie arched gracefully over the bed's edge before landing atop Sally. A pained wail from Sally was followed by a brief, ominous silence before the rest of her cry echoed around the room. If they were still in their "first child" parenting phase, both Bec and Smith would have sprung from the bed to offer help and comfort.

Bec sighed, lifting her head slightly and peering beneath her eye cover to survey the bed's sudden vacancy. Within a heartbeat, she mentally calculated the trajectory, force, and, judging by Sally's sobbing frequency and volume, potential injury. Resigned, she slumped her head back onto the pillow, fumbling with her eye cover. "Your turn, Dr. Craw."

Thirty noisy minutes later, Smith sat in the kitchen with a still-whimpering Sally on his lap, trying to feed himself some muesli. A theatrically apt parental triage had ascertained there were no real injuries. He forwent a much-needed coffee, knowing a hot liquid spill on her tender head would only set his youngest off again. Julie, meanwhile, was spooning cereal into her mouth while engaging a topless Barbie doll standing in her bowl. Watching the doll wade through the mushy cereal, he noticed it missing a shoe. He resisted the urge to inquire about its whereabouts, mindful that dividing his attention might reignite a squabble, especially with Sally's rival. The shoe would inevitably reappear in her poo, anyway.

"How's the patient?" Bec appeared in the kitchen doorway, rubbing her face.

"She's fine, aren't you, sweetie?" Smith gave her head a gentle rub and a light kiss. Bec regarded the Barbie sloshing through the cereal with mild interest. "What's on the agenda for you today?"

He was about to launch into a well-rehearsed speech, honed from a dozen similar weekend morning interrogations, detailing his jam-packed schedule and consequent inability to tackle his "honey-do" list. However, he didn't even get to start.

"The fence on the Allens' side needs fixing...remember?"

"Nope. I'm not doing that."

"Why not?" Bec straightened, adopting a semi-conscious stance of authority.

"He busted it, not me!"

"Oh, grow up. It's our fence. I'm so over your whingeing about Jim."

"I wasn't whingeing. I just..."

A dismissive wave of her arm was Bec's parting gesture as she shuffled back up the stairs to their bedroom. "Just get it done, will you please? We don't need the dogs fighting."

"Fighting! Hah! That dog of ours couldn't fight her own shadow and win." Realising that made no sense, he looked over at Julie who was constructing a disproving face, which signalled she knew what was coming. Smith lowered his voice.

"Anyway...it's..."

"Don't say it, Dad."

"It's the ..."

"Dad! Don't say it. I'll tell Mum." Julie lowered her brow.

"The ugliest dog God ever invented." He felt justified in propagating the oft-used insult given the lack of support he got from the dog yesterday while recovering on the kitchen floor. The three girls fell in love with it at the animal shelter or the foster home for dogs, or whatever it was called. They were supposed to bring home a dog. A normal dog. Not this snorting, press-faced, googly-eyed, fat little pug that walked around with its arse showing like a cat and with its twisted tail glued to its back. All his protests and arguments were in vain. They loved Smokey, so named because it screwed its face as though smoke was perpetually in its eyes. Well, that's the thought behind the name as far as he guessed.

Julie slammed her Barbie into her cereal in dramatic deference for her beloved pup. Cereal and milk slop went everywhere. She looked up at Smith in cautious defiance. Then, huffing loudly, she slid down from her kitchen chair and stomped off down the corridor to seek out her Mum, to restart the process of accusation, trial, and conviction.

Sally sat quietly, satisfied that she was getting so much attention from her dad.

For Goodness Sake, Just Fix It...

Arrayed across the sun-kissed Brisbane backyard, Smith's tools lay scattered on the lush grass. Taking a break, he surveyed his home. They'd made countless improvements to the house since they'd bought it shortly after getting hitched. Smith, a successful Brisbane-born salesperson, had met his wife Bec, a nursing graduate from Toowoomba, at a bush dance. Brisbane had seemed the ideal choice for the couple—city near the sea, close to the bush, and the perfect setting to raise their future children. Both Steve and Bec Smith were twenty-three when they tied the knot, working diligently to save up for their house deposit.

Smith's gaze wandered to the Allens' house. In their street of 1950s weatherboard homes with clay-tiled roofs, the Allens' two-year-old, blocky, white house stood out like a spin dryer in an old bookshop. The property they'd initially bought was perfectly serviceable, but they'd decided to flatten the house and build this towering monstrosity—a peculiar choice, Smith thought, for their otherwise modest neighbourhood. With its ludicrous blue roof, it looked more like an expensive beachfront property, complete with a painstakingly excavated wine cellar. The relentless noise and vibration of jackhammering had, for weeks, invaded Smith's peace, causing him constant irritation. Bec and Stacey had quickly become friends though, so every grumble from Smith was met with Bec's sharp reproach. It reached a point where a simple raise of her hand and a turn of her head translated to "Enough, please!" It's not forever, and I'm tired of your incessant moaning."

Stacey, the lone child of sheep farmers from Goondiwindi, had boarded at a private high school in Toowoomba. Her parents owned vast, sheep-fattening estates, but their lives were cut tragically short one night when a big kangaroo leapt out from a wild turnip patch on the roadside, deflecting their car into the only tree in the vicinity. Not long after their death, she met Jim Allen. After liquidating her parents' properties, he'd married into a considerable fortune. "Convenient timing, that," Smith muttered under his breath.

Then, there was the issue of the fence. Once the house was complete, Allen proposed replacing the old wooden paling fence with a white block one, offering to foot the bill himself. A block fence would be a better match for his house, he claimed. But Smith saw no need for a new fence, sparking a feud that ultimately involved the city council. He was certain the wives were conspiring behind his back to get the new fence approved, but he stood his ground. Eventually, Allen gave in, opting to plant shrubs along the fence to conceal it. However, his dog would often muscle its way through the shrubs, stirring up a ruckus whenever Smokey, the Smiths' pug, would saunter by the gaps between the palings. Smokey knew exactly how to rile up the Allen's kelpie and took great pleasure in doing so. On his way to the backyard shed, Smith couldn't help a half-smile at the thought of his dog's shenanigans, although he was puzzled as to why the Allens' dog didn't just jump over the fence. Bec was always on alert for any potential canine skirmishes. He remembered their most recent exchange on the topic.

"I don't want Smokey getting mauled by their cattle dog."

"Why would you call it a cattle dog? It's not a cattle dog. Allen wouldn't know a cattle dog if it bit him in the arse!"

"It came off Stacey's farm."

"It did not. He bought it as a present for her just before they bought that house."

"You sure?"

"Dead sure. That dog is just a conversation starter so he can talk about his 'bush background'."

Bec looked at him with that "you're hopeless" look. "You really need to stop this behaviour."

"What behaviour?" And that was that.

Returning from the shed with a crowbar, Smith heard a burst of laughter from next door. He had to admit that Stacey was a striking woman — clever, good-looking, and fit. He thought it was a real shame she wasn't a mum. They had tried to have children but without success, as Bec had relayed to him one day. He had suspected as much; money and careers were not hurdles for them.

He glanced down at the loose fence palings, dislodged by the relentless assaults of the kelpie on his pug, Smokey. Drawing a deep breath, he scanned his surroundings, feeling the day's heat colluding with the Brisbane humidity to make him increasingly uncomfortable. As he pulled off his shirt, the dog next door charged the fence with a bark. Smith stumbled backwards, tripped over his toolbox, and sprawled onto the grass, arms flung wide, face hidden, like a stuntman taking a fall in an action flick.

Another shriek of laughter — presumably from Bec on the patio — echoed through the yard, followed by a feigned inquiry, "Are you okay?" The dog was still furiously barking.

Feeling somewhat foolish, he grunted, "Yes."

Lying there for a moment, the short grass prickling his back, he heard the familiar sounds of Smokey's snorting and sniffing through his shirt near his ear. "Piss off, Smokey." He tugged his shirt down from his face just as the kelpie hurled itself at the fence again, barking madly. This time, the paling gave way and the assailant's head made it through the gap, snarling.

Smith scuttled backwards in surprise, moving awkwardly on his elbows and heels until he realised that the kelpie's shoulders were stuck. Smokey, the gutless pug, who had initially bolted for the house in terror, executed a masterful about-turn when she realised the kelpie couldn't get through the fence. With her fortune reversed, she charged the jammed dog, delivering a snorting, vicious bite to its ear and face before darting off, yelping as though she was the one who'd been attacked.

"You cheeky little bugger." Smith couldn't help but marvel at their dog's dramatics and cunning. Smokey continued her sprint, launched herself up the back stairs, and landed in Bec's lap. "Incredible."

The kelpie managed to withdraw his head with a whimper, retreating through the hedge.

"What the bloody hell's going on?" Jim Allen, just visible through the hedge, knelt next to his dog. Catching sight of Bec on the steps, he halted mid-expletive. "What's the deal, Bec?" he called out, unaware of Smith's presence.

"Just the usual dog drama, Jim. I think Smokey got a shot in at your dog this time."

"She sure did." He examined a small puncture beneath his dog's ear, which was just beginning to bleed. "Looks like a bite wound."

"I seriously doubt that. Our mutt can barely bite through her dinner." Smith hurried to interject, wanting to nip any talk of vet bills in the bud.

Allen, noticing Smith for the first time, frowned. Pushing through the hedge, he leaned over the fence to find his neighbour half-dressed, sprawled among tools. Seeing the displaced paling, he pieced together the scenario.

"Bloody hell, Steve. That bloody fence has given way again. Didn't I warn you?" His melodrama was cranked up to the max, clearly for Bec's benefit.

"It was your 'farm dog' that pushed through it." Smith's sarcastic emphasis on the dog's breed was intentional.

"If the fence were replaced like I wanted, no dog would get through."

"If the fence were replaced like you wanted, a Sherman tank wouldn't get through."

"Hey, you two, settle down, it's all good." Bec interjected. "How's your dog doing?"

The two men kept their eyes locked. "He'll be alright, Bec. Kelpies are pretty tough," Allen retorted, clearly a dig at Smith. Smith held his tongue, not seeing a point in continuing the argument.

With a smirk barely visible on his face, Allen retreated back through the shrubs. "Fix that bloody fence, alright?"

Choosing to ignore Allen's departing demand, Smith stood up and dusted off his trousers. He felt a hint of a bay breeze and decided to head back to the house for a drink.

"Don't think you're just going to leave that fence like that." Bec had her hands on her hips again. "You're lucky that dog didn't get through."

Smith heard Allen's sliding door close and winced at the thought of him eavesdropping on Bec's reprimand. He sifted through potential comebacks in his mind, but concluded none of them would be tactful. "Alright, okay."

Once he'd repaired the fence and tidied up his tools, he showered and reminded Bec that Rob was coming over to watch the game.

"Right, of course. Remember, I'm taking the girls ice skating."

"Oh yeah, that's right." Smith felt relieved it wasn't his turn to take the girls ice skating. It was ludicrous to him. Ice skating made sense if they lived in Iceland, but after the one time he'd been convinced to go with the girls, he spent the next day hobbling around with a bruised backside and an elbow that felt like it had been bashed by Thor himself.

Bec gave him a knowing smile. "It's good you have mates." She smiled again and started to walk away.

Smith was momentarily stumped. "Whoa, wait a minute..." He was suspicious of her casual comment. Although Bec got on well with Rob and Bill, Smith had only managed to knock a couple of tasks off his list, and he'd been expecting a less positive response.

"I mean it. I like it when you hang out with your friends. It lifts your spirits."

Smith wasn't entirely convinced but chose to remain silent. He stared at the spot where she had stood, half-expecting her to ambush him with a new list of tasks to complete before Rob's arrival. For the time being, he let himself believe that wouldn't happen. "Thanks." He could hear the girls dragging their ice skates down the stairs, chattering excitedly until their voices began to echo in the garage.

"Bye girls, have fun!" But they were already out of earshot.

"See ya!" Bec called cheerfully as she left.

He glanced back at the muted TV, an advertisement for the game flashing across the screen.

Something was definitely up.

Mates and Lovers

Steve Smith was the eldest of three children, brought up in Brisbane. He recalled his treks to primary school, with his mum watching from the letterbox until he vanished around the corner. Bill Leighton's house was en route, and they would occasionally detour through what they were told used to be a dairy farm, reducing their journey time. Despite the occasional shout of reprimand, it didn't faze Smith; getting yelled at was a daily occurrence at his own home. At times, they'd dump their school shoes into their bags, continuing barefoot. Regularly, Smith would scrape the skin off his big toe, with antiseptic dabs or splinter extractions forming an almost weekly ritual for his mum.

Bill's mum worked full-time. He'd get home before her, but he wasn't allowed inside the house, and no alternative arrangements had been made. Their typical old Queensland house was built on stilts with no built-in foundation. Smith would stop by Bill's place on the way home, and they'd often get up to no good, causing mischief that made him cringe in retrospect. On occasion, Bill would need to use the toilet but had no access to one. Smith would try to avert his eyes as Leighton squeezed under the floor rafters, dropped a poo on the higher side of the dirt, only to see Pal, his scruffy dog, gobble it up. It became a routine after a while, and he guessed Bill's parents never realised they had a makeshift toilet downstairs.

One day, they experimented with petrol, trying to light a campfire in the middle of Bill's backyard. That day, an old saucepan filled with petrol was kept nearby after splashing enough on the wood. When they struck a match, the head split, igniting the saucepan and singeing the wire of the Hills Hoist. The awestruck lads eventually realised the fire needed to be put out. Bill dragged the garden hose towards it, and as the burning petrol was displaced by the stream of water, a rivulet of fire trickled down the yard to the old, bare-wood paling fence. It caught fire effortlessly, and the flames spread across the dry grass at its base to a massive cluster of banana trees in the corner of the yard that hadn't seen any care for a decade. The trees practically exploded into a ball of flame, enough for Smith to dash home without a word or explanation to his dumbfounded mate, still holding the hose. He was at home, taking a gulp from a carton of milk, leaning against the fridge door, when he heard the fire brigade and promptly ignored his mother's call from the patio to "come and see the fire." That lunchtime, Leighton had already been disciplined by the deputy headmaster. His day didn't improve when his father arrived home from work and reacquainted his son with his belt. Leighton didn't take kindly to Smith's desertion. The next time they saw each other, Smith ended up flat on his backside sporting a split lip. Despite the incident, they remained friends.

Smith thought he had a strange childhood until he started high school and he met kids from a far wider geographic and social span. There were some strange stories there.

He did industrial chemistry at uni, then, worked in industry in various lab jobs in production and development roles until he felt the need to get outdoors. That was the end of his industrial chemistry career ambitions. He bumbled from one QC role to another and was considering a postgrad qualification in education when he met one of his former workmates in a pub close to home and some ideas were planted. It was lucky, because he really didn't want to be a teacher. One thing led to another and he started a role in selling laboratory instrumentation. He did pretty well at it and it was certainly "out and about." He enjoyed training customers in using the new equipment and met some nice girls doing it. He was with one of those nice girls at a dance "out west" when he met Bec.

There was something attractive and compelling about Bec and Smith couldn't keep his eyes off her from the second he saw her. She had a natural way of being, like she didn't care who was watching. She was pretty. The fact that she had mud half-way up her evening dress was part of it. It had rained the night before and they had no choice but to go ahead with the dance at the sale yards. It was a great time but a real mess. They ended the night walking through holding paddocks, just talking. Smith's date had caught a lift back to town as she was disgusted with the idea of dancing around in mud. It wasn't just talking with Bec; it was having fun while talking, something that Smith didn't think possible between two people who barely knew each other. They laughed and laughed and seemed to share the same curious sense of humour. Once they started "going out," they enjoyed being together most when they were out in the bush, which they did as often as possible. Some days it was enough to turn down an unknown dirt road and pull over where the bush seemed thick enough. They'd start walking until they were out of sight and earshot of the world and throw down a blanket and make love. Some horrible ant bites had in delicate places made for frantic interruption. It was during one of these incidents that he proposed to Bec while she was screaming in pain after a bull ant bite, prancing around stark naked. They laughed about it for years. She had to say yes about five times because he couldn't make it out whether she was crying from the bite or happiness. "Yes, you bloody idiot!" she finally screamed.

He and Bec were married in Brisbane after a short engagement. Bill Leighton was his best man. They were both Anglicans although that didn't seem to matter but they did "the church thing" because that seemed to be expected. Smith finally joined a good firm and they saved their house deposit quickly as Bec had been working as a nurse in Brisbane for a couple of years. They bought their house on the south side of Brisbane in a hilly area that caught the bay breezes.

Julie came a couple of years later and Sally a couple after that.

Bill ended up going to the same high school but as a boarder for the first few years. His parents had sold up and moved to buy a bakery in a small town "out west" and left Bill in Brisbane. Bill was picked on for the first two years until he started to grow and fill out to become the biggest kid in the school by grade twelve. They both played rugby from grade eight but it was the bush that called to them. They would go on outings with the school bushwalking club in the summer months and then take off by themselves, which eventually got them expelled from the club. They taught themselves abseiling and did some pretty scary rock climbing. Bill ended up marrying Anne and Smith was his best man. That was five years ago and two kids since for Bill and Anne.

Sniffing the Wind

"G'day mate," Smith answered, recognising Bill's caller ID. He slumped onto the couch, pleased to hear Bill's voice as Rob had cancelled last minute, leaving him to watch the game alone. "How ya goin'?"

"I'm good. It's a bit odd, though," Bill replied hurriedly.

"What's odd?"

"I was gonna ask you the same thing. Anything strange happening with Bec? Is she there?"

"No, she's out shopping with the girls. Nothing odd on my end." Smith fumbled and dropped the phone while switching hands. "Hold on. Actually, now that you mention it...maybe. Why?"

"I reckon they're up to something, Bec and Anne."

"Well, Bec was suspiciously agreeable today, considering I've done bugger all around the house."

"Hmm. Anne asked me when I'm going bush again with you."

"What's odd about that?" Smith could hear a splash as someone dove into the next-door pool, followed by a dog's bark.

"You forget? I'm practically banned from going bush with you!"

"Yeah, I remember. It's a bummer, mate."

"Anne's back now. I'll chat to you later." Bill hung up abruptly.

It was around two hours later when Bill rang again. "Your girls are over here, and Bec and Anne are having a chat out back."

"Shit, mate! Call the cops!" Smith joked, tripping up the stairs and cursing.

"Very funny. No, I mean something's happening."

"Then go ask them." Smith slumped onto his bed, the curtains billowing from the breeze.

"I will." Bill ended the call abruptly.

Smith was left open-mouthed, about to dissuade his mate from the high-risk venture of confronting the two wives simultaneously. The women were formidable when together, downright intimidating after a couple of wines. And Bill's behaviour was odd. Why would he be worried about the women talking? Smith shrugged it off.

Around thirty minutes later, Bec called. "Hi, darling. Can you come over here? Bill and Anne are putting on a feed."

"Sure. What's the occasion?" Smith was curious, if not slightly worried about what Bill might have done or said.

"Dinner. Food. Friends. Do we need an occasion?" Bec chuckled. "Hey, bring a change of clothes for the girls, and what's left of that Pav. And there are those lamb chops in the fridge we were going to have tonight."

"Yep, OK. Be there in half an hour."

Stitched Up

By the time Smith rocked up at the Leightons', they'd already cracked open a few cold ones. The four ankle bit-ers were wreaking havoc upstairs, carrying on like pork chops. Bec greeted him at the door, took the esky loaded with grog from his grip, hoisted it with difficulty behind her and pulled him into a one-armed hug, before ushering him into the heart of the house.

"G'day." Smith could smell the plonk on her breath, but she still smelt as good as gold.

"Alright, before we tuck into some grub, we've got a bit of a chinwag to get through." Bec was leading him out the back to the patio where the other two were parked. Bill was sprawled out, his bare feet taking a breather on a chair, while Anne was thumbing through some brochures coloured a mix of sky and sea blue.

"Hey there, Steve." Anne hopped up, gave him a hug and planted a smacker on his cheek. "Fancy a cold one?"

"Too right." This was Smith's first chance to eyeball Bill, who was pointedly ignoring him. "Alright. What's going on?"

Popping the top off a beer and slotting it into a stubby holder, Anne shot him a grin. "Why whatever do you mean, Mr. Smith?" Her attempt at a "southern belle" accent was pretty dodgy.

"Well, I've done bugger all at home. You two have been talking out back with His Lordship here." He hoisted his beer towards Bill. "And... Well... I've run out of things to say." Smith half-grinned. "But I reckon there's something fishy going on."

"Bali, mate. The girls wanna go to Bali." Bill didn't even glance up. Bec fiddled around restlessly. "And we get to play Mum and Dad." He looked up, his smile as strained as an old jockstrap.

Smith eyed him, curious about what kind of ordeal he'd been strong-armed into that would make him offer such quick-fire backing to this bonkers idea. He glanced at Bec and Anne, standing there, side by side, each clutching a wine glass.

"What's on the menu?" he asked, his voice as casual as he could manage. He needed time to think. The only time the girls had scarpered off together was a few years back for a stint in Noosa. That was bloody hard work. The kids were little tackers then. His job was basically to keep them alive. Now, it was a whole different kettle of fish. There were ballet classes for the girls, school prep... "Wait a sec...how long are we talking?" He'd put his foot in it now.

Bec let out a high-pitched squawk and threw herself at Smith, squeezing him in a hug. "Oh, you're a legend! The girls will be easy, I swear."

"Whoa, hold your horses! All I asked was how long?" Smith was half-wrestling to free himself from her grip and craning his neck to see the others. He was getting steamrolled.

"Seven days, mate."

"Seven flaming days!" Smith managed to sidestep between his missus and the wall to regain some control. He banged his head on a steel pot plant hanger. Bec and Anne gasped dramatically, though their concern was clearly just for show. He barely batted an eyelid. The reality of the situation was hitting him like a ton of bricks.

Upstairs, Sally let out a shriek. There was no follow-up wailing, so everyone ignored her.

"What do you reckon, Bill?" Anne lobbed the ball into her hubby's court. "Think you can handle the kids?"

"Too easy. You girls head off and have a blast. You've earned it."

Smith turned slowly to his mate who was looking at him with a ridiculously forced grin. He didn't understand what was going on. His mind raced through the logistics of such a trip; the weather in Indonesia this time of year and a host of other potential issues but nothing obvious fell out. He changed tactics. He turned to Bec. "Look, can we have a word?" He began walking towards the house, beckoning Bec to follow. She didn't. He stopped, shoulders dropped, and turned slowly. She crossed her arms and hardened her expression. It looked like she was going to get pissed off.

"Don't sweat it, mate. The girls have had this on the drawing board for weeks. We'll survive." That was our good ol' friend, Bill, again. He plopped back down with a shriek from the chair's leg scraping against the tiled floor, swigged his beer, and slumped his shoulders. Sally burst through the screen door with a bang and bolted to Bec in tears. Evidently, playtime was over. Julie herded the two boys out to join the adults, and just like that, the grown-up gossip was benched for the time being.

As always, Bill whipped up an army's worth of food. During dinner, only fleeting glances passed between him and Smith. Smith was determined to figure out how Bill was so at peace with the situation. It wasn't that he objected to the girls' trip. His gripe was about being steamrolled and not having a say in the decision. The girls chattered excitedly about the massages and manicures their friends enjoyed in Bali. They couldn't wait to take an elephant ride.

Once everyone had their fill, Smith rose slowly, stretching. "I need to drain the main vein." He tried his best to sound as crude as possible, signalling that a "men's conference" was in order. He threw a glance at Bill and gave a suggestive furrow of his brow.

"Yeah, me too." Leighton's chair echoed a familiar screech as he rose.

"Aren't you two adorable? Planning a little sword fight?" Bec was on fire with her quips.

Smith shrugged it off. He navigated through the house, steering clear of the restroom, and slipped out the front screen door, listening for Bill's footsteps. Sure enough, he was on his trail. The moment the door shut behind him, Smith turned and spread his arms wide. "Dude. What the fuck?"

"Shhh, keep it down." Bill threw a wary look over his shoulder to ensure the girls weren't playing spies. "I get it, I do. Anne's got me by the balls."

"No shit, mate?!" Smith kept his arms dramatically spread wide. "How? I mean, what did you do?"

"It's about what I didn't do." Bill's face suddenly sobered, which set off alarm bells for Smith, changing his tone to "careful inquiry."

"Everything okay?"

"Didn't you notice when you walked in?"

Smith dropped his arms, took a step back, and looked frustrated. "Notice 'what' when I walked in?"

"The floor."

Smith's annoyance was mounting, given this mysterious game Bill seemed eager to play. He cocked his head and looked away, feeling his patience waning. "For the love of..."

"Okay, the floor. I screwed up the floor order. They installed the wrong one." Seeing Smith about to retort, Leighton raised his hand for more explanation. "Anne chose the pattern for the new vinyl planks and was about to place the order, but I wanted to score a better deal. And I did. But I bungled it and ordered the wrong pattern."

"It looks fine to me," Smith tried to downplay the debacle.

"Are you nuts? What if you did that? How would Bec react?" Bill was starting to lose patience with his buddy's lack of empathy.

"Well, I guess..."

"Cut the 'I guess' crap!" Bill dipped his head as though ducking an incoming missile, realising he'd gotten a bit too loud. "Anne lost her shit. I mean, really. I've never seen her like this."

"How did you get the floor laid if it had the wrong pattern?"

"That's where I blew it. Anne had gone to the Goldie for a couple of days to see her sister and they came in and laid it. It was going to be my surprise to her. I was supposed to be there but after Trev and I moved all the furniture out we went to Jacko's to see his new ute." Bill looked at his feet. "Three rooms, all the halls, the dunny and the kitchen all wrong. They were just finishing when we came back. Man, I shit myself when I saw the sample Anne had in the kitchen."

"Why did you pay it if they messed it up?"

"They didn't. I did. I put the wrong pattern in the order. I did it by memory and they had it at their shop and...well I was sure that was it. The one they laid has a light brown background. I should have taken the sample and the order that Anne had written out. I forgot it."

Smith retreated a step, the full weight of the situation finally hitting him. "Mate, I see it now. Holy crap."

They stood in silence, the thrum of a V8 engine echoing down the street as Bill smacked a mosquito on his arm with unnecessary force. They were two blokes in a moment of solidarity with husbands throughout history who had botched a seemingly simple but crucial request from their wives.

A chill ran down Smith's back as he mentally swapped places with his mate. Seeing Bill like this was hard to swallow, but he got it. He recalled the fallout when he failed to refuel Bec's car after she'd asked him to. He'd said he did. Apparently. They ended up stranded on the highway and Julie missed her ballet recital while he was out fishing with Jonesy. His attempts to question Bec about her own ability to read a fuel gauge were shot down, earning him a week of palpable scorn.

"And what did Anne do?"

Bill stared at his feet again. "Mate, she..."

"So this whole Bali trip is because of your fuck-up, not some sudden bout of generosity?" Smith had connected the dots, but the implications were just sinking in.

"Yup." Bill hunched his shoulders in a schoolboy-like posture, as if bracing for a hit.

Smith stood there, staring at his helpless mate. He was dumbfounded at the manipulation the girls were exercising on poor Bill, and by extension, him. He was taken aback at how swiftly and enthusiastically Bec had seized the opportunity.

"So how does this involve Bec? And me?" Smith wasn't sure he wanted to know the answer.

"Yeah. Well. Anne gave me the silent treatment for a few days, only breaking it to express her loathing for the floor. Last Monday, she walked into the bathroom while I was shaving and announced she's off to Bali for a week with Bec. We were tasked with minding the kids."

"Who's 'we'?"

"Me and you."

Smith glanced over his shoulder, checking the hallway behind the front door for the girls. All clear. He rubbed his face and raked his hand through his hair. "What if I refuse?"

"Refuse what?"

Smith wasn't sure if Bill was playing dumb or not. "To go along with this ridiculous Bali scheme."

That's when Smith noticed the fear in his mate's face. Bill was easily twice as big and heavy as his wife. Anne was one of those petite women, and together they made quite the odd couple. At their wedding, with Bill by her side, Anne looked like the figurine atop the cake. They loved each other deeply and were best friends. He had never heard a harsh word between them. When Bill finished his accountancy qualifications, he proposed to Anne. A couple of years his junior, she was a Brisbane girl from north of the river. Her parents were decent folk — at least her mum was; her dad was a bit of a religious zealot, and Smith had only met him a couple of times. Anne was a top-notch woman. They had some rough patches, especially after making poor investments right after buying their house, but they worked through it. Smith realised the gravity of this upset for Bill. After finally settling their debts and starting renovations on their house, Bill pulls this. It was a breach of trust, in a way. Smith realised he had been out of line.

"Hey." Smith swung the top of his closed fist slowly to his mate's solid upper arm. "I get it, mate. I'm not going to make trouble."

"Thanks, Steve." It was rare for Bill to use his name; such was the gratitude expressed.

"I don't mean to be rude, mate, but are you guys good for the cost of the trip?" Smith was reflecting on the frugality they'd held to for so many years.

"No issue. Anne's mum is going with them and she's paying the lot. Even Bec's costs. She saw how cut Anne was, so she suggested it."

"She did? Anne's mum did?" So this wasn't Bec or Anne alone devising this foetid scheme. Smith was losing steam. It was a fait accompli.

"Yep."

Smith was thinking of how to ask Bill the next couple of questions that would better define this action of Anne's. Was it some sort of punishment or just compensation or was it really related to the floor at all? However, none of it made any difference. Bill had lost his mojo and he'd be ineffective as a wing-man in any such challenge to the girls.

He turned to the screen door as he heard a child running up the hall towards them. It was Julie. "Mummy said to ask if you two are gonna pick curtains soon?" It was an adult question in a little girl's voice through the screen door, but the point was made.

"Tell Mummy we are coming, please, Julie" Smith said in increasing volume as his daughter ran back through the house. "Well, mate we better go back and get this on." He turned to walk back into the house. "You really are a bloody idiot," he said with an honest chuckle.

"I know."

No Silly Stuff

In the world of business, it would have been hailed as a victory. Somehow, Bill mustered the courage to inform Anne that he and Smith had plans for the weekend before the ladies jetted off to Bali. The ensuing conversation was intense, but the arrangement was agreed upon. They were to return by Sunday late afternoon, ensuring the girls and Anne's mum could depart without a rush on Monday morning. With the news, Bill rang Smith.

"What were you thinking?" Smith had a counter-offer at the ready, but decided to keep it up his sleeve for now.

"Fishing. Brunswick Heads, mate."

"Yeah."

"Yeah. Any other ideas?"

"A night hike to the Lower Portals at Mt. Barney."

"That's genius, mate. But it's a no-go. Anne won't have me going bush with you. I told you."

Smith ignored him, already pulling up his tide tables, which also showed the moon phases. "Just checking now... Yep, the moon is perfect."

"Hey, are you even listening, mate?" Bill raised his voice. "I said Anne won't approve." A couple of years prior, during an abseiling expedition near Stanthorpe, a rock dislodged by the climbing rope had smacked Bill on the head. The blow had left him dazed and bleeding. Had it knocked him unconscious, he might not have survived, as he was still some way off the ground. He hadn't been wearing the helmet that Anne had made him promise to wear. After that, they were effectively "grounded" and hadn't gone bush since. Smith often teased his mate for being "under the thumb," but he knew the same could have happened to him.

"Maybe she won't find out."

Bill sensed a trap. Smith was egging him on, playing the "who's the boss" card. It seemed to be working, too. After the whole floor debacle, Bill was feeling pretty low. Eventually, he caved, realising he could please everyone: support the girls and spend the weekend with his mate.

"So we leave Saturday, hike in, sleep, then hike out? That what you're thinking?"

"Yep." Smith kept it straightforward. "No climbing, no risky stuff. Just the walk in and out."

Bill considered it. If they weren't climbing or rock-hopping in the gorge, it didn't seem too dangerous.

"'K. Yep. OK."

"Righto." Smith was processing the plan. "We'll take my Toyota, and we'll tell the girls we're going night fishing and returning late afternoon."

"We'd have to bring the rods and gear."

"Yeah, of course."

"Yeah."

"Yeah. Mate, this will be great. A day before the full moon. It's been ages since we've gone hiking."

Before Bill and Anne got hitched, Steve and Bill used to take what they called "moon walks." Under the glow of the full moon, they would trek one of their favourite bush trails, usually Mount Barney. Typically, the journey was ten to fifteen kilometres, and they would sleep at the lower portals before walking back the next day. It was a way to enjoy the outdoors without blowing an entire weekend. The girls claimed they were asking for snake bites, but the guys paid them no mind.

Things calmed down once the week started and the schedules of school and work took over. Smith had a half week trip to a training course in Sydney which ended on his return home, Thursday night. By the time he got home from the airport, he was tired and the idea of a walk the next night seemed hard. The discussion was had with the girls about their fishing trip. Bec had some concerns if it was rock fishing but that was deftly dismissed. It did, however, bring some tension to the planning chats between Smith and Bill. They would say they were staying in a tent near their fishing spot, which would explain their packs. It all seemed to be working out fine. They would leave mid-Saturday and be back Sunday afternoon.

Then, something strange happened.

It was a perfect Friday night, and Smith was back at his post by the barbecue. The moon they were counting on for the following night's adventure shone brightly. Bec brought out some chopped tomatoes, and Smith dumped them onto the sizzling hot plate.

"I've been thinking, love..." Bec began, leaning into him slowly. Smith wrapped an arm around her. "About your fishing trip tomorrow."

Smith did his best to remain nonchalant, but his senses were on high alert.

"What about it, sweetheart?"

"What about inviting Jim along?"

"Jim who?" Smith had no idea who she meant...

"Jim, from next door."

The suggestion hit him like a gut punch. It was unthinkable, absurd even. Plus, it was just downright weird. Bec knew full well that Smith could barely stand Jim Allen. Smith's mind raced. She must've caught onto their night walk. He conjured up a tiny smile and pitched his voice slightly higher.

"Darling, where on earth did that notion come from?"

"Well, I just thought it might help you two get along better."

Smith took a small step back, perplexed. "Really? That's surprising. He probably doesn't even know how to fish." He was doing his utmost to maintain his cool.

"Well, actually, Stacey says he's quite adept at fishing..."

"Sweetheart, there's a vast difference between holding a rod next to the water and doing what Bill and I do. Night surf rock fishing for large Mulloway requires serious skills. Honestly, I don't want to spend my night babysitting someone." Smith managed to bite back the words that were on the tip of his tongue: that Jim was an irritating know-it-all, and he would never willingly spend time with him.

"Well..."

"I have to ask, how did you come up with this idea? Was it you, or was it Stacey?"

"Actually, it was Stacey. She mentioned that Jim doesn't have many friends..."

"That's 'cause he's a pain in the backside." Smith decided it was worth letting that slip.

He expected to receive Bec's usual admonishing gaze whenever he spoke in such a way, but it wasn't there. She looked somewhat hurt, and concern clouded her features.

"Hey, are you okay, love?" Smith pivoted and pulled her closer to him. "What's going on?"

"Never mind. It's not a big deal. It was a foolish idea. I should've told Stacey that."

"No, hold on. What's really happening?" Smith gently lifted her chin. "Seriously..."

"Well, it's just that Stacey is so friendly. She's always proposing get-togethers and volunteering to watch the girls. And then there's your obvious disdain for Jim. It makes things difficult."

Smith had considered this, too. His negativity and resistance to change or consider new ideas had been brought up several times throughout their marriage. Sometimes, it worried him. He had learned tough lessons about things like Valentine's Day. Even though he and his mates unanimously deemed it a farce, the distress he caused — and consequently experienced — simply wasn't worth it.

Smith sighed and pulled her to him further. "OK, I understand and I'm sorry that puts you in a situation. I like Stacey, too. And she's great with the girls."

"So you'll consider it?" Bec's enchanting, moist eyes met his. She lifted her chin and planted a kiss on him, brushing a loose strand of hair off her face. Smith pondered where this was all leading. If the girls discovered they hadn't gone fishing, it would appear as if they'd concocted a massive lie to exclude Allen. The old saying "Oh, what a tangled web we weave" flitted through his mind, and he took a sharp inhale. He was beginning to understand the depth of that statement.

"Absolutely not. This isn't the kind of thing to do with Jim." Smith could feel his wife pull away slightly. "It's more for his safety, love. Imagine having to go next door and tell Stacey that Jim got swept off the rocks." He glanced at the pug as she waddled down the back stairs. "But I'll tell you what. I will brainstorm something that we can do together. Alright?"

Bec took it in stride. "Okay." She stepped back. "Are the chops almost ready?"

"Give it about five minutes, sweetheart." With that, she left. He decided not to mention this to Bill. This was his cross to bear. Anyway, everything would work itself out.

Over dinner, Bec informed the girls about their Bali trip and that they'd be staying home with Dad. They'd decided to keep the news until the last minute to prevent a fuss. The girls were unhappy about not going to Bali and about spending a week with Dad. As usual, Julie, the ringleader, brought up a list of insurmountable challenges: who would take them to school and preschool, who would make their lunches and dinners, who would iron their clothes, and so on.

✧

It's All Good, Mate

The house was curiously quiet on Saturday morning. Bec suggested that the girls might still be sulking about not accompanying her to the resort. The day was gorgeous; not a single cloud marred the azure sky, and the weather forecast promised a flawless weekend. Smith rose early to prep his surf rod and fishing gear. He'd been loading his camping equipment into his backpack before heading to Sydney. They planned to bring along just a few cans of soup, some cold chicken, and bread. Since Bec was also preoccupied with packing for her trip, Smith enjoyed a rare reprieve from her fussing.

His phone rang. It was Bill.

"Hey mate, how's the packing coming along?"

"All good. What's up?"

"Listen, I'm not sure if..."

Smith intercepted him after enduring thirty seconds of doubt-laden "what-ifs." He knew where this was heading. He moved away from the screen door to the other side of his Toyota. "Mate, are we going down to Sydney to hit up the girly bars?"

"No, but..."

"Are you cheating on your wife with that tall blonde from your office?"

"No, don't bloody..."

"Are you blowing all your hard-earned cash on the pokies?"

"No. OK, OK..."

"Look, mate, all we're doing is going for a walk. We've done it a dozen times. So what if the girls find out? It's not really a big deal."

"Are you trying to convince me or yourself? Alright, fine. All good, mate."

"You sure?"

"Yep. I'll be at your place around midday."

"No worries, cobba." Smith exhaled deeply and set his phone down on the hood of his 4WD.

He spun around and nearly jumped out of his skin at the sight of Julie's face squished against the screen door to the carport, her hands clutching the crossbar above. For a moment, he worried whether she'd overheard that conversation, particularly the part about the "blonde." He quickly rearranged his shocked expression and gave her a smile.

"Mum said to take the bait out of the freezer." Julie punctuated her statement with three quick puffs of breath against the screen, making a hissing sound.

"Tell Mum we're buying it on the way," Smith replied, looking out at the picture-perfect day. Now he was growing concerned about their grand deceit.

Their goodbyes were brief since they planned to return the following day. The fishing rods were securely fastened to the roof rack and the backpacks were ready to go. Bec was slightly puzzled about their early departure, given that it only took a couple of hours to get down to Brunswick Heads, but she didn't pry. The girls were still complaining about not going to Bali with their mum.

The drive to their starting point near Mount Barney was uneventful, with Smith and Bill exchanging stories about their kids and wives. Smith decided to share what Bec had suggested — inviting Jim Allen on their fishing trip. Bill yanked his foot off the dash and straightened up.

"What did you say?"

"I said no."

"Wait... just 'no'? And you got away with that? Bloody odd question."

"I know." Smith planted it and manoeuvred his 'Cruiser around an empty cattle crate, feeling a sense of achievement at the ease with which his car handled it.

"Does she suspect anything?"

"No."

"You answered that bloody quick."

"Look, Bill. Don't start that again mate. S'all good." But Smith was feeling that unease again.

"Yep. S'all good."

Bill and Smith reached the lower portals campsite around midnight. Between the drive to the starting point and the near-four-hour hike, they had put in a full day's work and were excited about the adventure. First, they stashed their fishing rods in the bush since leaving them on the car was a no-go. The moonlit walk was picturesque. The lunar glow was so intense it felt almost like daylight. They only used their torches when the foliage became dense and even then, only in brief flashes to avoid ruining their night vision. The air held an unusual chill for a January night. They encountered no snakes, and the towering golden orb spiders — notorious for spinning their webs across paths — were few and far between.

They rolled out their swags and surrendered to a well-deserved sleep, the creek's waters lulling them with their boulder-skipping song. Dawn arrived with a riotous chorus of parrots squabbling on two young eucalyptus trees nearby. The cacophony was almost unbearable.

"What a bloody racket," Bill groaned.

"Tell me about it."

"I'm gonna get a fire going."

"No worries, mate." Smith easily slipped back into slumber, waking an hour later to the cosy crackle of the fire. He wriggled out of his swag, standing groggily. Bill, clad only in his underpants, sat on a small boulder next to the fire. The babbling creek's music was once again audible. Despite it still being summer, the gorge held a chill as the sun had yet to pierce the tree canopy.

"Got the billy on."

"Good on ya, mate." Smith ambled to the clearing's edge for a pee. Finishing up, he claimed a boulder on the opposite side of the fire, squinting as smoke swirled into his eyes. The surroundings were familiar; they had camped there many times. He shivered, missing the warmth of his swag.

"Tea or coffee?" Bill rummaged through his pack, looking for the right packet.

"When did I ever drink tea?"

Bill grunted in affirmation, finally finding what he needed.

"And no powdered milk. Black. Unless you've got real milk." Smith reached around to extract his aluminium pannikin from his pack and tossed it over to his friend.

"Black it is then."

Smith observed Bill carefully doling out the condiments. Bill picked up Smith's battered, dented pannikin, scrutinising it like a museum exhibit.

"How old is this thing? Did you swipe it from Noah's Ark?" Bill was in high spirits, and Smith was glad to see it.

"Give it a rest and make the coffee." Smith was desperate for his caffeine fix.

Bill shifted uncomfortably on his chosen boulder. It was an inconvenient height and rather uncomfortable. A quick scan of their surroundings reassured him they had chosen a decent camp. He used the billy stick to retrieve the billy from the fire. As Smith got up to retrieve something from his pack, he heard a brief grunt, a metallic clang, followed by a scream. In the few seconds he'd looked away, Bill had attempted to adjust his position on the rock, lost his balance, knocked the bottom of the billy against the rock, and spilled much of its near-boiling contents onto his "nether region."

"Faaaaaaarrk!" Bill's scream of pain snapped Smith out of his mid-step freeze. "Faaaaarrrk!" Bill screamed again, scrambling to stand. It took Smith a second to realise what had happened. The scalding on Bill's upper thigh had already turned his skin pink.

"Quick! Into the creek, mate!" Smith hollered, darting around the fire as the first wave of intense pain hit Bill. He yanked him by the arm, directing him towards the icy creek. "Off with your jocks... No, wait." Smith's lab safety training for liquid burns kicked in, though it didn't exactly cover scalded nuts.

"Faaarrrck!" Bill slammed his foot into a rock, stumbled, and plunged into the frigid creek. "Jeeeesus Christ!" he bellowed. It had taken a mere half-minute to go from the scalding billy to the creek.

"Sit down!" Smith ordered, realising he needed to take control of the situation before Bill reconsidered. If Bill attempted to exit the creek, he wouldn't be able to stop him, and he might receive a stiff arm in the process. He pushed Bill down into the water. Bill twisted a bit and sank into the creek up to his chest, inhaling sharply as the cold water engulfed him.

"Oh, jeez. Oh, jeez. Bloody hell."

For the first time in what felt like ages, there was silence. He figured Bill's howling must have scared every bird, reptile, and mammal within a mile into flight or stunned silence.

Bill was gazing down into the water. He looked up at Smith, an expression of fear rather than pain on his face — fear of what was to come, considering their remote location. He started to rise from the water.

"No, mate, stay put. Need to pull the heat out."

"I didn't scald my tits, mate." Bill was alluding to the water's depth that Smith had shoved him into.

"Oh. Yeah." He assisted Bill in sliding over to a shallower part closer to the edge where the current was stronger. Up close, the creek's noise was surprisingly loud.

They stood and sat there for a couple of minutes, exchanging occasional glances.

"Smart thinking, heading for the creek, mate."

"Yeah. What did you burn exactly?" He asked. Bill looked up at him. "I mean, I didn't see it happen."

"My balls, mate. My balls. And my legs."

"Shit. Is it still burning?"

"Just starting to hurt now." Another silence descended. "We'd better have a look."

"What do you mean 'we'? They're your balls, mate. There's nothing I can do for you." Smith attempted to infuse some humour into the grim situation, though he was half serious.

Bill shot him an annoyed glance.

Surrendering, he said, "Alright, let's get you up and see how it looks out of the water."

The big man rose carefully, his body shivering and covered in goose bumps. The scalding on his upper thighs just below his jocks was evident once he emerged from the water. A small patch of red just below his belly button indicated that his mishap was remarkably precise. A small bit of belly had started to form, but he was still fit. He began to peel off his jocks.

"Whoa!" Smith protested instinctively.

"What?" Bill thought Smith had seen something alarming.

"I mean, mate... the last time I saw your willy was in grade 10, and I don't need a repeat performance." He glanced at Bill, noting his pained expression. "Oh, shit. Alright."

Bill slowly slid off his wet jocks down to his knees. He stepped back, allowing Bill to wobble on the smooth rocks underfoot until he regained his balance.

"Bloody hell."

"What? What?" Bill was now panicking through the pain.

"It looks like it missed your dick and got your balls."

"What?"

"Seriously. Your balls are cooked red but your dick looks good." He realised what he said on the instant as Bill let out the smallest of chuckles, despite his predicament. "Piss off. You know what I mean." He looked up at Bill. "Does it hurt?"

"Yeah, mate. Seriously hurting now."

"What is?"

"…balls."

"Have a look yourself."

Bill spun around in a futile attempt at modesty, and Smith caught a glimpse of some activity happening beneath the bent curve of Bill's neck. "Ah, shit, that hurts!" He grimaced, swivelling back to face Smith.

"Back into the creek, mate."

Thirty minutes later, they'd laid out a swag, and Bill was splayed out naked, knees bent as though he were about to give birth in the bush. A wet handkerchief delicately covered his privates. Waves of pain washed over him, and his balls were raw, yet luckily unblistered. "Should've ditched those jocks earlier," he murmured.

"Perhaps." Smith cast his gaze around their all-too-familiar campsite. The clock had ticked past nine, and they should've begun their return trip by now. "Mate, we'll have to hit the road soon." Their wives were leaving for Bali in the morning, and the blokes had sworn they'd be back by five in the afternoon. The issue of who would babysit the kids had suddenly become their most pressing concern. Well, that, and saving Bill's scalded nuts.

"Shit balls!" Bill practically shrieked. "Bloody hell!" He gingerly touched his scrotum, sucking in a breath through clenched teeth. "How in the bloody hell am I supposed to walk out?"

The two knew they wouldn't get mobile reception until they were near the car. "Get off your arse and see if you can walk."

Bill eyed him with a worried expression, reaching back for his trousers that he'd discarded the night before. "Help me with these."

"Why?"

"I reckon it might help."

"Scared the cattle will see your bits?"

"No, you bloody dolt. Just reckon it might be more comfortable."

"Well, first just try standing up."

The next few minutes made it clear that Bill wouldn't be walking anywhere quickly. The burns on his scrotum were particularly severe alongside his legs, likely where the boiling water had pooled. An attempt with his jocks on offered marginal improvement, but it still hurt continuously.

Bill plopped back down, assuming his burnt-balls birthing position. He slowly extended a leg, trying to unstick the pink skin of his scrotum from his inner thigh. "Ah, bugger this for a joke." He winced, sucking in another breath.

"I've got a plan." Smith hoisted himself up and stumbled around a bit. "I'll head out to the car now, get a hold of the cocky who owns these paddocks, and ask him to open the gate. I can drive right here if we can get that gate open. We'll have Bec find his number. I've got it in my book at..."

"Shit, no." Bill cut him off. "No, don't call Bec." He winced again. "Only the last gate is locked, remember? You bring the

'Cruiser in. I should make it to that gate by the time you walk out and drive back."

"It's a good couple of klicks, mate. You sure you're up for it?"

"Gonna have to be." Bill winced yet again.

"I'd better get moving, then." Smith started to pack his backpack. He headed to the creek to fill his water bottle, then began readying Bill's pack.

"Thanks, mate. Listen..." Bill hesitated, looking up at Smith, who had slung his pack over his shoulder and was fumbling for the belly strap. "No, seriously."

He paused, focusing on Bill. "What's up?"

"When you tell Bec, don't mention what happened in case she blabs to Anne."

"Why not?"

"Because she doesn't know we went bush." Bill finished, wincing yet again.

"What the hell did you tell her?"

"I said we were going down the coast for some fishing."

"So did I." Smith shrugged, indicating his puzzlement.

"But she warned me not to get hurt. She would not have allowed me to come. What do you think she's gonna say when she hears about my boiled nuts?" Bill seemed seriously concerned.

"You bloody drongo," Smith guffawed. "You think rock fishing's free from risk? Mate, think again."

"Nah, not as much as here."

"That's utter baloney!" Smith felt an urge to steer the conversation. "Look, mate. Here's the sum of it. We had planned a fishing trip but switched gears. Ended up spending the night in the gorge. You singed your private bits and that's about it. You're not in any real trouble. If anything, folks will feel sorry for you." He gave a nonchalant shrug. "As long as your manhood's functional post this mishap."

"Bugger off." A spark of humour finally flickered in Bill's voice.

Smith, taking on a caretaker's role, ensured Bill had all he needed. He had unloaded as much gear as he could into his own backpack to lighten Bill's load. Walking around to his mate, he crouched down, his hefty pack causing him to wobble. Extending a hand, he got a firm shake in return. "Take care of yourself. Meet you at the locked gate and don't go beyond it. Don't play hero; I'll come for you. But don't dawdle. Your pace will be less than speedy."

With a last look at his mate, Smith hefted his pack and started off. "You know what?" He didn't stop walking.

"What?"

"You're a complete nitwit. Who manages to scorch their balls while brewing coffee?"

"Bugger off."

"Drongo!"

And off Smith went at a brisk pace.

The trek back to his Toyota was record-breaking. Luckily, the bull was nowhere in sight. Just as he was nearing his car, he decided to try his mobile. As expected, reception was scarce, with just one bar showing up. Leaning on his pack for support, he dialled his wife. Her voice, barely audible, filtered through. Reception wouldn't improve until he was about twenty kilometres closer to town.

"Bec? Bec, can you hear me?"

Nothing.

"Bec?"

"Steve. Hi." She sounded energetic. "Had a fabulous night. Want to say hi to the girls?" She was already veering off topic.

"Bec! Bec! Wait."

It was Sally's voice, barely discernible. "Hi, Dad." She sounded fatigued.

After a few minutes of exchanging pleasantries and expressions of love with his daughters, he was back on the line with Bec. The line was still far from clear.

"Bec, can you hear me?"

"Yes. Are you heading back?"

"No. Well, yes. But... is Anne there?"

His wife's voice changed. "No, she's left. Why? Is everything okay with Bill?"

"He's fine, but he's injured."

"Oh, my God. What happened?"

Smith toyed with the idea of spinning Bill's tall tale. "Did you and Anne talk about where we went?"

"No. Steve, is Bill okay?" Her voice was filled with growing anxiety.

"He's alright but he's hurt. He should be on his way now."

"On his way? He's not with you? Where is he?"

Smith realised he needed to brief his wife on their predicament. He explained the situation as concisely as he could.

Silence from the other end. "Bec?"

"You were supposed to be fishing." Bec's voice had dropped several decibels.

"Hey, this isn't my doing! I didn't boil my wedding tackle. All Bill had to do was walk in and out." Smith momentarily felt guilty for throwing his mate under the bus.

Another pause.

"I won't be covering for you with Anne."

"I don't expect you to."

Another pause.

"How serious is it?" The line was getting worse, and Bec began to talk faster. "Do we need to call an ambulance?"

"No. I'll get some ice and take him home first."

"Can he even walk that far?"

"I don't know, but I can tell you this, he won't be sprinting across that bull paddock near the campsite."

"Oh, lord, Steve. You blokes... Fine, I'll inform Anne. Not sure how she'll react, though."

"I gotta bolt. Just don't pin this on me with Anne," Smith blurted, instantly regretting his silly request.

"Oh, you're definitely part of this. Don't you worry."

Smith swiftly ended the call with a brisk goodbye, not keen on being hung out to dry over the phone. He completed the short stroll to his car.

After negotiating five gates and three creek crossings, he reached the final locked gate, spotting Bill's half-emptied backpack hanging from it. 'He's made it this far,' he mused, 'so far, so good.' He hopped out of the car and scanned the area.

"Bill!"

"Over here!" A yell echoed from the creek, hidden amidst the trees. "Down here."

Smith descended to the creek, finding Bill seated in the water. He seemed in pretty rough shape.

"Mate, this is bloody agonising."

"I've got the car."

They made their way toward the Toyota. Bill had discarded his undergarments way back. Helping him into the car, Smith was confronted with the severity of the burn. It must've taken an immense amount of courage to walk such a distance in such pain.

"Mate, I'm not so sure you shouldn't be heading to the hospital."

"I know." He drew in a sharp breath as the pain flared up again. "Did you chat with Bec?"

"Yes." Smith left it at that, striding over to the driver's side after slamming the rear door shut, aware that Leighton was eyeing him.

"Well, what did she say?"

"I'm in deeper hot water than you."

In the end, they didn't make it home. Smith veered off to Beaudesert, escorting his injured friend to the hospital, while booking himself a room at the nearest Motor Inn. He had a sinking feeling that the next call home wouldn't be pleasant.

A New Person at Work

Steve Smith bounded up the stairs from the store into the office. He'd just had a chat with the two storemen about a few customer complaints related to their packaging of spare parts. Early in his sales career, he'd learned the best way to talk to these guys: be straightforward, but respectful. As a technical salesman responsible for the company's revenue, it irked him when the packaging wasn't done well. Once, after a bout of apparent indifference from the storemen, he'd lost his cool in front of both of them. That single incident led to months of petty hassles from their end. He'd soon realised that winning against them was a lost cause, and their work was integral to his success. A good-natured afternoon of drinking on his dime had helped smooth things over, and since then, they'd been reasonably cooperative.

As he stepped into the office, he was greeted by the refreshing chill of the air conditioner. While making his way past the printer, he came to an abrupt halt upon seeing his boss.

"There you are, Steve."

The comment barely registered with Smith. His gaze was captured by the woman standing next to his boss. He felt his mouth might have fallen open, but he couldn't be sure. His eyes involuntarily swept over her stunning figure before returning to her face, one of the most beautiful he'd ever seen. For a few heartbeats, he forgot who or where he was.

Realising he was blushing, Smith made sure his mouth was closed. His gaze, unsure of where to rest, darted to the printer, pretending that had been his intention all along. He finally gave up and looked at his boss. "Hi, James."

"Steve, I want you to meet Veronica Jacobs. She'll be taking over from Jill next month."

Smith's eyes swung back to the woman in front of him. Good heavens, she was breathtaking. Tall, impeccably shaped, with shoulder length, brown hair that perfectly framed a face worthy of any fashion magazine cover. Her tanned neck exuded femininity and athleticism, while her shoulders and breasts looked as if they had been sculpted from marble. Her low neckline suggested an enticing mystery. Not even Raphael himself could paint a more magnificent portrait. Smith found himself wondering what a woman of such remarkable beauty was doing in an industrial sales office.

This wasn't a new sensation for him. He'd experienced this reaction before and with only certain women. He'd attempted to discuss this peculiar affliction with his mates, but the conversation had inevitably devolved into ribaldry. He felt a twinge of guilt that he had never felt this way about Bec. She was lovely, sure, but not breathtaking.

Then Veronica was approaching him. Smith admonished himself internally. Pull it together! If she were brandishing a broadsword, preparing to cut him down, he couldn't be more taken aback.

She closed the distance between them, Offering her hand, keeping it close and low. "It's nice to meet you, Steve." Her voice was soft and melodic, instantly disarming him.

Smith accepted her hand, feeling cool, soft skin and a gentle yet firm grip. Her smile showcased a set of flawless teeth, accentuated by a dark red lipstick. The first hint of her perfume overwhelmed his senses as he moved into her personal space. She smelled like a tropical paradise, a heady mix of frangipani and fruit. He felt an almost magnetic pull towards her.

"Steve." His name was all he could get out. He managed a tight smile. He flicked his eyes to his boss who was already resisting a suggestive grin. Smith managed to push out another word. "Welcome." He steered his eyes back to this lady in front of him. She had released his hand but not stepped back. This close to her, he could barely breathe.

It wasn't a sexual thing, at least not on the instant. It was being in the presence of someone so femininely stunning and so absolutely perfect that he was intimidated. The effect was like what happens when you're bushwalking and the trees open to a magnificent elevated vista that takes your breath away. It was like that.

He realised his boss was talking. "...will be taking over from Jill as I said, so I'll need you to go over your customer base with Veronica. Whenever you have some time today or tomorrow." Jill was the logistical heart of their office and they collaborated frequently. She'd confided in Smith about her plans to leave before the company was aware. She excelled in her role and the customers adored her.

"Absolutely." Smith replied, still trying to reboot his systems after the interaction.

Before he knew it, they'd departed. Smith watched the captivating woman saunter away, moving with a feline grace. As they rounded the corner, disappearing from sight, he snatched one final glance at her.

He began the familiar ritual of self-chastisement that typically followed such encounters. Luckily, these weren't frequent. "God-dammit!" he muttered to himself repeatedly, his shoulders drooping as he heard someone thud up the stairs. Brad, the storeman, peered through the glass pane in the door, then flung it open, marching in with a triumphant smirk.

"Not bad, eh?" Brad nudged Smith as he sauntered past, a handful of labels clutched in his hand. The lingering aroma of male sweat that Brad left in his wake served as a sharp reality check for Smith, akin to a beleaguered boxer taking a whiff of smelling salts.

With a day full of customer visits scheduled, Smith took advantage of the opportunity to leave the office earlier than initially planned. He descended the back stairs and walked through the store, shaking his head at his own foolishness as he drove out of the carpark.

The day rolled on as any other would. Following a call from Bec to pick up milk and bread, and a request from Bill to borrow his chainsaw over the weekend, Smith returned home. Upon arrival, he found Bec tending to some newly planted flowers in the front yard. He approached her, computer bag in hand and arms laden with groceries, and chuckled at Sally's frustrated attempts to wrestle the hose from her mother.

Bec wasn't having any of it. Seeing her husband approach, she turned the tables on their daughter, feigning a loss of control over the hose and spraying Sally, causing her to shriek and scamper away. A perfect execution of playground justice, Smith thought, sharing a laugh with Bec.

"How was your day, darling?" Bec asked, wrapping her arms around his neck.

Wary of a potential hose-down prank, Smith replied, "You keep that bloody hose..." His sentence was cut short as his thoughts drifted back to Veronica Jacobs, incited by Bec's inquiry about his day.

"What was that?" Bec asked, momentarily stepping away from Smith to keep an eye on the mischievous Sally.

"Nothing." Smith answered, realising he'd lost enough composure already. An overwhelming urge washed over him; to drop to his knees and confess his helpless ogling of the new employee. To admit his need for psychological help to understand why he was so affected. To reassure Bec of her beauty, his love for her, and his unwavering fidelity regardless of any distractions at work. To gaze into her eyes and pledge his loyalty to her for a thousand years more. Yet, he said nothing.

"Steve. Are you OK?"

Smith started to snap out of it. A monosyllabic response wasn't enough. "Those bloody store guys are driving me nuts." It was a good save and it allowed for a visual sweep of his front lawn and back to Bec. "It's OK. I'm fine."

Smith walked up to his front porch with Sally on his back while Julie struggled to lift, or rather, drag, his work bag up the front path. His mind reverted. "How the hell am I going to work with this person?"

With dinner had and the washing up done, the girls were in their shared bedroom playing. Smith walked in and kissed and hugged them both. He was going to do the same when they were in bed but he loved their soft hugs when they were winding down for bed and they smelled absolutely wonderful in their clean pyjamas, fresh from a bath. He regarded it as his grounding experience for the day.

"Oh, yeah." Bec walked to the fridge and turned with an envelope in her hand. "Work letter came for you. Sorry, I opened it thinking it was a pay slip. Jill is leaving, huh?"

Smith took the letter and another couple of unopened window envelopes. His work mail came home because he worked from home half the time, which was the reason for the girls sharing a bedroom. The third bedroom had been sacrificed, as Bec had described it, as his home office. The office staff was supposed to put the mail in a courier bag but someone had whined about the cost and it now came in dribs and drabs through the post. "Yep. Seems so." The letter was an invitation for a get-together at the pub local to work to say goodbye to Jill. Fair enough, too. Jill had been a solid performer for almost twenty years.

He put the envelope down without reading it. "Saw that at work, ta."

Bec was currently without a job. Following her nursing career, she retrained as a speech therapist. Up until she became pregnant with Julie, she'd been working at a medical centre, assisting stroke patients. Though the work didn't particularly appeal to her, she knew its importance and thus persevered. Several of her patients made significant progress, which was a rewarding aspect. Around six months into her pregnancy, she and Smith decided it was time for her to quit. This was a sound decision since her water broke a month earlier than expected. Consequently, she was bedridden at home until they took her to the hospital to induce labour. Everything went well, and Julie arrived safely. Smith often recalled to his friends, "That was the most freaking stressful thing I've ever done."

"And you didn't even do it," was Tom's predictably unsympathetic reply, uttered between sips of beer at a past barbecue. "In fact, given how cute Julie is, I question whether she's even your kid." This was standard bloke humour, triggering chuckles from the rest.

Smith's phone rang just as he was flicking envelopes onto a stack of papers next to his bread. It was Bill, calling back to say he didn't need the chainsaw after all, due to a misunderstanding about which tree his wife, Anne, wanted cut down.

"That massive gum tree in the back?" Smith dramatised his surprise.

"Yeah, that one."

"Geez. That'd be a real challenge to fell it into your yard," Smith added, channelling his inner woodsman.

"Yeah, no, not happening."

Their conversation continued, and then Smith hung up.

By the time Smith and Bill finished clucking over the absurd tree-cutting request and exchanging their routine stories of triumphs and life lessons, the girls were ready for bed and eagerly waiting for their "Daddy story." These were improvised tales based on a subject that the girls alternated in choosing. This left Smith with no preparation and demanded his ability to wing it. They only earned a story after they finished their reading. Bec loved the idea, her only concern being that some tales were a bit too thrilling or scary for bedtime. So, Smith kept his stories soft and mild.

"What's tonight's Daddy story about, Julie?" Smith asked, adjusting Sally to avoid aggravating an old football injury.

Julie drew a deep breath, shot Sally a cautionary look to ensure her sister wouldn't intervene with her own topic, and declared, "A magic horse."

"Alright, and what's the magic horse's name, Julie?"

"Veronica."

Smith opened his mouth to start the tale, but stopped abruptly when Bec re-entered the room. He quickly dismissed the image of Veronica Jacobs that had sprung to mind.

"But that's a hippopotamus," Bec corrected, settling onto the bed and slipping off her shoes.

Sally burst out laughing at her older sister's apparent error. Julie crossed her arms and huffed, clearly unimpressed.

Smith began berating himself internally. He was stunned that a brief encounter with a woman could infiltrate such a cherished part of his daily routine. Now, Bec was giving him a puzzled look.

"OK, a Daddy story about a hippopotamus called Veronica. Here we go."

"No! A horse!" Julie just about screamed it.

"Yes, my mistake, Julie. A horse named Veronica," Smith admitted to his wife with a wince and raised eyebrows. He then began to weave the story on the fly, using that soothing paternal voice that always lulled the girls to sleep. It was a good Daddy story and both girls were asleep in his arms within minutes.

Carefully extracting himself from the children, Smith tucked them into their beds, and they were back asleep in no time.

After brushing his teeth, Smith found Bec in the kitchen.

"Don't you remember Veronica?" Bec asked as she threaded dental floss between her teeth over the sink. "You must have read that story to the girls a dozen times."

"Of course, 'The Hippo That Wanted to Be Famous,'" Smith said while filling the kettle.

"OK, yeah. You just looked like you'd never heard of it."

"Right." Once again, Smith scolded himself and walked back into the kitchen. "By the way, we won't be going to the Leightons this weekend. No tree dropping happening."

"I heard. I don't think you're being very helpful," she replied, arms crossed. "We... You... could save them a couple thousand dollars. I've seen you with that chainsaw. You know what you're doing."

Smith was astounded at how quickly his wife had received word about the tree. He shook his head. "It's precisely because I know what I'm doing that I can't cut down that tree, Bec. It's dangerous. I thought they were talking about a different tree. Bill did, too. It wasn't me who said no; it was Bill."

"Yes, I know. OK, OK, I understand."

Smith sauntered over to his wife and drew her gently but firmly towards him. She rested her head on his shoulder.

"Who's Veronica?" Bec asked softly.

"What?" Smith was further horrified at how the situation had infiltrated his home life. "A hippo. Why?"

She nestled further into his shoulder. "Don't know. You just seemed to have a reaction to the name."

Suddenly, a wave of stories, advice, and horror tales about husbands mismanaging matters concerning other women flooded

Smith's mind. The unwavering rule echoed in his thoughts, "never, never admit anything." The reasoning being that even the smallest slip in a story can create a huge problem, and no man can survive such a conversation with his wife. But, defying that advice, he felt compelled to clear the air. His relationship with Bec had always been open and honest, and the idea of it being anything less terrified him.

"A hippo. And the person taking over from Jill in logistics," he answered, wondering if using "person" instead of "woman" was a mistake. Yet, he'd never met a man named Veronica.

Bec's slight stiffening signalled she'd processed his answer. She shifted her feet, but her head remained on his shoulder.

"She started today," Smith added.

Bec slowly raised her head from his shoulder, shaking her shoulder-length hair out of her face. "What's she like?"

"Not sure. Only started today. James wouldn't hire anyone who wasn't competent..."

"That's not what I meant, and you know it," she interrupted, forcing a smile. "What's she like?"

At that moment, Smith realised he had already mishandled the conversation. The only way through was "full disclosure." He briefly considered a few possible responses before deciding on honesty.

"She's actually one of the most beautiful women I've ever seen," he confessed. He resisted the temptation to soften his declaration and merely gazed at his wife with an unreadable expression.

Bec's expression remained unchanged, her smile steady. "Well, I hope she's as good at her job as she is attractive to you." She freed herself from his loose hold, turning to walk towards the fridge. "Coffee?"

Smith was taken aback by the "to you." "Not just to me. To any guy. Or girl for that matter. I'm just being honest. James caught me off guard with her. I only spoke to her for about twenty seconds." Smith halted, aware that he was starting to ramble.

One of the girls coughed, causing both parents to hold their breath, waiting to see if it would continue. Julie was just recovering from a chest cold; any nighttime cough was worrisome given her history of childhood asthma, which she seemed to have outgrown, fortunately. Bec turned to Smith. "It's not about what this woman looks like, Steve. What concerns me is your lack of honesty."

Smith's incredulity began to grow. "Not honest? Not honest about what? I met the woman today. I didn't hire her or even interview her. You asked me about her, and I answered honestly. If I had said she was 'ugly as sin,' you'd have eventually found out that wasn't true, and then..."

Bec interjected, "No, I mean honest about you thinking about her." Her forced smile had vanished, replaced by a hint of hurt.

"What? Just because her name is the same as a hippo's, how is that dishonest?" Smith's frustration began to show, feeling an unjust accusation being levelled at him.

The kettle clicked off as Bec set down the coffee container and walked out of the kitchen, muttering something purposefully unclear.

Leaning against the kitchen counter, Smith came to the bleak realisation that he'd already made a royal mess of things. He felt drained and foolish, yet a sense of injustice lingered. Only now did it occur to him that Bec had detected the subtlest change in his demeanour and had followed that clue, leading to the confrontation. He regretted not having handled her feelings more tactfully. Shaking his head, he heard the ironing board being set up in the laundry room, followed by Bec's footsteps approaching the kitchen. His arms folded instinctively.

Bec re-entered the kitchen. She stopped, her hands hanging at her sides, and looked up at him. "Sorry." It was almost a chuckle, but there was a hint of pain in her voice. She stood there, her eyes beginning to moisten. It was exactly what he needed to hear. Smith stepped forward, enveloping her in his arms and pulling her head to his shoulder. He held her close.

"No, I'm the one who's sorry." Smith kissed her head. "I'm sorry for being such an idiot sometimes." His apology was simple, but sincere.

"I get so jealous sometimes. I'm sorry." She adjusted her arms around his back. "Thank you for being honest with me."

The only thought that came to Smith's mind was, "What on earth?" He was stunned by the events that had transpired both at work and at home. He'd heard of men who had affairs with women at work, men who seemed to bear the disgrace with grace, their demeanour unaltered, handling the disapproval of their colleagues with an unfaltering stride in their daily routines. Yet, he couldn't even handle meeting a woman without everything falling apart. In a bizarre way, he felt less manly. His normally average life perspective felt like a bystander observing his own car wreck.

I Can Fix That

$\mathbf{S}$teve Smith wasn't bad with his hands. He was able to fix most things he attempted. He just didn't attempt a lot. He didn't have a great set of tools, so his repairs were typically rudimentary and often not pretty. Much to Bec's chagrin, his favourite saying was "Function is beauty." That meant "it doesn't matter how it looks...as long as it works."

Bec Smith managed to tolerate this peculiar quirk. She knew it was tied to her husband's ego, so she approached the matter with careful communication. Most tasks on Smith's "honey-do" list, like squeaky doors or loose cupboard handles, would be handled almost instantly. Other chores, like trying to start the lawnmower, might take a few weeks of contemplation and occasional cursing at the offending inanimate object. Then there were some projects that were complete disasters, despite their apparent simplicity. The "leaky gutter saga" was one such episode.

Living in a verdant part of Brisbane, the Smiths' home was surrounded by large eucalyptus trees. Their leaves, carried by the wind, would land on the roof and clog the rain gutters. Cleaning them out was a hassle that Smith avoided due to the height of the house, which was daunting to him. Over time, the decaying leaves would produce organic acids that corroded the thin steel gutters, causing leaks. Despite Bec's repeated pleas, Smith never attended to these leaks. To him, the dripping gutters were low priority since most of the rain was still effectively drained.

However, a couple of holes had formed in the gutter running along the porch next to the front door. The entire family had experienced the annoyance of being dripped on. The trickling water, carrying rust and dissolved organic material, stained the tiled landing by the front door. When Bec brought home a liquid concrete cleaner, Smith dismissively perused its ingredients, then demonstrated its ineffectiveness as Bec watched, arms crossed, with a disapproving scowl. Smith vowed to find a solution, dropping some chemical terms like "sequestration" and "chelation." Bec retorted with a loud "whatever!" before stomping off.

Smith was steadfast in his resolve to fix the leaks himself. He reasoned that the task simply involved purchasing a section of gutter, cutting out the corroded part, drilling a few holes, inserting some rivets, applying sealant, and voila! How hard could it be? He found the idea of hiring a roofer to replace a short bit of gutter, that he could access from the porch with a ladder, to be ludicrous. The job wasn't beyond him; it was just about understanding how gutters were installed, finding the right clips, recruiting a mate to lend a hand, and they'd be kicking back with beers a few hours later, probably a thousand dollars richer. Despite Bec's repeated requests, Smith's response never wavered.

That all changed last November.

It was Melbourne Cup Day. For the first time in years, after dedicating herself to being a mother and putting socialising, hairdressers, and manicures into the "not important for now" bucket, Bec accepted an invitation from her friend, Stacey Allen, to attend the races. She relished these events: the cheeky banter with her girlfriends, the flow of champagne, and the opportunity to doll herself up with a beautiful outfit and, of course, a hat.

As Bec made her grand entrance down the stairs, Smith and their daughters, Julie and Sally, were loitering in the hallway.

He let out an appreciative wolf-whistle, while Julie and Sally voiced their awe with a chorus of "oohs" and "ahhs." Bec basked in their compliments, looking radiant in a brilliant white dress smartly trimmed with dark blue lace, strappy, shiny dark blue stilettos, and a large, tasteful hat adorned with a blue bow. The morning's hours spent at the hairdresser were evident under that hat. She smelled divine. Smith, ever the protective dad, warned the girls not to get their kiddie-grime on Mum's pristine dress, earning an appreciative smile from Bec. He couldn't care less about horse races, even the Melbourne Cup and knowing this, Bec seized the opportunity for a playful afternoon with her girlfriends.

However, unbeknownst to the family, something sinister was developing. It hadn't rained for over a month in Brisbane, which was quite unusual for that time of the year. The water in the gutter above their front door had evaporated into a slimy, thick sludge, teeming with organic matter and heavy with rust. It seeped slowly towards the hole in the gutter, taking over an hour to form a droplet. Any grime that could dissolve or be carried by the droplet was present. As the droplet grew, it eventually broke free from the gutter and began its descent. Bec, oblivious to the droplet's existence, walked out of the house, turning to bid her family goodbye just in time for the filth-laden droplet to land on her dress, right above her left breast. While Bec felt the impact, Smith saw it first. His horrified expression relayed the tragic news to Bec before she even had a chance to look. Dropping her handbag, she stormed past him and the girls towards the hallway mirror.

"Steve!!! For God's sake!!!"

Smith froze. He knew he had seriously dropped the ball. Immediately shifting into damage control mode, he ushered the children behind him as he approached Bec, who was rooted in front of the mirror, a look of pure horror etched on her face.

"Can you..." he started.

"Shut up," Bec cut him off, teetering on the brink of an eruption.

"But what if..."

"I said, shut up!"

Smith stood there, mouth agape. Julie, oblivious to the stain — a brown blotch dotted with black spots — continued to gush over how lovely her mum looked, assuming Bec was giving herself a "last check" in the mirror. Fearing his daughter might get caught in the impending explosion, he quickly shushed her.

Bec remained in front of the mirror. Smith watched her. Nothing changed. He knew he had to do something.

"A corsage," he suggested.

"What...?" Bec's temper was on a hair trigger.

"A corsage. To hide the stain," he proposed, bracing himself for anything from a stream of expletives to a slap. "It's in the perfect spot..."

"Perfect? Perfect?" Bec was building up to her boiling point. "There's nothing bloody perfect about this, Steve." Then, silence. A heavy fifteen seconds passed. "Yes."

"What did you say, love? I..."

"I said yes." For the first time she glanced at the girls who were wondering what was going on. She looked up at Smith, her brow dropping in intent. "Get me some of that maiden hair fern from under the back stairs. A few fronds. Some of those native flowers — the small white ones near the back fence."

Smith began to feel some reducing tension. "What about some of those...." He stopped as Bec walked up to him. Her hat rim passed over his head as he put her lips to his ear with one perfectly manicured hand on his shoulder.

"Just do as I say, exactly as I say, Steve, or I will kick you in the balls, right in front of the girls. Now get going." Smith let go of the girls and shot out to the back yard after finding the scissors in the kitchen. By the time he returned, Bec had found some white lacey ribbon and pins. A couple of minutes later, Bec was back in front of the mirror, more relaxed. Smith was tempted to say that her new adornment looked nice but he didn't push his luck.

Bec said goodbye to the girls and pushed past Smith being careful to walk around the "drop zone," lest she take another muck-laden deposit to her dress. Smith thought she might turn to make reference to the gutter but she continued to Stacey's next door.

Unexpectedly, weeks passed before the issue of the dripping gutter resurfaced, mainly due to the persistent dry spell causing the gutter to dry out. It wasn't until after Christmas, when torrential rains lashed the area for days, that the problem became more prominent. The tiny hole in the gutter had expanded, and the once-dripping water had become a stream. The girls found amusement in this, taking turns shoving each other into the makeshift waterfall. By early February, Bec was on Smith's case, reminding him he still hadn't fixed the gutter. For the first time, she issued threats about hiring tradesmen to handle the task. Smith, who now felt slightly more confident in his ability to undertake the job, brushed off Bec's threats as if his newfound knowledge alone would fix the leaky gutter. That was yet another tactical blunder on Smith's part.

Fast forward to mid-March. Smith had travelled to Sydney for technical training from Monday to Wednesday, a trip that had been planned well in advance. Additional sales training was scheduled for Thursday and Friday. On the first day, it was announced that the sales training was cancelled as the trainer from the USA had fallen ill. Smith promptly emailed his travel agency to arrange an early flight back home on Thursday morning. He was about to text Bec about his change of plans when he thought it'd be a pleasant surprise to show up a couple of days early with presents.

The flight back to Brisbane felt brief as he sat with Veronica Jacobs, who had accompanied the team to Sydney for an admin meeting. They chatted throughout the entire flight. Smith had grappled with his inability to handle Veronica's presence. He found her immensely attractive and, having gotten to know her, also warm and personable. His fantasies about her might have been more manageable if she were aloof or mean, but instead, she was perfect, stunning, friendly, and capable. To him, she was like a million-dollar supercar, beautiful to look at but forever out of reach. They parted ways in the long-term parking area, and Smith continued home.

Arriving just before 11 am, he was in high spirits as he pulled into his driveway, only to screech to a halt in disbelief at the sight before him. A scaffold was set up across his front porch, with two blokes working on the gutter. They were young, probably in their mid-thirties, shirtless and tanned, both with long brown-blond hair. One had his shorts snagged by his tool belt, revealing a starkly white bum. Smith could've blushed. The taller one with the exposed backside turned to look at him, then casually dismissed him. Smith felt like an outcast, silently scorned by a group of "Coast boys" prepping for a surf session. They were already well into their work. Smith backed out of his driveway and parked in the street, behind the tradie's ute bearing the logo "Roots Roofers."

Exiting his car, he locked it and headed up the driveway, taking the side path to the back of the house. There, he found Bec chatting with Stacey over the back fence. When Stacey greeted him with a smile and a wave, Bec turned and, with a hint of surprise, acknowledged Smith's early arrival.

"Oh, Steve. You're back," Bec stated rather flatly.

Stacey chuckled, backing away. "Well, I'll leave you two to it then."

"Sure am." Smith approached his wife, wrapping his arms around her in a close hug, planting a kiss on her cheek, and hugging her again. "I missed you."

"Missed you too, love." Bec's voice was warm and close in his ear. She smelled and felt divine. As he began to loosen his hold, sensing she wasn't ready to let go, he hugged her tighter. This exchange continued a couple of times until he finally conceded, "OK, OK, I get it." He dropped his hands to his side, standing somewhat slack until she relaxed her grip and stepped back. Bec adjusted her hair. "So. You saw my little project underway, did you?"

"I did, yes." Smith, crossing his arms, was resolute in drawing out a clear admission of guilt from his wife for acting solo in a domain he considered his.

"It was supposed to be a surprise." Bec's tone was indifferent, her hands now resting by her side.

"It certainly was," Smith responded, still smiling.

"I mean they were supposed to be finished before you got back." Bec shifted her feet and absent-mindedly scratched her arm.

"Ah, I see. I wasn't supposed to catch you red-handed hiring male strippers moonlighting as roofers, then."

"Steve!" Bec, struggling to suppress a smile, sported a quizzical expression. "Look, we don't have to do this. You've had over a year to fix that gutter, and it's still leaking."

"So you called in Magic Mike and his rooting mate. Who names their business that, anyway?"

"They came highly recommended."

"By whom? The local Cougar Club?"

"Wha..." Bec stood there, mouth agape. "Did you just call me a cougar?"

Smith heard a giggle from next door and realised that their neighbour Stacey hadn't ventured far. It seemed Bec must have forecasted his reaction to the fixed gutters, and Stacey was keen on hearing the ensuing fireworks. "Stacey, you stay out of this!" Smith called out, not truly irked, although he couldn't see where Stacey was behind their shrubs.

Bec began to retreat. "When you've cooled off, we can discuss this like adults." Smith sank into a garden chair, and a short time later, Bec returned with two open stubbies of beer. She handed one to Smith.

"It's 11 am, and a workday," he protested half-heartedly. Nevertheless, he accepted the drink, a smile creeping onto his face as they clinked bottles.

"Yeah, I know. But you look like you need a drink. Jealous man. Move over." She nudged her way beside him. Bec was grinning, and Smith mirrored her smile. Part of him wanted to continue the stand-off with his wife, to argue about not being consulted, about not sourcing multiple quotes. But the bottom line was that he had failed to do what he'd promised to: fix the gutters.

"Not jealous," he retorted.

"Definitely jealous."

"Not jealous, eh?" Smith said, suddenly curious if Bec was feeling as frisky as he was. He gave her a sly glance, the one he usually reserved for those rare, out-of-the-blue "You in the mood?" inquiries. Recognising his look, she returned his grin.

In response, Bec snuggled closer, planting a passionate kiss on his lips. He reciprocated, the sun warming their faces and bodies. Pulling her leg across his lap, he left no room for doubt that he was already in the mood. Hand in hand, they made their way inside the house. Smith stopped, turning to his wife. "Hey where are the kids?" He realised he'd not seen them since he was home.

"At Anne's while this work is being done." She smiled. "Come on."

As they tiptoed towards the bedroom, Smith halted their progress in the hallway. With the front door closed and the sounds of the workers directly outside on the scaffold, Smith pinned Bec against the door. She mutely protested they might hear, but Smith ignored her. He began kissing her neck and was rewarded with a deep breath and a quiet moan. She pulled open his belt and fly and felt him while his pants slipped down off his butt. He lifted her skirt and she shuffled down her panties. At one stage, they froze when Bec's elbow hit the door quite hard and the workers went quiet. They giggled quietly. Then he was in her and she was biting his ear. They realised their predicament was impractical and skipped off to their bed, where they finished lovemaking. It was a wonderful welcome home that started in a most curious way.

As they lay in each other's arms, Bec broke the silence. "So... what was that about?"

"What?"

"You know what." She teased him with a mischievous smile. "That front door escapade."

Smith shrugged, looking away. "Dunno. Nothing, I guess."

"I don't believe you," Bec prodded gently, her hand on his chin. "Tell me."

"I guess..."

"Yes?"

"I guess I was marking my territory," he finally admitted.

"Against me or the boys?"

"Oh, so it's 'the boys' now?" Smith couldn't hide a twinge of jealousy, despite his smile.

"No, silly. But seriously, tell me."

"Just letting them know that I'm the luckiest bloke alive to make love to a woman like you."

Bec beamed at him. "Right answer. But you do know they had no idea we were there, right?"

"Of course, they did."

"Silly." Bec nestled into Smith's neck, both of them drifting to sleep in their birthday suits on the rumpled sheets.

Smith was roused by an odd tapping sound.

"Um…hey folks…" It was one of the roofers attempting to get their attention discretely.

Shaking off sleep, Smith noticed a hand waving through the window. The blinds were raised and the thin curtains billowed in the breeze, offering a view into their bedroom. While Bec's leg covered his privates, one of her breasts and her buttock were on full display. It occurred to Smith that the workers shouldn't be near their bedroom window if they were working on the leaky section of the gutter. She's having the entire front gutter replaced, he realised.

In a twist of poetic justice, the roofers had shifted their scaffold and unwittingly walked in on an eyeful of naked entwinement. They were tactfully suggesting Smith and his nude wife might want to cover up.

"Darling, hey, darling, wake up." He whispered into her ear.

"Hmmm?"

"Wake up, love."

"Hmmm. I'm awake." She nestled further into his neck.

"How much of the gutter are they fixing?"

"Why?" Bec asked, her body tensing ever so slightly.

"Because they're peeping through the window at you now."

For a few moments, nothing happened. Then, with a shriek, Bec sprang from the bed, grabbing the sheets. As they were tucked under Smith, she stood stark naked for a moment before scampering out of the room, squealing all the while.

Smith covered up and began laughing. He told the blokes on the scaffold that they could keep going now; that "all was clear." Bec swung her head back into the room, still blushing, now wrapped in a towel, glancing cautiously at the window. She was aghast at Smith how he so calmly had held her out as a visual spectacle to the tradesmen.

"Steve. What the fuck?" She retained part of a smirk but was a little annoyed and definitely puzzled.

Smith lay back with his hands behind his head and smiled.

"I said...what the fuck?" Bec put strong emphasis on the last word.

"Well. I didn't ask them to come."

"Holy shit, Steve! What sort of shitty thing is that to do?" She was getting annoyed.

Smith looked at his wife. Maybe he had gone over the line with this. I mean, letting blokes see his nude wife. Maybe he was a weirdo.

The Crush

Navigating the complex realm of chemical analysis instrumentation is no walk in the park. Recently, the release of innovations from their parent company in the US necessitated Steve Smith to deepen his understanding of relevant chemistry and physics. Their company's technical community was abuzz with anticipation, poised to launch a new kind of online analyser. This innovation not only offered a unique position in their industry but also ventured into the intricate sphere of online process control and digitisation (or digitization, as their American counterparts would spell it).

A ten-day training trip to New Jersey loomed, wrenching Smith away from his family. The thought of leaving his young children behind gnawed at him. While he loathed the cramped domestic flights in economy class, Smith found the more spacious international business class somewhat bearable, primarily due to the potential for sleep. Being over six feet tall, he never quite "folded" comfortably in economy class. His Pacific crossing, however, was far from uneventful.

Boarding the Qantas 747, Smith was greeted like royalty as he ascended the stairs to the upper deck. Having stowed his bag in the overhead compartment and exchanged pleasantries with a few flight attendants, an attractive stewardess offered him a drink. He jestingly commented about it being "5 pm somewhere" and accepted the champagne. After making room for the passenger accessing the window seat, Smith attempted a cordial greeting, only to be met with an aloof disregard.

Undeterred, Smith tried to strike up a conversation. "G'day mate," he began, not waiting for a response. "I plan on catching some shut-eye for quite a while once we're in the air. Would you prefer this aisle seat instead?"

Taken aback by Smith's directness, the fellow passenger — an American, judging by his accent — curtly declined, never once making eye contact.

Slightly put off by his briskness, Smith persisted, explaining his plan to pop a pill and sleep for hours on end.

Again, the man declined, this time finally turning to look at Smith.

"OK, no worries," Smith replied, deciding the man was simply one of those who preferred to keep to themselves. On the plus side, the spacious business class seating would keep them comfortably distanced during the flight. Despite his gruff demeanour, Smith couldn't help but feel a twinge of concern as he noticed the man's heavy breathing and hefty frame, signs of the strain from the small climb to the upper deck.

Breakfast was served, living up to the high standards Smith expected of Qantas. He then settled down to watch a movie. His wife Bec had made him promise not to watch any new releases "she might enjoy," as they regularly went to the cinema for their monthly "date night." She was not keen on him spoiling her movie choice by having already seen it. After a few instances of Smith's "been-there-seen-that" response to movie suggestions, Bec had put her foot down. Smith had since learned to sit through a repeat viewing patiently, feigning ignorance if he'd seen the film previously.

After reviewing the presentation he was to give on his Asia Pacific business, Smith put away his computer and set up for his intended long sleep. He asked for a second blanket, which was cheerfully provided by the flight steward, located his eye cover and earplugs, popped his 10mg of benzodiazepine and wondered if he would hallucinate when he woke. It had got him before. Once, on his first trip to China, in business class, with both the aisle and window seat controls in the middle, he had woken into a sedated stupor and tried to bring his seat upright. He was frustrated with the unresponsive controls and was trying the "up" and "down" buttons repeatedly, thinking he'd got a dud seat. He noticed the elderly Chinese woman to his right moving up and down, thought it curious, but dismissed it. He still didn't put it together as she reclined again. Once Smith realised what he was doing he almost jumped out of his seat, horrified with the sideshow alley ride he'd given her. The expression on her face was priceless.

He was soon asleep.

Smith heard something that could only be described as a lady rousing on him. For a short time, it was accommodated into his dream until he realised the sound was coming from outside his head, around the earplugs. His mind was still foggy when he pulled down the eyepatch. What he saw made him almost scream until he recognised it was the face of the bloke next to him, only inches above his own. As he focused, he could see the bloke's face and his entire body semi-horizontally above him. His face was bright red and he was shaking. An involuntary "what the fuck!" escaped from Smith's mouth. It was then he saw the flight steward to his left standing next to the both of them and he connected the voice as hers. She was berating this American to "get off" Smith. Smith finally put it together. This idiot had attempted to get across his reclined self to get to the aisle and had tried to support his weight on the armrests as he went across. He'd either slipped or he didn't have the strength to hold and move himself across. He'd become stuck, barely able to stop himself from falling onto Smith. Smith lifted his arms out from the blanket as the bloke dropped a knee between his legs, just south of his wedding tackle. He pushed up and began to take the bloke's weight, probably just before he collapsed. His hands pushed into a soft pair of man-boobs before his force up seemed to make any difference. Smith was alarmed to feel that the bloke, once he felt supported, relaxed near the point of exhaustion, dropping the mass of his over-weight upper body onto Smith's arms.

"Holy shit!" Smith grunted. He finally made out what was, to that point, the flight steward's instructions.

"Sir, you need to get off him," again came the reasonable demand, but it fell on deaf ears.

Stirring from his drug-induced stupor, Smith found the situation absurdly humorous. "Oh, it's fine. I'm quite comfortable," he mumbled, though the reality was far from it. It was then the man fainted. His head dropped onto Smith's nose and and he suddenly found himself in a precarious situation. He was bearing the brunt of the man's considerable upper body weight, his breathing shallow and rapid, if present at all.

Turning his head to catch the steward's eye, Smith gave his uninvited bedfellow a solid bonk. "He's just fainted," he grunted. "You've got about twenty seconds before this bloke and I become much too intimate." As two male stewards made their way through the gawking passengers and began to haul the unconscious man off him, Smith barked out a warning.

"Stop! Stop!" His left arm, trapped against the armrest by the man's ample chest, was about to snap. "My arm!" Sensing the urgency, the stewards halted their efforts, reconsidering their strategy. They lifted rather than rolled the hefty passenger onto the floor, with Smith rolling back as soon as the weight was lifted. "Bloody hell!"

As a steward checked on Smith, the fallen passenger let out a panicked moan, regaining consciousness. As soon as they determined he was mentally coherent and physically stable, they guided him to the service area to recover. After a couple of minutes, the flight steward returned to Smith, the crowd of onlookers now dispersing.

"I'm so sorry, sir. That was unacceptable behaviour," she said.

"Ah, it's fine," Smith dismissed the concern while he adjusted his seat back to upright. "Poor bloke just found himself in a spot of bother."

"That's kind of you, sir. But such actions are indeed dangerous and not permissible."

Smith, curious, asked, "Why is that, apart from the obvious?"

"Such a fall can result in broken ribs or punctured lungs, among other injuries. You were lucky to be strong enough to handle it," she explained.

"I'm just grateful he didn't break my nose or my arm," Smith confessed.

After attending to a call, the steward returned, offering, "Mr. Smith, we'd like to offer you a first-class seat for the remainder of the flight to Los Angeles."

"Oh, that's kind but unnecessary," Smith replied, basking in the attention. "Why not give it to the other fellow? I'm perfectly fine here."

The steward smiled and left. Shortly after, the purser approached Smith.

"Mr. Smith? I'm James Cross, your purser." He extended his hand, which Smith took. "I understand we put you through quite an ordeal."

"No, you didn't," Smith emphasised, deflecting blame from the flight crew. "The bloke who decided to use me as a workout mat did." Despite the fatigue creeping into his eyes, Smith managed a smile.

"Very generous of you, sir. I understand Mandy offered you a first-class seat?"

"Yes."

"May I assist you there, Mr. Smith?"

Smith smiled. "Really, best if that other bloke goes. I'm fine here."

The purser seemed disappointed and then looked pensive. "Of course, Mr. Smith. It's just an unusual...."

It was then Smith realised he should take up their offer, which was easier for both him and the American. He did and relocated to first class, with their assistance. The Yank was still sitting in the servery as he walked towards it, then sauntered down the stairs.

The flight was otherwise uneventful and Qantas first class was excellent. He decided to ignore Bec's imploration about watching this or that movie and enjoyed what he wanted on the larger screen. He'd be happy to see it twice.

Transiting through LAX was almost an autopilot exercise for Smith. He spent time in the airline lounge and reaccustomed himself to being back in America. He was advised that his flight to Newark had been delayed which would result in a late arrival to his hotel. When finally he boarded the flight it was dark and he was tired. He took his aisle seat a couple of rows from the front. It was an older aircraft and while the business class benefits were apparent, a really comfortable seat wasn't one of them. He did his best to relax. He ate, set himself up with a small blanket, earplugs and an eyeshade. The earplugs he used were not the airline issue; he had some from one of the Gladstone customer sites. When inserted well into the ear canal, they were super-effective. He could hear almost nothing. Smith nodded off immediately.

He woke with a start, not sure how long he'd been asleep. A quick glance at his watch reminded him he'd not set it to Pacific time. The window shade was not closed and when he craned his neck and carefully leaned over the sleeping woman in the adjacent seat, he could see the Las Vegas lights. Damn. Not a good sleep. He needed a wee. Standing, he saw that everyone in business class was asleep; everyone except him, he lamented. The almost silent experience with earplugs still in place was surreal given his proximity to screaming jet engines. There wasn't the slightest bump or vibration to be felt. Smith staggered towards the toilet. Adjacent to the aircraft door, with her seat back on the aft wall of the toilet, sat their quite senior flight steward. She was reading, legs crossed. He was surprised and a little miffed that she didn't look up as he passed. He opened the toilet door, trying to be as quiet as possible. Once inside, he secured the door, lifted the toilet seat with a besocked foot and opened his pants fly zip. He felt worn out. He began to wee and felt a sizable fart coming down as he relaxed. A considerable seismic sensation in his backside was noted with ambivalence. After finishing his tinkle, he pressed the flush button, zipped himself back up and...

"Oh shit." Smith froze. A feeling of dread overcame him. His backside was at the level of the flight steward's head and what separated them was not a bulkhead. It was the thinnest of walls. Did she hear that fart? He washed his hands, dried them, composed himself and then opened the toilet door. He took his time closing the door and took the first careful step past the steward. She was looking up at him with an unmistakably admonishing expression. Smith averted his eyes, terribly embarrassed. Oh God. He made his way back to his seat, being cautious not to so much as glance in the direction of the steward. Fumbling with the insufficient blanket, he wondered why stuff like that seemed only happen to him.

He cringed when he thought of the next meal service...

Can't Believe You Did That...

After wrapping up the U.S. training and returning to Brisbane, Smith took a few days to recover from jet lag. The following week was filled with preparation for a significant presentation he was leading at a chemical plant in Brisbane's industrial area. It was effectively the Asia Pacific launch for the new on-line analyser. The weekend rolled around, packed with typical family activities. His daughter, Julie, had run a fever on Friday night, but was better by morning. They decided to take a drive down to the Gold Coast for one last April swim before the water turned too chilly. They had to be back that night as Bec's sister and her family were visiting on Sunday. He enjoyed their company; Bruce was a good bloke and they relished a drink and a barbecue.

Sunday morning arrived, and Smith was up early tidying the backyard. The Barrys had twin boys, about three or four years old, who were a lively handful but heaps of fun. Julie and Sally found them too boisterous; any playmates not interested in dolls and Barbies were apparently a bore.

The Barrys showed up late Sunday afternoon. Bruce had an esky in tow, while Mel carried a pavlova. The twins dashed past without a word, each eager to claim the best toys first. They typically ended up disappointed by the predominance of "girl stuff" in the house, but the half-built cubby house in the mango tree out back usually served as a decent diversion.

The afternoon went well. Bruce and Mel operated a small earthmoving company, and they had just invested in a new piece of machinery. Smith didn't recognise the machine's name but nodded and made supportive noises nonetheless. The twins eventually grew restless. With a couple of beers in his system, Smith offered to find some toys that might pique their interest, leaving Bruce to supervise the steaks and sausages on the grill.

Smith headed upstairs to the girls' room, trailed surreptitiously by the twins who had correctly surmised that something of interest might be in the offing. The girls were off elsewhere. Once inside the room, the twins began eagerly rummaging through the "old toy" box, which probably should have been discarded years ago. Most of its contents were summarily dismissed. Smith fetched another box from the cupboard, a move that had the twins flocking around it like puppies at a food bowl. The differences between boys and girls were already glaringly obvious.

Robert, the more outgoing of the twins, pulled out a curious object with a large suction cup on the end.

"What's this?" he asked.

Smith grinned, remembering the toy. "It's for babies to play with in the car. It sticks to the window." The spinning toy part was missing, leaving it resembling a colourful drain plunger.

"We're not babies," Sam retorted, sounding slightly offended even at their tender age.

Robert seized the toy from Sam and, reaching as high as his tiny stature would allow, tried to whack it onto the window. It was clear he hadn't grasped the concept of the suction cup. Smith pressed the toy onto the window, and the twins' eyes lit up at the novelty. Both stretched their arms out towards it, but were unable to reach. Smith thought better than to lift them up; he was certain they'd hit the deck if the suction cup gave way. He glanced around for another smooth surface to adhere the toy to.

The boys, growing more boisterous and demanding, were quick to vie for his attention. Acting on impulse and aiming to amuse, Smith moistened the suction cup with a bit of spit and, to his surprise, managed to stick it onto his forehead while kneeling. The moment he let go and pulled a silly face, the boys squealed in delight. They both lunged for it, narrowly avoiding poking Smith's eye in their enthusiasm. Despite their tugs and pulls, the resilient suction cup held its ground. Smith got into character, crawling around and making mock unicorn noises as both boys hung onto his makeshift "horn." To his delight, he found he could engage with boys as well as girls — his experience having been limited to the latter until then.

This playful chaos continued until Sally and Julie stormed into their bedroom, taken aback by the unexpected sight of their dad cavorting with the troublesome twins. They dashed back out, loaded with tales of how Daddy and the boys were wreaking havoc in the room.

A few minutes later, the twins too wandered off, leaving Smith alone with his new forehead attachment. He yanked it off, the suction breaking with a "pop," and marvelled at its unexpected strength. He retrieved his beer from the kitchen on his way back to the backyard, running into Bec at the back screen door.

"I was wondering…" Bec halted mid-sentence, squinting and raising her hand towards Smith's head in disbelief. "What on earth…?" Her expression suggested Smith had suffered a head injury. "What on earth is that…?"

"What?" Smith wiped his face, assuming he had smudged crayon or something on it.

"On your forehead? What...? Did you hit yourself?" Bec was trying to put the pieces together.

Smith, growing a bit annoyed, retorted, "What?"

"Just go look in the mirror, will you?" she advised.

He obliged, turning to the hallway mirror. Staring at his reflection, he uttered an exasperated, "Oh, shit."

Bec followed him, asking, "What is it?" She sounded genuinely worried, thinking he had hurt himself. The unusual shape...

"Oh, shit." Smith turned to face Bec. "It's the window stick-on toy for the car," he said, his expression deadpan.

It took a moment for Bec to process this. She looked at him as though she was about to expire, and then burst into laughter right in his face, doubling over in uncontrollable hilarity. She stopped, turned back to him, and erupted in laughter again, this time so hard that she collapsed to the ground, hysterical. Gasping for breath, she managed to spit out, "Steve, you bloody idiot!" Smacking the floor, she let loose another shrill cackle, now in tears from laughing so hard.

Mel walked into the house, uncertain whether the sounds she heard were from uncontrollable laughter or hysterical crying. At first, seeing Bec on the floor, she was concerned, but quickly realised her sister was rolling with laughter.

"What's so funny?" Mel asked, trying to understand the situation.

In response, Bec pointed to her husband from the floor, in between bouts of laughter. Her face was soaked with tears.

Mel turned to Smith, who stood there emotionless. An intensely coloured, perfectly round bruise adorned the centre of his forehead, hard to miss like a traffic light. Approaching Smith, Mel suppressed her laughter, still uncertain of the cause of the spectacle.

"Suction cup...toy...idiot..." Bec managed to gasp out between laughs, "Oh, I'm gonna wet myself!"

"Oh, no," Mel began giggling. "You didn't." Her giggles soon escalated into a full-fledged fit of laughter.

Smith returned his gaze to the mirror. In just a short time, the bruise had darkened to an intense brown-black. He found himself estimating how long it would take to fade.

"That's so..." Mel trailed off, searching for the right word.

"Stupid...!" Bec hollered from the floor, her laughter reaching new heights.

Moments later, Bruce, the twins, and the girls all rushed into the house, attracted by the uproar. The girls joined in the laughter, simply delighted by the infectious joviality. Smokey, the family pet, darted through their legs, misjudged a leap, and toppled face-first over Bec, adding to the chaos. The twins, seizing the opportunity, scampered off to raid the girls' room.

Bruce, however, didn't laugh. Instead, he found himself empathising with his fellow man. Two women laughing hysterically at another man's misfortune was a sight all too familiar. He shot Smith a commiserating look; his friend was standing there with a half-smile, clearly in damage control mode. Smith was less than a day away from the most important presentation of his career, a fact that Bec seemed to have forgotten amidst her fit of laughter.

"Mate, you look pretty silly," Bruce commented, trying to lighten the mood.

Smith looked at himself again. This was a real problem. Glancing down at Bec, who was still rolling on the floor, he extended a hand. "Come on you, get up off the floor."

About ten minutes later, they were back at the barbecue, which Bruce had wisely turned off before rushing inside. The sight of Smith reignited fits of laughter in Bec and Mel, while Bruce shook his head, smiling. They attempted to compose themselves. Smith let out a resigned sigh.

"Yeah, OK, I get it. Now how do you want your steak?"

"Medium, thanks. Same colour as that dot on your head, I think!" Mel couldn't help but chuckle, prompting another round of laughter from Bec. Wine spilled out of their glasses.

Bruce attempted to steer the conversation towards a solution. "What do you think you will do?" he asked, his tone serious.

Mel interjected before Smith could respond, "About what?"

A brief silence followed, during which Bec fought to keep a straight face. Bruce pressed on, "Steve has an important presentation tomorrow morning."

"You're fucking kidding..." Mel caught herself, casting a guilty look towards the kids for her slip of the tongue.

Smith turned to them, opening his arms wide, the BBQ tongs flicking some fat over towards Smokey. "No, not kidding. For real. So any suggestions gratefully received." The bruise was now almost black but no less well defined. It looked, by any person's account, ridiculous.

"How did it get so intense?" Mel was truly inquisitive. "It's like..." She stopped herself.

Bec shouted, "A whopping hickey!" Mel burst out laughing again, wine spraying from her mouth over one of the twins' legs. "You bugger!" She was referring to Bec's timing.

"Mummy! Yak!" was the protest from Sam.

"Like if that's not what you first thought." Smith dismissed their continuing mirth. "Come on. I need help."

"OK. Sorry." Bec looked at him. "You're right. This is serious." Bec stopped, easily able to burst out laughing again but controlling herself. "Can you postpone the presentation?" her question still came as a chortle.

"Nup." Smith flipped a steak, causing a flame around it and a loud sizzle. "Yanks here for it." Smith had called both of them earlier that day at their hotel to welcome them back to Australia.

"What about foundation?" Mel suggested. "Could that work?"

"Maybe. Depends how dark it's going to get." Bec nodded. "But that's our best bet."

"How 'bout a bandage? Like you cut your head or something?" Bruce shifted in his chair. "If the makeup idea doesn't work."

All ideas were amassed and they set to finding a solution so that Smith could get to sleep without the matter on his mind. Much to the amusement of Sally and Julie, the ladies set upon him with foundation. By the time they'd finished with him, Smith looked like he had a piece of a doll skin grafted to his forehead. They both stood back and shook their head.

"It's his skin." Bec concluded. "'Skin's no good."

"Yep."

"OK, let's get it off."

Once the makeup idea was abandoned, Bruce moved in. He asked Bec for some sticking plaster and some mercurochrome. A small dab of antiseptic escaping from the side of the intended bandage placement and a large enough plaster strategically off-set the absurdity and symmetry of Smith's bruise. Smith excused himself to assess the remedy in the hall mirror.

"Yep. I can make that work."

Voluntary Disconnection

"So you're sure you're okay with this?" Bec Smith stood with one hand on her hip, the other reaching out inquisitively, trying to coax out any latent hesitation her husband might be harbouring.

"As I said this morning, yesterday, and last week — yes, Bec. I am okay with it." Smith avoided his wife's gaze, knowing his tendency to smile when trying to maintain a serious facade. He flipped his watch onto his wrist and fastened the buckle. A shout from Sally in the hallway was met with a stern "Hey!" from both parents.

"Gotta go, darling." Smith took his wife by the hips and kissed her on the lips, then the cheek. "See ya." He felt surprisingly light-hearted that morning.

"Bye, darling." Bec held her sceptical expression a beat longer, ensuring Smith saw it. "I hope you're not doing this for me, Steve."

As he walked out of the room, Smith retorted playfully, "Of course, I'm doing this for you, Bec. Which husband ever got his nuts chopped off for himself?" He shot her a cheeky grin before disappearing down the hall.

During his commute, Smith tuned into the radio news, appreciating the clear, cloudless day. When his phone rang, he glanced at it, hoping the caller wouldn't ruin his good mood.

"Hey, mate." He was relieved to hear Bill Leighton's voice on the other end.

"What's happening?" Smith asked casually.

"Not much here, but I heard from Anne this morning you're joining the ranks of the neutered."

"Jesus, what the fuck do those girls not talk about?" Smith was referring to his wife and Anne Leighton's unabashed sharing of supposedly confidential information, the latest tidbit being his impending vasectomy.

Leighton, who had undergone a vasectomy about eighteen months prior, asked, "Local or general?"

"What?"

"Are you getting a local or general anaesthetic?"

"Dunno. Haven't got that far." Smith asked for Leighton's experience, and soon they were bantering about the procedure. The conversation ended with some crude humour, leaving Smith chuckling to himself.

The morning at work flew by. Being a Friday, they went for a pub lunch and a couple of beers. Smith took the opportunity to ask his colleague Clint Hastings, an electronics technician, about his experience.

"Your kids are teenagers now, right?" Smith asked.

"Yep. Fourteen and sixteen." Hastings replied, mouth full of coleslaw.

"Got the snip?"

Hastings paused, mouth agape, "That's a personal question, isn't it?" His joke was clear, but he played it straight. "Mind your own fucking business."

Smith knew he wouldn't have cared about the question. He remained expressionless. "So? Have you?"

Hastings had resumed chewing and was no longer looking at him. "Yep."

"Local or general?" Smith pushed out the question in a monotone drawl, playing down his interest in it.

"Local. Why? Getting the snip?"

"Maybe."

"You mean yes."

"Why yes?"

Hastings stopped mid-chew again. "Yes, because you're the sort of bloke who would do it."

Smith jerked back his head a bit. "What does that mean?"

"Means you're the sort of bloke who would agree to get it done."

Curiously, Smith felt embarrassed and a little annoyed.

Hastings went on. "Considerate. You're a gentleman, mate."

"Nothing to do with it." Smith was trying to distance himself from that label.

"Sure it has." Hastings leaned towards him. "Many blokes wouldn't even consider it. Like it affects the sanctity of their dick or something."

Smith nearly snorted beer through his nose. "Jesus…" He shook his head to protest Hastings's incorrigibility.

"So why you getting it done?"

"Didn't say I am."

Hastings rolled his eyes over the top of his next forked mouthful. "OK… then…why are you thinking about it?"

"Bit of a personal question, isn't it?"

Hastings shook his head as if to shake snow off it and screwed up his brow. "I just told you, shithead."

"No, you didn't. You told me that you had it done. That's not nearly as personal as why you got it done."

"Man, you got hangups."

Smith smiled. "Nah. Really. It's just that I wanna get Bec off the pill."

"And you hate frangas."

"And I hate frangas." Both men nodded knowingly.

Hastings lifted his beer so as to toast his workmate. "Fuck frangas."

Smith lifted his beer and they touched glasses. "Yeah. Fuck frangas." He drained the contents of his glass. "Your shout, snippy."

Hastings was on his way to the bar, laughing, before Smith's empty glass hit the table. "You're a 'general' bloke for sure." It was shot out like an insult as he swerved around two big blokes in the next table.

It was weeks before the subject came up between Smith and his wife but there wasn't a day that went by that both didn't think of it. It was one of those quiet, calm week nights with the girls asleep and nothing on TV. Bec had walked in with her nightgown purposely open and Smith double-took and then it was "on." They were in bed together touching, talking, whispering and…

"I wonder what it will be like?"

Smith had his lips gently around his wife's erect nipple. He didn't disengage so his question came out muffled. "What?"

"After your…you know…after your procedure."

Smith blew his wife's nipple out of his mouth with a dry, lippy exhalation and pushed himself up onto his hands. "Boy, you know how to kill a mood, don't you?"

Bec brought her hands over her face and did a peek-a-boo through them.

"Sorry." She pushed it out through a forced smile. "I guess I'm learning about this, too."

Smith rolled off her. "You don't have to know anything about it. It's my balls under attack." He smiled.

"Can you quit saying that?" She rolled onto her right arm, struggling to pull the sheet over herself with Smith having it pinned beneath him. He remained immobile.

"Hey, I'm not the one with the issue here."

Bec glared at him, shaking her head in disapproval.

"What?" Smith was oddly amused by the exchange.

"I'm having trouble grasping why you're so okay with this."

Smith raised his hips off the sheet, allowing his wife to drag it up over her shoulders. This move revealed his now-flaccid penis. He gestured towards it, as if it were a spectacle.

"See what you've done? He's hearing all this. He's afraid he's about to be chopped off."

"Steve!" Bec protested, "Can you cut it out! I'm serious. I want to know."

Smith raised a surrendering hand. "Alright, alright. There won't be any difference."

"You're sure?" Now, concern seemed to cast a shadow on Bec's face. "I mean, there's no risk...well...you know..." Her hand trailed off, vaguely gesturing toward his penis.

"What? You mean that I won't be able to get a hard-on if the operation goes south?"

"Well...yes," she nodded.

"None. They aren't going anywhere near my dick. And I'll still be able to make a mess."

"Yes, I know that you'll still ejaculate. I read about that," Bec informed him in a straightforward manner.

"So, what's the problem? You'll be off the pill, we can make love anytime we want, and we won't have any unplanned kids." Smith rolled onto his back. "'S'all good," he declared, flashing a satisfied smile.

Bec scooted over to her husband and kissed him. She nestled her mouth against his ear. "Thank you. I know you're doing this for me," she whispered.

"You're welcome." His last word hitched to a squeak as her hand found its way to his penis. The touch made him jump a little. "Now, you're very welcome."

It was another month before Smith managed to snag a referral for the vasectomy. He booked an appointment at the local medical centre, notorious for offering nothing more than a ten-minute consultation. This, however, suited his purpose perfectly. He didn't wish to indulge in a lengthy discussion. His strategy was simple: get in, get out.

He'd opted for a local anaesthetic rather than being put under completely. Enough blokes had weighed in on the matter to assure him of a diverse range of responses:

"No worries."

"Don't be a wuss. You only need a local."

"Mate, you're off your rocker if you don't get a general. My brother-in-law…"

"Local. Sore balls for a couple of days. No drama."

"Why the bloody hell doesn't your missus get snipped if she's the one wanting off the pill?"

And the like…

Naturally, Bill Leighton had dared him to go for the local, "Just so he could see how he stood up to it, versus having your balls seared off."

With the urologist's referral in hand, he scheduled the appointment for the following week, cashing in on a cancellation. Although some business travel prevented him from undergoing the procedure immediately, he was eager to lock in a date. His sudden urgency was perplexing. Bec voiced her thoughts on the matter before dinner one night.

"Maybe you're just trying to get it over with, to stop dwelling on it."

"Yeah, probably."

Bec started the kettle. "So, how soon after can you use it?"

"Dunno. Didn't ask that. I suppose we'll have to wait for it to clear through before you quit the pill."

"What pill?" Sally entered the room, her large doll being hauled by its leg, and Smokey, the family dog, playfully tugged at the doll's arm. Smokey growled, imitating a triumphant lioness on the Serengeti.

"No pill, darling. Just some adult talk."

Smith opened his mouth to speak but his wife interjected. "No...no...nooo..." A look of scorn crossed her face.

"As if I was about to bring up that topic," Smith retorted, mirroring her expression.

"Talk about what?" Sally whirled her toy, Missus Chips, around her legs, Smokey having relinquished his hold.

"Nothing, darling." Bec knelt down in front of her child. "Just some adult talk."

Julie trudged in backwards, dragging a box full of toys into the kitchen and leaving it in the doorway. She pivoted towards the fridge.

"Hey, don't leave that there. Your dad will trip over it."

"Cheers." Smith raised his hands in surrender. "Like I'm the clumsy one in the family."

"When is Daddy going to the hospital?"

The parents exchanged a glance of mutual blame, each accusing the other of being careless with their words within the kids' earshot. Knowing they wouldn't want to lie to their girls, they had to handle this tactfully.

"In a couple of weeks."

Julie swivelled to face her father. "Are you sick, Daddy?"

"No, I'm not sick."

"Why you going to hos-pital?" Sally, unable to pronounce the word correctly, was visibly confused and annoyed that she'd likely been the last to hear about this family development.

"Mummy will tell you," Smith called back at the family as he walked from the kitchen, box of toys in hand, throwing a playful smirk at his wife.

It was a day before Smith's specialist appointment, about which he felt no concern. "I've read about it. Nothing to worry about," he assured Bec. "Just a meet-n-greet with the bloke who's going to neuter me."

"Steve! Can you please stop that?"

"Alright. Just trying to lighten the mood."

After rummaging through a pile of bills on their shared desk and cursing his way to the referral letter, Smith left for work late, allowing time to make his appointment. He checked in at reception.

"Steve Smith to see Dr Harrison."

The receptionist returned his greeting with a smile and handed him a four-page form, which he filled out absentmindedly. He returned it, receiving no acknowledgement.

"Please take a seat, Mr Smith. Dr Harrison will be with you shortly."

Walking back to his seat, Smith found it strange that the doctor was addressed as "Dr", not "Mr". He thought most surgeons preferred "Mr."

Just as he settled into his chair, another woman called his name. He sprang back up, took a step, swung back to his seat to retrieve his mobile phone from the table, and walked toward the woman. As he neared her, she extended her hand confidently.

"I'm Dr Harrison. Pleased to meet you, Mr Smith."

Smith froze for a fraction of a second. "A woman? A woman performing vasectomies? Blimey, why would a woman want to do that? She's going to see my privates. Why would any woman choose this?" His momentary pause ended. He shook the woman's hand.

"Pleased to meet you, Doctor."

His brief panic continued as he followed the doctor into her room.

"Please, take a seat, Mr Smith."

"So, Mr Smith." She scanned his paperwork. "You were referred by your GP. Doctor... ah... Singh, as I see... yes, Dr Singh."

"Yes, it's time for the snip," Smith said, aiming for a nonchalant tone. He wasn't being paid to be serious here; that was the doctor's job.

They navigated the usual "are you sure you want to do this?" discussion. The doctor then leaned back from the paperwork, turning her attention fully towards him.

"Now, Mr. Smith. I need to organise an anaesthetist for you." She continued writing. "It has been over ten years since your last general anaesthetic so you can choose either a general or a local anaesthetic."

Smith was ready for that subject. "Which do you prefer, Doc?" He thought there was some sense in the question.

The surgeon glanced down at her feet, then up at Smith, arching her eyebrows. Her tone was stoically flat. "Mr. Smith, I have no preference. My job is to sterilise you through a surgical procedure in which I excise a section of your vas deferens and tie it off. Whether you're a conscious spectator to that or not doesn't concern me."

Feeling somewhat embarrassed, Smith mumbled his choice. "Local. Thanks."

"Alright, fine. My assistant will be in touch to set a date, or you can discuss it with her today."

Smith looked at her, puzzled and for the first time, a little frantic. He craved some form of reassurance from the doctor, something like, "Well, you seem like a sturdy bloke; a local should be fine for you."

But before he could rid himself of this thought, the doctor was standing with her hand outstretched. "Goodbye, Mr. Smith."

Then he was outside her office, facing the receptionist. Three women occupied the waiting room, the youngest a pretty lady no older than twenty-five.

"We need to book a time for your vasectomy, Mr. Smith," the receptionist announced, her voice carrying to every corner of the room. The complete lack of discretion was unappreciated. Smith pulled a face of annoyance that the receptionist didn't bother to acknowledge. The date was set for three weeks later. He left without receiving any semblance of gratitude for his business and received a nonchalant glance from the woman nearest to the door.

"What a bloody circus." He grumbled to himself once outside.

A few days later, Bec Smith almost dropped a plate of potatoes and nearly stepped on the dog in response to what she heard. The girls were waiting at the dinner table in the living room.

"Steve! No... no... no, you can't just have a local anaesthetic!"

"Why not? They're my balls!" Smith forced out the last words in a whisper, trying not to alarm the girls. "Move over, Smokey."

After setting the plate on the table and asking Sally and Julie to serve themselves, she returned to the kitchen. "But why would you do that? Why endure that pain?"

Smith put on a mock terrified face and held his hands to his cheeks. "Pain? You didn't mention pain!"

"Steve! I'm serious." She overlooked Julie dropping a small piece of chicken in front of the pug, assuming it was too small to have a bone, and dismissed it. "What's wrong with a general anaesthetic?"

Smith sidestepped her to reach the table, where he leaned over Sally to cut up her meat. Sally watched her dad upside down as he did so. "Why opt for a general if it's not absolutely necessary?" Smith kissed his daughter on the head before walking to his chair.

"What's a general?" Julie was quick to question, but her query was brushed off.

"Take off, Smokey." Smith slowly swung his leg to nudge the dog away, who deftly avoided his foot. "I swear, I'm gonna step on that dog one of these days." The pug scuttled from under the table, its nappy slipping down its rear.

"Mum, Smokey's nappy is coming off," Sally pointed out. Smith shot Bec a look that wasn't well received. He had been trying to get the dog fixed, but Bec had explained to the girls what was happening and they seemed unfazed, not connecting the dots to the fact that the same process might happen to humans.

"Perhaps the mutt should trade places with me." Smith gestured towards Smokey, out of the girls' earshot post-dinner. "When are we going to get her fixed?"

Bec loaded the cutlery into the dishwasher. "After you are. Let's handle one procedure at a time."

"What? You're equating my vasectomy to the dog's desexing?" Smith was baffled by the comparison. "Really?"

His wife brushed off his jest with a wave of her hand. "Don't be ridiculous." Bec studied him, trying to discern whether he was joking. "We'll get her fixed as soon as possible." She couldn't think of anything else to add.

Smith watched the pug scamper off, nappy secured in place. "You realise she'll be attracting every scruffy mongrel within cooey," Smith called out to ensure he was heard in the next room.

Bec rushed in, admonishing him. "Shh, for heaven's sake."

"What?"

"Do you want to initiate the birds and the bees talk with our girls right now?"

"Don't be absurd, Bec."

"Just be patient. I'll get her fixed as soon as possible, but money's tight, as you know. So, we're keeping her indoors for now while she's in heat."

"I thought the pound only gave out rescue dogs that were already desexed?" Smith's memory of the pug's adoption from last year was fuzzy.

Bec shut the fridge door. "No, remember it was a foster dog arrangement, not a rescue dog situation."

"Foster dog? So someone else owns Smokey?"

"What?"

Smith altered his query. "What's a foster dog place?"

Bec pushed a chair toward the table, accidentally thwacking her husband's knee. "Okay, that's the end of this conversation. I'm not having..." She caught herself speaking loudly and lowered her voice to just above a whisper after a glance toward the lounge room. "I'm not having the girls fretting over losing Smokey."

"Yeah, yeah, alright." Smith was growing as impatient with the conversation as his wife. He figured he'd have to tolerate a dog in a nappy occasionally. It was better than her first period. Bec had to explain the blood to the girls then have an unnecessary vet visit resulting from their worry, which was a waste of money. Smith was certain he'd been told that the pug had been fixed, but he'd never checked for a scar. He shook his head and wrote off the whole situation as eccentric women's business he wasn't going to meddle with.

It had only been a few weeks since Smith began organising his vasectomy, although if he was being honest, the wheels had been set in motion back in February with his initial GP consultation. Finally, it was D-Day or rather, V-Day.

Bec parked the car in front of the hospital's outpatient department. "Are you sure you don't want me to come with you?"

"I'm good, Bec." Smith opened the car door and pushed it open with his foot. "The nurse will call you when I'm ready to be picked up."

She leaned over and kissed him. "Be careful, love. I love you."

"I love you, too." Smith kissed her again. He swung his legs out and stood up, leaning back into the car. "Oh, and you need to bring a jar when you pick me up."

"A jar? For what?" Bec looked puzzled.

"My balls."

Before she could protest, Smith shut the door, stifling her response. He waved her away, her head shaking.

"Alright," he thought to himself, taking a deep breath. "Let's get this done."

As he ambled towards the reception area, the words of a storeman echoed in his head. "Bugger that. Why doesn't your missus get the snip if she's off the pill?" That sentiment had been shared thrice, albeit in varying phrases. Smith questioned if he was being "too obliging."

The reception desk wasn't hard to find, and the lady there was as pleasant as could be. Smith abstained from any attempts at humour, feeling notably deflated. He was directed to another waiting area where he received a wristband and was shown to a cubicle with a hospital bed, adorned with a familiar blue gown. A male nurse entered, introduced himself and ran through a series of identity verification questions.

"Leave your bag on the bed, and we'll keep it safe. Once you've got your gown on, I'll be back to prepare you." With that, the nurse exited, pulling the curtain wide open, leaving Smith to note the absence of privacy. Popping his head back in, the nurse added, "Split at the back." Seeing Smith's confusion, he clarified, "The gown. The opening goes at the back. And don't forget those booties." Then, he was off again.

Smith donned the gown, puzzled as to why the opening should be at the back. He was there for urology, not proctology. He found himself missing Bec, who would've chuckled patiently, perhaps even sympathetically, at his jest.

The male nurse reappeared, wheeling a trolley laden with kidney-shaped bowls covered by folded towels. He closed the curtain behind him.

"Alright, let's get you prepared. Are you shaved, Mr. Smith?"

Smith recoiled in surprise. "What?"

"Downstairs? Shaved?"

Smith found the question absurd. The nurse would find out soon enough anyway. He's messing with me, he thought.

"Nope."

"OK." The nurse's response was almost melodic. "Let's get this protective sheet under you and get it done."

Smith hadn't even considered the prospect of shaving his nether regions. Years ago, Bec had suggestively offered to do it for him, which he'd hesitantly agreed to. The result was a rather fruit bowl-esque spectacle. The prickly regrowth a week later had been uncomfortable, causing constant squirming. That was the last time he'd done that.

"Can I do it myself?"

The nurse clutched the razor to his chest dramatically. "Mr. Smith, I'm hurt. I've been shaving balls for years." He slowly lowered his gaze to meet Smith's, maintaining a grave expression. "You know what they say in the movies." He clenched the shaver tightly. "We can do this the easy way or the hard way." His expression remained unwavering.

Smith's level of discomfort was on the rise. Despite the absurd stand-off, he complied and found himself laid bare, balls being tenderly lathered in warm water. The nurse's actions were nimble and professional, and before long, Smith was smoothly shaven and prepped for surgery.

With the nurse gone and his freshly shaven area dried, Smith contemplated calling his wife. He missed her. But he thought better of it. A missed call could trigger an alarm and have her calling back, worried. The curtain rustled, and a tall man in a grey suit entered, introducing himself as the anaesthetist.

"I'm not having anaesthetic." Smith began to get more concerned about his surgery.

Selecting his words with precision, the anaesthetist explained that Smith would receive an injection in the back of his hand, administering a "soothing drug" to make him slightly "dopey" for a more relaxed surgical experience.

Smith offered a nervous chuckle. "The only thing that could calm me down now would be a dozen beers."

Catching the humour, the doctor jested, "Oh, you'd be surprised by the cocktails we offer." Clearly, he was trying to beat a swift retreat, but Smith wasn't about to let him off the hook and amped up his cheeky banter.

"Hey, Doc," Smith called. The anaesthetist, already heading out, turned back slowly. "When my pants are off and you're about to stick that needle in my hand..." The anaesthetist raised a hand to cut him off.

"Let me guess, Mr. Smith," he interjected, removing his glasses. "You're going to ask me not to say 'just a little prick'." Standing a bit straighter, he revealed a sly grin.

Smith sunk back, deflated. "Heard it all before, Mr. Smith," the anaesthetist chortled on his way out.

Reeling from that verbal lashing, Smith was feeling quite deflated. When they came to collect him, he was surprised to be led on foot to the operating theatre. He passed a long corridor to his right and thought that way out was his last chance to bolt. They'd never catch him and he could jog home, bare arse and all, he thought. Then he was in the operating theatre.

The intimidating array of equipment and bustling medical professionals paying him no mind unsettled him. He wanted them to all stop what they were doing and acknowledge, by acclimation, the magnanimity of his actions in voluntarily having his virility disconnected. But, nothing. Helped onto the table, he was asked the identity verification questions again, and his booties were removed.

He felt incredibly vulnerable, akin to Anne Boleyn kneeling before the executioner. More personnel and gear encroached, boxing him in. Out of nowhere, the anaesthetist reappeared and started talking to him. His feigned pleasantness grated on Smith, who was in no mood to play nice. He was frightened.

The cocky anaesthetist confidently took Smith's hand, turning it so the back was exposed. After swabbing it, he unveiled the needle. Smith inwardly groaned, craving some explanation as the sting intensified. It was definitely more than just "a little prick." He waited for the knockout effect, but he only felt slightly "disconnected."

Suddenly, he was gripped by panic. He should've chosen general anaesthesia. He tried to psyche himself up — "Don't be a wuss," but to his shock, he heard "wuss" escape his own lips. He realised he was speaking aloud. He froze. The surgeon was now positioned near his hips, her face masked. He attempted a smile, perhaps she reciprocated, but he didn't register it. His panic ebbed slightly because she was standing still, not near his feet. Then it dawned on him; his feet weren't the subject of the surgery. Bloody hell! She was there for his wedding tackle, which now swung freely with his legs propped up. The doctor began a dialogue about something. He wasn't sure if it was a comment or question for him. Overwhelmed, he felt everything was moving too fast. A theatre nurse appeared to his left, gently touching his chest. The surgeon was examining his manhood, akin to a chef contemplating which side of a fish to fillet first. Cold liquid ran down his balls. A sting, harsher than he'd ever felt, cut through the "dopey" drug. Another sting, a burning sensation, then another sting. "Bloody hell, it hurt like a bitch!" The pain amplified, unrelenting. Then abruptly, it stopped. The surgeon glanced up at him, then back to her work. She proceeded to the other side.

"Sweet bloody hell!" slipped out from Smith's lips. Then, the pain ceased. His balls felt cold. Or perhaps they were missing entirely. How the hell could he tell? In his distressed state, Smith instinctively held his breath, just like one does when ripping off a Band-Aid.

A nurse's gentle pressure on his neck broke into his thoughts. "Breathe, Mr. Smith. Breathe." Her hand again pressed into his neck, but he wasn't listening. Whatever was happening down there wasn't fine by him. Then he felt something being tugged, something that had never been yanked before. It was as if something was threading through his ball sack, the other end tethered to his earlobe.

Next, he heard the anaesthetist's voice and saw his face looming overhead. "Mr. Smith, you need to breathe or I'll have to administer more anaesthesia." A light slap on his face punctuated his statement. Smith felt like he was about to faint. He wished to be anywhere but there.

Suddenly, he heard, "OK, he's fine." That same weatherman's voice. Evidently, Smith had resumed breathing. The memory of his vasectomy faded from there. He'd heard tales of some surgeons showcasing the excised snippet of the patient's vas deferens, but he had no recollection of such a presentation.

Coming to, Smith found himself in a different room devoid of curtains, a light blanket draped over his legs. His mind was foggy. A senior nurse was repeating his name, rousing him back to consciousness. An unfamiliar sound caught his attention. It sounded like a fart — a colossal one at that. An involuntary smile crept onto his face. He was emerging from the anaesthesia, still clueless about the fart's origin but fairly confident it wasn't him. He surveyed the room, noting a few elderly ladies. Two of them were dozing, but the one across from him was staring directly at him. She seemed not quite "back" yet.

Smith was unperturbed by her vacant gaze until she released an enormous fart, quite possibly the loudest he'd ever heard. Halfway through, she seemed to snap out of her stupor, realising the noise was her doing. She looked shaken and somewhat upset, yet for some reason, she didn't tear her gaze from Smith. Despite his best efforts to suppress it, laughter bubbled up from within him. The nurse seemed torn between scolding Smith and comforting her flustered, flatulent patient. She chose the latter.

"Let it go, Mrs. Matthews. Let it go," the nurse comforted, patting her on the hand. Just then, one of the other ladies let loose a formidable fart, adding fuel to the fire for poor Mrs. Matthews, who responded with an even longer, louder fart. Looking apologetically at the nurse, she finally diverted her gaze. The scene was too much for Smith, who was now crying from suppressed laughter and seriously risking a rupture of his fresh stitches or even an accident of his own.

The nurse gently released Mrs. Matthews's hand and walked over to him. "Mr. Smith, you need to be careful. You have fresh stitches."

"Uh…" Smith was just about to burst with stifled laughter, unable to utter a single word. Yet again, Mrs. Mathews released a fart, this one shorter and of a higher pitch than the last. The expression on her face was a strange mix of mortification and ecstasy. Smith could only look up at the nurse, tears streaming down his face, on the verge of snorting. It was as though he was caught in a no-man's land where farts, instead of Axis bullets, were whizzing past. He was trapped. All he wanted was for the relentless barrage to cease. The nurse proceeded to move down the ward towards the other women.

A second nurse entered the room and gave Smith a puzzled look, taking note of his tear-stained cheeks and watering eyes.

She focused on him for a moment, swept her gaze around the ward, took a few steps back, and then turned to face Smith once again. Leaning over him, she placed her hand on his arm.

"These ladies have just had colonoscopies. They've been pumped full of gas to facilitate the camera," she explained, looking at him to ensure he understood.

"Oh," Smith finally received his answer, "Oh."

Leaning closer, the nurse whispered, "My first couple of weeks here, I nearly wet myself trying to stifle my own laughter."

This comment caught Smith completely off guard. He grinned up at her.

"But seriously, if you don't stop laughing, we'll have to stitch you up again."

Smith could only shrug in a "what am I supposed to do" manner.

"We've called your wife, Rebecca. She should be here shortly."

Smith appreciated the professional use of his wife's name. "Thank you."

From the other end of the ward came another fart. Smith did his best to ignore it, but it was a struggle and his eyes were watering. The stifled laughter was causing his testicles to ache. He needed to blow his nose. Mrs. Matthews had now caught on to Smith's levity. She tried to cast disapproving glances at him, but her efforts were interrupted by two high-pitched, somewhat soggy, chirps. Smith lost it completely, a snot bubble expanding as he burst into tears.

Just then, Rebecca Smith arrived. Seeing her husband red-faced and teary-eyed, she covered her mouth and felt a surge of emotion herself.

"Oh, Steve," she dropped to hug him, smothering a sob. As she lifted up to hold his cheeks, she asked, "Are you okay?"

"Yeah. But we need to leave now," Smith wiped his eyes, akin to a dog bolting to the car after a vet visit, fearing a longer stay.

After a quick ID check and a round of observations by the nurse, and with a growing pile of used tissues on his blanket, Smith assured Bec that he was okay and promised to explain later. This confused her more than relieved her.

"Explain what?" She worried there might be a problem with his surgery.

Helping himself onto a wheelchair brought by the first nurse, who gave Rebecca a broad smile, Smith waved away her puzzlement at the nurse's comment, "You've got a live one there..." The nurse handed Bec the "home pack" of painkillers and post-surgery instructions before walking off towards the other end of the ward.

Bec was still distressed, wondering why her husband had been crying.

"Let's go," he said, as an orderly pushed him out to the pickup area and waited with him until Bec pulled up in the car. Smith thanked the orderly. His testicles were starting to throb.

As Bec drove off, Smith dried his eyes and carefully blew his nose once more. After a sharp wince at the first speed bump, he gingerly repositioned his groin.

Bec pulled over into a loading bay and looked over to him. "Seriously, Steve. Are you OK? You were crying in there. It was terrible."

"Yes, Bec, I am OK." He explained what had happened in the recovery room.

Bec Smith was perplexed. The last thing she expected to hear was how he was laughing uncontrollably after being sterilised. She abandoned further questioning at that point. "Oh, my God, Steve. You could have hurt yourself. I'm so glad you are ok."

Ahead of their arrival home, Smith volunteered information about the surgery. Smith told his wife that he didn't feel a thing. It was a lie to put her at ease. Maybe sometime later he would tell her. However, now he could propagate the bullshit he'd heard about "vasectomy by local anaesthetic" to any bloke who asks. It was a tradition and he'd earned his stripes.

"No problem, mate. It was easy."

Chainsaws and Promises

The mid-year westerly winds had come through Brisbane a few times. They were the distant effect of cold fronts that had moved across the lower six degrees of latitude of Western Australia, pushing heat into the south and cold in from the western Queensland desert. It was a dry, gusty wind that turned the self-consciousness of the loss of a summer tan into the embarrassment of fine flaky skin as it dried out. Steve Smith was at their back door overlooking the Allens' yard being mechanistic and low key in response to Bec's questions.

"What do you think?"

Smith looked across at the tree at the back of the Allens' house, right next to the fence. The wife-to-wife request was made for him to drop it as it had died and they thought it may fall and be a safety risk.

They had walked down to their back yard. "Who thinks that?" It was the first question Smith asked his Wife when the possibility of him helping was considered.

"Don't know." Bec was hanging newly washed clothes onto their ancient Hills Hoist. She turned away, tactically, to hide her disdain for the line of questioning that had commenced.

"I can assure you, that tree will be safe for years, if not decades. It's a Grey Gum. Hardwood. Last leaves only just dropped."

"Well, you're a walking, talking 'Funk & Wagnalls', aren't you?"

"I'm just saying there's no urgency."

Smith eyed the towering tree sceptically. Dropping it from the base would be a nightmare. He was reminded of his youth when he spent weekends with his mate, Jack, at his parents' property north of Brisbane. They'd routinely use their chainsaw to cut firewood or clear fallen logs. One day, Jack hit some concealed barbed wire which snagged a tooth on the chainsaw, hurling the snarling blade forward then up towards his forehead. The chain brake kicked in just in time, the blade merely grazing Jack's head, but it was still enough for a few stitches. Jack's mum had a fit, and his dad arranged for them to have lessons with Bob Brown, the owner of the saw mill in the next town. He knew Jack's grandfather from way back.

Brown was a stocky, creased-faced man who looked like he'd stepped out of another era. Initially, he assessed the boys with a steely gaze, deciding if they were worth his time. However, Smith and Jack demonstrated enough respect and eagerness to convince Brown to "show them the ropes." They brought along their Stihl sixteen-inch bar chainsaw, which Brown hefted as if it were a child's toy. The old man effortlessly yanked the pull-start cord without having to throw it to offset the compression. The chainsaw roared to life. For the next half-hour, Brown passed on his wisdom about safe chainsaw use, including how to cut scarfs, strainer post stays, mortises, and more.

Upon seeing the boys' genuine interest, Brown was quite generous. At one point, Smith nervously requested something of him. Brown cast him a brief smile and beckoned the boys to follow him to a corner of the now-quiet mill. They waited beside a massive saw bed as he returned carrying an enormous, bare metal saw that looked like a motorbike, minus the wheels, with a massive chain bar attached. They instinctively stepped back in awe. Jack made the ill-judged request for Brown to start it up. The old man promptly set the saw down, extended a weathered, muscular hand in farewell, and briskly dismissed them before they could properly thank him.

Years later, after much practice, Smith was adept at handling a chainsaw, particularly during a fencing job in Muckadilla after finishing university. He treasured the skill, and despite seldom using his own saw, he kept it in pristine condition.

Bec Smith approached, her pyjamas draped over one shoulder as she sought an open spot on the clothesline. Wet laundry brushed past Smith's head. "Honestly, Steve," she said with a hint of exasperation, "I don't know if you really believe you can't cut down that tree, or if you're just being difficult because it's Jim Allen's property."

Smith waited for the rotating clothesline to clear his view of Bec. "I'm not being difficult, Bec. I'm telling you that tree needs a professional. Someone certified in roping and tree lopping. That's what they need to do. It might cost them about $1500, I reckon."

Smith wasn't being a dick. He was no lumberjack but he had dropped many dead trees in his time and it took a lot of skill to know how and where to cut the scarf and make the drop cut. Only once he blew it while cutting strainer posts, leaving the chain bar jammed as the tree fell smashing the saw as it slid off its base. His fellow workmates on the fencing crew took the piss out of him for days.

He had studied the Allen's tree and convinced himself that its boughs were orientated such that it didn't seem to have a favourable weight bias that could be used to drop it where it was safe to. He knew how to drop it. There wasn't much space in the Allens' yard between the yard fence and the pool fence even if it could be made to drop the right way. He just wasn't sure. Then again, over the Allen's back fence was a lovely Indian family, according to Stacey Allen, and he pondered if he could make the mistake of dropping the tree on their stereo to quieten their sita music.

Bec told Stacey that Smith didn't think it was safe and that we recommended they get a tree lopper in. Smith regarded the matter closed.

A couple of weeks later, the unthinkable happened. On an early July Saturday morning, a typical crisp day that promised nothing but sunshine and a light breeze, the piercing sound of a chainsaw invaded their peaceful home. Smith, in the midst of brewing coffee, set the grinder down and sauntered over to the screen door. The sight that met his eyes elicited an under-the-breath curse. Jim Allen and some other bloke were by the tree, chainsaw in hand.

"What's that?" Bec, with little Sally attached to her like a barnacle, ambled over to the door. She reached out to open it, but Smith, in a reflexive attempt to prevent her from doing so, pulled the handle from her grasp. "Bloody hell, Steve!" Bec's face oscillated between shock, irritation, and a sense of being slighted. She knew her husband's abrupt action was rooted in some sort of competitive bravado towards Jim Allen, something she had seen him succumb to many times before.

With a disapproving glance at Smith, Bec sighed, "You were supposed to help Jim." She attempted to untangle herself from their two children.

"Looks like he's got help," Smith retorted, sidestepping his wife to retrieve milk from the fridge. He had spotted the brand and size of the chainsaw and surmised the bloke with Allen likely had no idea what he was doing. He predicted a disaster in the making.

Bec looked noticeably distressed by the developments next door, prompting Smith's concern. He stepped beside his wife and peered through the screen door. "What's the problem, Bec?"

The piercing whine of the chainsaw restarting drowned out any reply Bec might have given. Smith didn't want to watch the impending disaster unfold. Having concluded that he wouldn't offer his help, he felt the matter was closed and exited the kitchen.

"Steve!" Bec called after him.

Turning back, Smith spread his arms wide. "What?"

"Aren't you going to help?"

Smith recoiled from the demand, which he perceived as emotional and illogical. "No. Why would I?"

Bec, now free from the clutches of their children, stomped towards him. "You know you're more experienced with a chainsaw." She made a face, imitating him in a mocking tone, "That's why."

Smith realised he needed to sit down with his wife. He led her by the hand to the living room and gently nudged her onto the couch before joining her. After a pause, he spoke up.

"Bec, I'm not sure what's going on here. I assessed that tree and concluded I couldn't safely fell it." Smith's voice became softer, slower. "I know you conveyed the same thing to the Allens."

"I told Stacey," she corrected him.

"Yeah, same thing."

Bec shook her head. "You should have talked to Jim."

"It's his tree, his yard. If he wanted my help, he could have asked," Smith retorted, becoming increasingly bewildered by the conversation.

Bec shook her head again, visibly upset. "No!" She choked on a sob midway through her outburst. "No, Steve." She leaned back on the couch, pulling her hand away from his and let it slump into her lap.

Smith was really feeling unsure. He was going through a score of mental subroutines, the script of which was installed when his parents made a boy. There was nothing in the library of tactical responses appropriate to a wife going nuts over something that has no interest to you and should have even less to her. However, Smith was well aware something was up and he wanted to find out what it was, for curiosity's, if not his survival's, sake.

"Bec, I can see you're upset. Can you tell me why?" He held a caring gaze into her eyes until she responded.

"You just don't care, Steve."

Smith thought that was a step in the right direction, although he wondered what his wife was still upset about. "About what?"

"About things I ask you to do."

Smith shook his head ever so slightly as he processed his wife's statement, still wondering what was going on. He knew the obvious next question but wondered if he dares ask it. He went for it. "Like what things, Bec?"

He expected a tirade of tears and accusations but she didn't provide it. "Like when I ask you to help my friend."

Smith re-initiated his analytical processes and came up with only one response. "Which friend?" He ventured further. "Stacey?"

"Yes."

"About the tree?"

"Yes."

Smith felt he was getting somewhere but he didn't like where it seemed to be headed. His wife was still upset but he dared not leave her alone, especially if that required walking away. "You talking about me not helping with the tree?"

"Yes."

Smith mused over the situation, wondering if his wife's upset really hinged on this. He grumbled under his breath, "But I think I already addressed that."

"You said you wouldn't do it," she reminded him.

"That's right," Smith replied, mentally remaining on high alert since the conversation still felt hazy to him. "Remember, I said I wouldn't do it because I didn't like how the tree was weighted. It's too close to the Patels' property and our fence."

"Then why is Jim doing it by himself?" Bec's gaze bore into Smith's, a silent plea for him to treat her question with gravity, or he might have burst into laughter.

Smith found himself at a loss for words. Well, he had words, he just doubted their usefulness. The root cause of this emotional upheaval was still unclear to him, and he doubted "you didn't help" was it.

The chainsaw's ear-splitting cry filled the air again, and Bec looked at her husband, her expression inscrutable.

"What do you want me to do, Bec?" Smith knew it was the absolute worst question he could ask, but his patience was wearing thin with both the situation and their circular conversation.

"Go and help them."

Smith instantly knew he was right. That had been the worst question, and her answer the worst possible outcome. He briefly considered the merits of swiftly filing for divorce, bidding the kids a quick farewell, patting their ugly dog, and hitting the road forever to avoid the horrendous request his wife had just made.

"So you want me to ask them if they want some help?"

Bec pivoted towards Smith, her knees brushing against his. "Of course not, Steve. You know Jim will just say no. I want you to go over there and use your expertise with your chainsaw to prevent someone from getting injured."

Smith leaned back, perplexed. "Bec, I know you're upset, but this is not making any sense. I can't just strut over there with a chainsaw and take over."

"Why not?"

Smith stifled an expletive. He shook his head, realising he needed to change his approach. "What about your great Uncle Sam, or whatever his name was?"

"You mean Shane."

"Shane. Right, yeah, Shane." Smith shifted uncomfortably, his backside starting to numb. "Didn't you tell me how he stubbornly refused to ask for help when stacking hay in his shed after he fired his farmhand? He did it all by himself, three days with no sleep, right?" Smith hoped he was onto something.

"Yes, he didn't ask for help and nearly worked himself to death."

"Yes, but who tried to get him help?"

"Great Aunt Beatrice."

"Exactly!" Smith felt like he was floundering. "But why couldn't she get help for him?"

"Because everyone she asked refused."

Smith gently took her hand. "No, because she asked the wives, not the husbands."

Bec snapped her hand out of his. "What are you implying?" She furrowed her brow for the first time in their conversation. "That I shouldn't have spoken to Stacey?"

"That's right." Smith felt like he was walking on a tightrope, uncertain of his next step.

"That's the most stupid, irrelevant analogy I've ever heard."

"But it's real-world."

"In your world, you mean." Bec shook her head, looking at him incredulously.

"In anybody's world. If Jim Allen wanted my help, he could have asked me." He sat back a bit more. "And if I said 'no', nobody would be upset, especially not you." Smith decided to add a footnote. "If Allen did get upset, it would only mean he was as weak as piss."

"You're being absurd, Steve. This isn't an Amish community where only the men discuss such things. I can have a discussion with my friend next door."

"...Stacey knows how to use a chainsaw and drop a tree?"

Bec tightened her jaw and glared at him.

Smith stopped the discussion going to where it oughtn't with a raise of his hand. It was evident that Bec had promised his help where it was neither needed nor sought. She wanted to be helpful and wanted to be seen to be helpful to her friend.

Smith felt he had dragged sense back into the discussion and had potentially rebooted his relationship with his wife for the day. Bec Smith began to fidget, indicating her intention to rise from the couch. However, he felt he needed to push on despite the chainsaw screaming next door.

"But here's the point of all this Bec." He slid a little closer across the leather lounge. Not knowing where the girls were, he lowered his voice. "I think Jim Allen is a smart arse and I'd not expect him to ask me for help with anything." Bec Smith stiffened and her brow came down a little. "I don't like him but I'm really happy that you and Stacey..."

Bec Smith bursting into tears was not expected. "That's the problem with you, Steve. You put your stupid pride ahead of me. You don't support me when I ask you to do reasonable things that I feel are important. I'm...."

Smith realised then that he missed the whole point of the issue. It was not about the tree or Bec or Jim Allen. It was about Bec being listened to and respected that she could make sensible choices. She knew he and Jim Allen didn't get along and simply wanted that to be put aside in the interests of helping a friend. He sighed gently while Bec shuffled away from him after he put out his hand to comfort her. "Bec, I..."

Smith's appeal was interrupted by the unmistakable cracking sound of a dead tree splitting and falling, followed by a loud "crump" as it hit the deck. He rushed to the screen door to see both Jim Allen and his mate standing back from the tree which was felled squarely into the Allen's yard with only a few thin dead branches reaching their pool fence. It was a perfect drop. Smith was aghast. Bec joined him but didn't open the door. For the first time he got a good look at the bloke's chainsaw. It was a small, old McCulloch. "How on earth...??" he asked himself.

Bec Smith pushed out from under his arm bracing onto the wall and walked away, flicking her eyes at him with the slightest frown. "Hmm. Maybe you wouldn't have been able to."

Smith opened his mouth to respond but closed it. It was a wholly unsatisfactory ending to a great big waste of their time and emotion. He'd lost ground with the women that he loved and probably lost trust as well.

Foetid Confidences

Steve Smith was exasperated with the notification from his wife, within a few minutes of his arriving home from work, that there was "something of concern" to discuss after the kids are in bed. The kids had left the table to brush their teeth. "Wish you'd give me a hint what it is." He didn't like this sort of thing. Why even say anything?

"After the kids are in bed."

"OK." It really wasn't. It was annoying.

It was hours later, after a challenging bedtime routine involving two made-up stories, a read-aloud book, and a fair share of wailing. Both parents were worn out. The girls were riled up about something, so much so that their "manners dinner" had to be abandoned. That was a ritual they completed as a family every now and then where the girls were given an opportunity to show off their very best manners with a formal table setting. They were given twenty points each to start and lost points if they transgressed the rules of excellent dinner etiquette. Infringements such as lowering their mouth to their fork, tipping their soup bowl towards them and the like were what they were picked up on. If they stayed above ten points they'd get a special treat. The girls usually rallied to the challenge but tonight it was a total mess. Sally became frustrated and threw a roasted potato at Julie after she laughed at her younger sister's minor infraction. Steve and Bec Smith regrouped in the kitchen following the protracted goodnight ritual.

Bec set the kettle to boil. "Coffee?"

"Yep. Thanks. Decaf."

"I know."

Smith watched his wife, anticipating her movement towards the table with their coffees. He joined her before she could take a seat.

"How 'bout a bikkie?"

"Sure." She rummaged in the pantry, then plonked a pack of Scotch Fingers in front of him.

He held one above his coffee. "Dunking approved?"

"When have you ever needed approval for that?"

Their shared smile was comforting.

Smith took the lead. "So, what's on your mind?" He had no clue what was going on, whether he'd screwed something up, or what needed to be decided.

Bec, too, dunked her biscuit in her coffee.

"Careful..." Smith cautioned, concerned her biscuit was submerged for too long.

"Oh, come on...I know how..." The soggy end of her Scotch Finger snapped off and splashed onto the table. "Dammit!"

Smith grinned, wisely keeping his amusement to himself.

Bec jumped up to clean up her spill. "Got a disturbing phone call today." She wiped the mess and tossed the remains into the sink. "Very disturbing."

He regarded his wife with a neutral expression. "From who?"

"Whom."

Smith maintained his poker face. "From whom?"

Bec settled back into her chair, taking a moment to get comfortable. She looked at her husband. "Sarah Gilbert."

Smith's expression didn't change, though he was taken aback. "Oh, yes?"

"Yes." Bec's gaze didn't waver from her husband's eyes.

"What did she want?"

"Can you guess?"

"No. Why would I know what Sarah wanted?" Smith had a hunch but hoped it was off the mark.

"Really?"

"Bec, I have no idea why she'd have called you." Smith struggled to keep his composure. "Why did she?"

Bec finally broke eye contact with her husband. She took a sip of her coffee, still looking at her mug. "I hope you're being honest with me, Steve."

"Honest about what? You haven't said anything."

Bec looked at her husband. "Sarah rang to ask me if you'd ever said anything about Chas." She fiddled with the mug handle. "About Chas fooling around with other women while travelling on company business."

It was precisely what Smith had suspected. "What else did she ask?" Smith was surprised to hear his own question.

"That was it."

Smith was adamant he wasn't going to be embroiled in this mess. Chas Gilbert was the lead instrument technician in his division, spending nearly forty percent of his time at customer sites across Australia, New Zealand, and Indonesia. He was in his mid-forties, highly competent, a hit with the customers, and a complete sleaze. They frequently travelled together, but Smith often departed from the site or hotel well before Gilbert, whose instrument commissioning or repair tasks usually took longer. Gilbert was a self-proclaimed "ladies' man," to put it politely. He had frequently boasted to Smith about his numerous "conquests." Smith knew Gilbert was married with two kids. He had met Sarah Gilbert several times — during airport drop-offs, occasionally at work, and at various company functions, including the annual Christmas party. Over the years, Smith had tolerated Gilbert's distasteful "conquest" stories, hoping his lack of reaction would eventually bore Gilbert into silence.

He finally confronted Gilbert one night at a hotel bar in Townsville during one of Gilbert's boasts. He was saying that he had screwed a waitress at the hotel in Gladstone during his last service trip. Smith finally made it clear he didn't want to hear any more about it and that he, Gilbert, should not think such stories were appreciated. He wanted to say a lot more. In fact, he wanted to smack Gilbert in the face. However, he had to work with this pig of a man and knew that he had a strong customer following. He did ask if Gilbert had shown poor judgement in sharing these stories with customers as there were times when customer entertainment, with or without Smith, was warranted. Gilbert had denied any such thing and criticised Smith for thinking that of him. Smith recalls the gall of the man on that evening.

It wasn't just Gilbert's celebrated infidelity that Smith found hard to stomach. For Smith it was, at times, hard to hold faith to his own wife and to his vows. Especially while travelling and "double-especially" while travelling through Europe as he had done on certain new technology commissionings in Eastern Europe where he was asked to help. It wasn't the girlie bars that were a challenge. It was in the hotel bars where business-women would dine and drink alone. It was so easy to catch an eye or a smile from an attractive woman. Those instances would go harmlessly into the "wank-bank." It was only once he was caught out by a tall, pretty, brunette, Romanian woman who approached him without him even seeing her in the bar. She was well within his personal space when she told him that she wasn't a prostitute, that she'd been watching him, that she knew he was married as she was and that she said nobody would be the wiser if he wished to spend the night with her before she flew to Bucharest the next afternoon. He turned her down and felt sick to his stomach that he came so close to going to her room with her. In reality, he never knew how close he was to following her that night but it still scared him.

What truly sickened Smith was the implicit understanding he had with Gilbert, an unspoken agreement that he'd keep Gilbert's infidelity under wraps, despite occasionally interacting with Gilbert's wife and kids. Smith struggled with this. In fact, he found himself secretly hoping for a customer complaint about Gilbert's inappropriate behaviour, a justifiable reason to sack him. Until such a time, Smith felt stuck maintaining this toxic secret.

"What did you say, Bec?"

"I told her the truth."

"And what was that?" Smith was careful not to make a misstep.

Bec looked exasperated. "I told her that I hadn't heard anything of the sort from you." She regarded her husband with an odd expression.

Smith took a moment to reflect. There was absolutely no way he was going to let a colleague's immoral behaviour jeopardise his relationship with his wife. "No way in hell," he vowed.

Bec was studying her coffee again. "So, what's going on, Steve?"

Smith had been expecting this question. Now, he was faced with the quandary of what to tell his wife. Could he trust Bec not to share with Sarah what he revealed about her husband's actions while away on business? Should he tell her anything at all? Was Gilbert even guilty of the misdeeds he boasted about, or was he just a blowhard? Was it out of line for Sarah to ask Bec such a thing? Smith needed to distil this down to fundamental principles. He looked deeply at his wife. "All you need to know, Bec, is that I've been faithful to you." He paused, then placed both hands on the table, readying to rise. "Wonder what's on TV...?"

Bec threw her head back, coffee spilling as she struggled to free her fingers from the mug to better express her astonishment. "What the hell, Steve!" She now had the use of both hands and threw them up in protest. "You can't just leave it there!"

Smith sat down again. "Yes, I can."

"This poor woman called me today. She was crying on the phone. It was dreadful, Steve. What was I supposed to say?"

Smith tried to muster a smile. "You're supposed to say exactly what you did, Bec. That you never heard any such thing from me. And that's the truth." He paused. "Now can we—"

"No, we can't!" Bec interrupted, suddenly conscious of her raised voice. "Is he cheating?"

Smith knew that the slightest change in his tone or the most subtle twitch of his face could spell disaster. He loathed being in this predicament, feeling disgusted by the entire situation. "Screw this," he told himself. Yet, he knew he should say nothing, not even a denial, and certainly not a lie.

"Bec, once again, all I want to say is that I have always been, and will always be, faithful to you."

"God, Steve." Bec stared at him intensely.

There was so much more Smith wanted to add, but he didn't dare.

"But she called me, Steve." Bec was not angry, but her emotions were starting to show. "She hardly knows me. That poor woman must've been desperate to do that."

Her statements hung in the air, but Smith let them fall, untouched. He wanted to criticise Sarah for contacting Bec, but he held back, aware that such a path could lead to darker places.

"So you're just going to sit there and feed me that line?"

"No, I'm also going to say I'm sorry you had to go through that." Smith bit back his words, despising every moment of it.

"Well, so am I."

Bec appeared quite upset. "Is this the sort of thing you blokes do while on...what was the phrase...'company business'?"

Smith looked at her with as much empathy as he could muster, trying to understand what she might be feeling. He wished he could remind her that "she knew better."

"I'm not going to disrespect you by lying or stuffing you with pointless details, Bec. I'll just reiterate that I have always been and will always be faithful to you."

Bec regarded him even more intensely. A lengthy silence passed. Her eyes welled up with tears. "Thank you." It was all she could manage without breaking into sobs.

She stood up, collected the coffee mugs, and walked towards the sink.

"Thank you for what?" He asked hesitantly.

"For reaffirming your commitment to me and our marriage."

At that moment, Smith understood how shaken his wife must've been from Sarah's call. She was likely empathising with Sarah, sensing the looming shadow of betrayal. The feeling of not knowing, yet having unspoken confirmations of her suspicions. The isolation of the deceived. Smith was suddenly hit by the bitterness of his situation. The very thing he feared had transpired. The thoughtless actions of a disloyal colleague had wormed their way into his relationship with his wife. There was no honour code here. There was no agreement with Gilbert to keep his indiscretions confidential.

"Bec..." Smith extended his hand to his wife, who was still by the sink. "Please, come sit." He pulled her chair a bit farther out. "Please..."

Bec looked at her husband, uncertain if she wanted to follow his request. She slowly walked over to the chair and took a seat.

Smith sighed. "You're my wife, and we're in our home. I love you. I don't want any secrets between us." He reached out and touched her hand, but made no attempt to grasp it. "Ask me anything, and I'll give you a straight, honest answer." He had to reassure himself with the same "screw it, why shouldn't I" sentiment. He considered limiting the range of inquiries to the current issue, but dismissed the thought. If there was a time when he was truly vulnerable since marrying Bec, this was it.

Bec looked suddenly apprehensive. She started to speak, but stopped herself.

"There's no game-playing here, Bec. Truly." Smith reassured her.

"No, Steve." Bec flipped her hand over and grasped his. "I trust your judgment."

Smith managed to keep his physical response in check. He smiled. Not a happy smile, but a loving one.

Chas Gilbert and his loose morals could bugger off out of his kitchen.

Romantic Dud

Smith shoved his laptop aside in the Qantas Club lounge in Brisbane, cradling his head in his hands. After a restless night, he was due for a commissioning gig at a sugar mill outside of Mackay the following morning. He appreciated these mills — friendly folks, captivating machinery. Pushing himself up, he brewed a coffee, returning to the closing paragraphs of his novel. It wasn't half bad.

For years, Smith had been lauded for his technical and business writing prowess, becoming the go-to guru for advice or coaching. He cherished writing, harbouring a marked disdain for the underwhelming literacy skills presented by recent — and some not-so-recent — graduates. His curiosity was piqued by the idea of crafting a novel, often daydreaming about the process while flipping through books in airport newsagents. Romantic novels, with their immense popularity and minimal research demands, seemed an enticing choice. Historical pieces would entail significantly more work. Smith considered the possibility of tackling a syrupier love story, but that would require actually reading a couple to gauge feasibility.

The thought of discussing this venture with anyone didn't sit right with Smith. Yet, he'd already semi-written several stories in his head, laying out possible content. Sure, it was a somewhat cynical endeavour, but who would be the wiser? With his ability to whip up vivid prose, he reckoned penning a romantic novel couldn't be too challenging. Perhaps a pseudonym was in order. No self-respecting woman would read a romance authored by an allegedly "neanderthalic" male. He had surveyed several romance writing websites, finding valuable guidelines for crafting a "sigh-worthy" novel. His brain whirred with potential heroines and scenarios. At times, he chuckled at the simplicity of it all. Publishing was another hurdle, but he was getting ahead of himself.

As Smith mulled over the prospect, he slowly began to believe that he could actually complete a novel. He decided to keep his endeavour a secret from Bec and his mates to avoid their potentially disheartening laughter. If successful, the potential financial gain would undoubtedly win them over.

In a month, Smith crafted a promising start — fifty pages that met his exacting standards. He found it easy to dive back into the story after a hiatus, producing ten pages at a stretch without difficulty. Handing over his manuscript for a woman's perspective seemed like the next logical step. Among his options were Bec's friends or his female colleagues. It was during a chat with a lab colleague, Vanessa Rountree, that he mentioned his project. Vanessa was bright and bubbly and had always enjoyed their company banter. The odds of a misunderstanding seemed minimal if he asked her to read his manuscript. He decided to take the gamble.

"You're what? You're writing a novel?" Vanessa fiddled with a sugar container lid in the staffroom. It was well before work and they were alone.

"Yes."

"Really?"

Smith wondered if his revelation was poorly judged. "Yes, really. Does that seem surprising?"

"Not at all," she spoke loudly against the coffee machine's noise. "Just didn't think you'd have time, I guess."

"That's reasonable," Smith thought to himself. And to Vanessa: "Do you like to read?"

"God, yes. If I could do nothing but lie on the beach and read all day, I'd be in heaven."

"Oh. Perhaps you'd like to read what I have so far?" Smith put it out there. "I'd like to know if I'm on the right track before I do more."

"Love to." She wiped up after them and returned the milk to the fridge. "How much have you done?"

Smith took a swig of the usually poor-tasting coffee. "Five chapters so far."

"Yep, for sure."

"It's a romantic novel." Smith was waiting for the laugh but it didn't come.

Vanessa seemed surprised. "Really?"

"Yes. Is that a problem?"

"'Course not. Good on you for being different." Vanessa smirked.

Smith was relieved. "Do you read many romantic novels?"

"Never read one. So it will be interesting."

They continued on for a minute then exchanged salutations. Smith sent it to her private email later that day.

He was excited about her assessment but, at the same time, somewhat trepidatious and embarrassed given some of the soppy content and the chapter three sex scene. He wondered if he had done a sensible thing in sending it to her. He was put at ease a few days later.

Vanessa walked into his office in her brilliant white lab coat. She sat down, crossing her hands in her lap. She was smiling.

"So!" she started loudly. "Aren't you a surprise?" Her eyebrows were up.

Smith led with his chin. "So you thought it was OK?"

"Yeah. I thought it was good." She fanned her face with her hands, smiling. "Bit raunchy for me, though."

"Oh, too much?"

"Don't think so. Just didn't expect it, I guess."

She leaned forward, thumping her thighs in applause. "You might have a winner here. I must admit it's hard to believe you wrote it. You being a bloke I mean." She smiled. "I don't usually gravitate towards this genre, but I reckon it'll work."

"Not overly sentimental?"

As she rose to leave, she responded, "Not in the slightest."

"Thanks heaps for giving it a read. Your feedback means a lot."

At the door, Vanessa spun around, her expression turning serious. "One more thing, Steve…" she cautioned. "Don't share this with any other ladies at work, or you'll be up for sexual harassment." Her laughter erupted before she added, "I'm not joking!" She exited the room, fanning her flushed face. "Phew!"

Feeling rather smug, Smith decided to do more editing and then present his masterpiece to Bec, without revealing anyone else had read it.

It took him another month to complete another round of edits, expand the first couple of chapters, and add two more. He printed it — double-spaced.

Bec appeared both intrigued and impressed by his dedication, given his workload. His aspiration to become an author caught her by surprise, as he'd never mentioned it before. Smith refrained from revealing the genre, allowing the story to speak for itself. The title, *He'd Never Agree*, gave little away. When she inquired further, he playfully retorted, "You'll find out when you read it." He requested she keep it private due to copyright concerns — even though he didn't fully understand that issue himself. Bec agreed, albeit slightly bewildered.

More than two weeks passed, and Smith's frustration mounted as Bec hadn't started reading it. Finally, he implored her to at least begin the first chapter. Apologetic, she promised to complete it within the week.

About ten days later, long after the girls were asleep, Smith was on his way to the bedroom when Bec intercepted him. She bore a smile and clutched the folded manuscript.

Smith's anticipation bubbled up. "So, what did you think?"

"Who really wrote this?" Bec asked, her smile hinting at incredulity, as she brandished the pages.

"I did."

"Really? No one else assisted you?"

Smith began to loosen up. "Nope. All me."

Suddenly, Bec marched towards him, the manuscript smacking against his chest with such force it made him stumble back. Her smile vanished, replaced by a fierce scowl.

Her voice was husky, laced with indignation. "You can write this, but you can't pen me a Valentine's Day card, shower me with flowers, or make me feel special? Now I know you simply choose not to."

With that, she stormed past him into the kitchen. "You're an arsehole Steve!"

And thus ended Steve Smith's foray into romantic novel writing.

A Bad Reaction

The drive home from Bill and Anne's barbecue was eerily quiet. Bec Smith was peeved at him. Smith had made a few grumbling remarks about other drivers that night; ordinarily, Bec would "tsk" or "tut," but now — silence. The kids, sensing the tension, had toned down their backseat shenanigans, straining their ears to eavesdrop on their parents. Eventually, sleep claimed them.

A mere minute after Smith had yanked the keys from the ignition, his wife was out the back door, one of their slumbering offspring draped around her neck. Her icy gaze as she glided past his still-closed door was a trailer for the frosty evening he was about to endure. After a brisk shower, Bec feigned sleep, leaving him to tuck the girls in after a brief bedtime story.

As he wriggled into the sheets, his wife tactfully put some distance between them. He huffed aloud and surrendered to sleep.

Sunday morning unfolded in muted tones. The girls were busily engaged in the lounge room, and the Allens' dog was making a racket. Smith decided it was best not to comment; he wasn't keen on becoming the trigger for any imminent outbursts.

Bec Smith emerged from the ensuite in her robe, a towel swaddling her head, and sauntered past him. Smith, stationed on the bed, reached out to caress her thigh. She shied away abruptly.

"Don't touch me, Steve Smith."

His arm dropped like a stone, and he buried his face in his hands. "Oh, for heaven's sake." He straightened up, letting his hands rest on his lap. "Alright, alright, I'm sorry... I..."

"Sorry?" Bec interjected, stepping in so close he had to crane his neck to meet her eyes. "You're sorry?" She took a swift step back, as if he was about to reach out again.

Slowly, Smith rose to his feet, planning to lean against the dresser, but thought better of it. That decrepit heirloom, long overdue for a dump, was on his "to-fix" list. The repair quote was exorbitant, so Bec suggested that "stabilising" it would do. The rickety antique clashed with their tastefully decorated room, much like their neighbour's ostentatious "beach mansion" amid modest weatherboard and clay-tiled homes.

Smith swivelled to face his wife. "OK, look, maybe I did cross a line."

Bec nodded. "You sure did." She perched on the bed. "Such lovely folks, and you just had to act the absolute galah."

Smith inhaled sharply, taken aback by Bec's harsh assessment of his behaviour, and more so, her apparent support for Anne Leighton's parents. It was time to mount a defence.

"Are you kidding? Nice people?" Smith paced to the farthest corner of the bedroom. "Maybe Anne's mum, but that bloke is..."

Bec interjected, "My best friend's father and your best friend's wife's father." She shook her head in disbelief. "And you couldn't just rein it in."

"Bec, I've been biting my tongue for years around that... that... loony." Smith knew he might be relegated to the couch, but he had already said too much to backpedal now. "I've been a loyal mute while he repeatedly harangues me about his church and his God." Smith lowered his voice. "Bec, I'd simply had a gutful. And what gives him the right to shove his beliefs down my throat? Every encounter with those two, he's at it again."

Smith moved to the bed and gingerly settled beside his wife, making sure to mind his hands.

They sat there in silence for a short while.

"You can't be so aggressive, Steve."

"I wasn't aggressive."

Bec Smith turned to him and quietened her voice. "You told him he was a nut-job fuckwit or something like that." Bec seemed not concerned with her use of swear words. "And everyone heard it. How is that not aggressive?"

"Aggressive would be if I shoved him."

"Don't be absurd." Bec paced out of the bedroom, calling Sally and her sister to come to the kitchen for breakfast.

Nothing more was said on it; for now, anyway. Smith considered through the events of the previous evening. They had been invited over to Bill and Anne Leighton's place for a BBQ. Smith thought twice about going as they'd seen a lot of the Leightons of late. But the girls played so well with their kids. They arrived a little early and Smith reminded himself he was driving as he'd had a couple of full strength beers in the first half hour. He'd enjoyed a few good laughs with Bill over some of the jokes one of their mutual acquaintance had sent them. The bloke was not really liked by either of them but some of the stuff he sent around on email was really funny and totally inappropriate.

It was a lovely Saturday afternoon with a slight bay breeze. The Leighton and Smith kids and another set from their neighbourhood were playing well and the wives seemed happy. Bill Leighton opened another beer and asked about the surf rod that Smith was making. Before the response came to his lips, they curled when he saw Anne's mother and father come into the back yard through the side gate. Smith recalled himself glancing away as Leighton waved a hello to his in-laws. Anne greeted them warmly in embrace.

Smith's reflections were interrupted by Sally appearing at the bedroom door. She was panting on purpose to convey an instruction. "Mum said breakfast is ready."

"Ok, thanks, darling." He followed his daughter down the stairs, the pug coming the other way, then executing an ungainly, panting u-turn on the stairs to come in behind them, like she was herding her humans to breakfast.

Smith pushed his thoughts of the previous day aside and joined the family for breakfast. The girls were pretty quiet for a Sunday morning; perhaps still sensing tension between their parents.

Much later in the day, while Smith was knee-deep in tools in the garage, he heard the crunch of tyres on his driveway. Bill Leighton. His visit was a surprise, and Smith ambled out to greet him.

"What brings you here?" Smith was still cheesed off at his best mate. "Or have you just come to continue playing the wuss?"

Leighton paused at that before stepping out of his car. He hadn't so much as glanced at Smith since switching off the engine. "Don't." He pointed at Smith, a feeble attempt at a warning.

"Why the hell not?" Smith was now uncomfortably close. "What do you reckon?"

"Reckon about what?"

"Your lame attempt at diplomacy last night."

Smith watched Leighton's jaw tighten. "You could've handled yourself better. Don't blame me if you're in the doghouse."

Smith propped his foot against Leighton's front tyre. "Are you seriously telling me that last night was entirely my fault?"

Leighton offered a wave to Bec Smith as she appeared on the porch and then retreated indoors. "You bet. You knew what Dick's like. You couldn't zip it."

Smith was dumbfounded. "And you knew his game, too, but did nothing to muzzle him. You let it all fall on me."

They both realised their escalating argument was growing too loud, too quickly.

Leighton toned it down. "Steve, you don't understand the bind I'm in with Dick."

Smith snorted, trying unsuccessfully to stifle a chuckle, causing Leighton to bristle. "Look at the size of you, mate. You could fit two of him inside you. You're being a bit of a sook."

Leighton was irritated by Smith's irrelevant comment. "You know what I mean."

"No, I don't know what you mean." Smith wasn't about to let his mate off the hook that easily. He slammed Leighton's car door shut, signalling that he was inviting him inside.

"Hold on, Steve." It was the first time Leighton had used his name during their conversation. "I want to sort this out before Bec gets dragged into it."

"She's already in it, mate." Smith was still avoiding his best friend's name. "She's been breathing down my neck since we left your place."

Leighton glanced at a noisy motorbike roaring past, a ruckus that seemed excessive for such a tiny vehicle. He turned back to Smith. "Look, I know my father-in-law can be a tough nut to crack. And I know he's fervent about his religion and..."

"Fervent?" Smith cut in. "That's not fervent, mate, it's self-righteous, ignorant, and..." Smith cut himself off and took a deep breath. "He feels entitled to steamroll anyone who doesn't see eye to eye with him." Smith scanned the porch to see if Bec had re-emerged. He faced Leighton again. "And you knew full well he was going to provoke me, and you let him." It was a charge Smith had weighed carefully. "You let him because you thought I'd cop it sweet and not kick up a fuss." Smith was surprised Leighton had let him speak uninterrupted. "And you knew I've dealt with his garbage before." Smith dialled back his voice. "Mate, what did you think was going to happen?"

Leighton regarded his mate intently. "I thought you'd be a good mate and keep your cool."

Smith noted the "good mate" comment, subtly dragging Anne Leighton into the conversation. The two men locked gazes for a tense few seconds before Smith responded.

"Well, you thought wrong." He turned and silently gestured for his mate to join him for a coffee, leading the way to the front door without waiting for a reply. Leighton trailed him into the house.

Bill wasn't a metre into their hallway when Bec Smith pushed herself to him, giving him a hug. "I'm sorry about all this."

Smith threw his arms into a dramatic enquiring stance as his wife walked past him. He was left looking at his mate who could not hide the smile anyone would sport after a hug like that from Bec. He turned and walked dejectedly towards the kitchen.

The girls, hearing Leighton's voice in the house, ran in to see if he had brought the kids with him and ran out just as fast, without salutation, when they found he hadn't.

It was strange in the Smiths' kitchen. Smith wanted to confront the issue but sensed that he'd be shut down if he did. His best mate seemed to be taking some solace from the presence of both of them, like a détente had commenced.

Bec started. "We enjoyed ourselves last night, thanks Bill."

"No, we didn't." Smith had no choice.

"Steve, must you?" Bec was feeling her way.

"It's OK, Bec." Leighton shifted in his seat. "I think..."

"OK, OK, stop it." Smith had had enough.

"I need to set some things straight." Smith lifted his hands, scanning between the two potential objectors, but no protests emerged. For a moment, he felt lost in this complicated triangle. He was sitting with his wife and best mate, trying to mend the fractures in their relationships. Mostly with Bec, but the issue with Bill Leighton hadn't even been addressed. Not that Bill had gotten a word in edgeways. The last time Smith saw Anne, she was attempting to placate her distraught mother. Her reaction to Smith's so-called attack on her father was overblown, he thought, and perhaps manipulative. There were so many potholes on the path to resolving this fiasco. He suspected an apology to Anne's father would be demanded. That was one step too far. He had repeatedly asked the man to stop his sermonising and judgmental demands; there was no way he was going to apologise for calling him out as a bigot, a born-again zealot, and a nuisance. Smith remembered enduring similar tirades at earlier gatherings, the first of which had been at Mary Leighton's christening party years ago. He wondered why he was the one constantly under siege, despite showing no interest. The conclusion was simple: Anne's dad was a jerk. His stealthy approaches had always ensured no one else heard his words, and Smith now wished he had been equally discreet.

Smith drew a breath, checking for eavesdropping kids who had a knack for staying out of sight but within earshot. The coast was clear. He eyed Bec and Bill Leighton, the latter attempting to play the innocent bystander, which was less than helpful. "Alright, I won't pretend that what happened was a picnic. And I'm not going to pretend I was forced into it either." Smith started his defence cautiously. "I'm not even going to say I don't regret it. But I want to explain my side." He felt like he was addressing a tribunal, trying to avoid charges. "Firstly, Bec, what's your take?"

"Well, it's not about me."

Smith had anticipated her response. "Actually, it is. You've been treating me like I auctioned off one of the kids. So, yeah, I think it involves you."

Bill Leighton shifted in his seat. "Steve, I'm not sure—"

"Get in line, Bill." Smith didn't even glance his way.

Smith looked at his wife with as much tenderness as he could muster, choosing his words carefully. After a few more seconds, he ventured, "OK, let me try this. Bec, I reckon you saw me acting out of character, supposedly attacking a harmless old man without provocation. I can see why you'd be unsettled." The last part was the first semblance of a rebuttal.

Bec regarded her husband, finding solace in his empathy and relief that she wouldn't have to adjust to a new, volatile version of him. But her best friend was upset, and she wasn't sure how to mend that fence. "What about Anne?"

Leighton started to respond but was interrupted.

"No, Bill, I'm talking to Steve." Leighton's mouth clamped shut, and his hefty hands landed on the table.

Smith sat back in his chair assessing the situation to that second. Again, a wave of resignation came over him.

"I owe Anne an apology, it was unjust," Smith conceded, finally gaining the upper hand in this regrettable mess. Bec seemed to ease up, allowing Smith a moment's respite. He asked his eldest if everything was alright, just a casual diversion.

Bill, however, sent everything spiralling. "Your apology won't be addressed to Anne."

Smith's gaze hardened at his friend, horrified. No way he was saying sorry to Leighton's father-in-law.

"I will if you will."

Leighton was taken aback.

"What are you saying, Steve?" Bec's confusion was evident.

"It means, love, that this knucklehead could've put his father-in-law in his place before I had to." He nodded at Leighton, gambling on his reaction in front of his wife. Smith was all in now. "So, I'll apologise if Bill does."

"What do I have to apologise for?"

"You knew Dick was a nuisance. You knew it wasn't the first time I had to endure it. Actually, you knew it really pissed me off." Smith ducked as if expecting reprimand for the crude language. The girls were clearly out of earshot or they'd be insisting on Dad's swearing "penance." He faced Leighton and Bec. "So, I apologise; you apologise." Smith leaned back, arms crossed. It wasn't just a tactical move; the entire situation was ludicrous. He was tired of it.

Bec was growing uncomfortable. Her priority was to broker a concession for Anne, left at the barbecue grappling with her mother, who was, in turn, handling her dad. Bec was getting nowhere.

Leighton had been boiling until Smith's "I will if he does" bit. Getting an apology from Smith, a formidable task to begin with, now seemed hopeless. Leighton was out of his depth, daunted by the folks he had to placate. Damn! Maybe Smith was right. Maybe he should've intervened, stopped Dick, and faced the ensuing storm. His father-in-law was a royal pain. Thankfully, Dick's "finding God" occurred post-marriage to Anne, else Leighton might have bolted. He pondered his situation: two upset in-laws and a saddened wife.

Standing, Bec began to fill the kettle. "This is absurd. We're grown-ups trying to resolve a petty argument." She placed the kettle on its base, turning to face the men. "Steve, you've got to do something," her voice quivered with uncertainty.

Smith saw his wife's distress. Not good for resolution. He uncrossed his arms, sitting upright, preparing to speak when the girls burst in. Bec shooed them out, permitting TV time.

"Please try to understand my perspective," Smith began in a calm, measured tone.

Bill let out a near-inaudible sigh.

"Dick's entry into your backyard made me wince. No ill will, but he lived up to expectations." Leighton glanced at the Smiths before eyeing the biscuits Bec set before him. "He greeted me, then started attacking my 'lack of spirituality' — same game plan as before. I tried to divert the conversation, even walked away, but he followed."

Smith monitored Bec's reactions; they would dictate his approach. He turned to his mate. "Ever think there might be a few kangaroos loose in the top paddock?"

"Who?" Leighton's redundant question irked Smith.

"The Pope, who do you think? Dick, your father-in-law. Is he a sandwich short of a picnic?"

"Steve!" Bec interjected. "Uncalled for!"

Smith assessed her reaction. Show or sincerity? "It's a valid question, considering the grief I've copped from him — repeatedly. Well, Bill? What say you?"

Bec was both animated and anxious about Leighton's impending response.

Leighton, tactful yet detached, replied, "I don't think there's any mental illness, Steve."

Stumped, Smith sank back. Bec signalled Leighton with tea and coffee options, allowing him to select by pointing, to avoid distraction. He chose coffee, signalled for milk, and sugar. With a brief smile, Bec turned to prep. "I'll have coffee too, Bec," Smith addressed his wife's back, not having been granted choice. He looked at Leighton without turning. "Why does he treat me this way?"

"He doesn't do anything to you." Leighton countered, irritation creeping in.

"Then what does he do?"

"He merely offers guidance to those he believes need...spiritual direction."

Smith was aghast. "You can't be serious, mate." Struggling to articulate his dismay, he leaned forward. "Are you implying Dick's justified in being a prick because I need saving? Is that it?"

Leighton mirrored Smith's posture, faces barely a foot apart. "Maybe you do need saving."

Smith looked to his wife, busy serving coffee and cream-filled biscuits. She didn't respond.

"Have you lost your bloody mind, Bill?"

"Steve!" Bec's reprimand was less about the swearing — likely overheard by the girls — and more about rising tensions.

"Sorry, Bec, that was my bad. I was only joking." Leighton's apology dwindled to a whisper.

Both men reclined, Leighton slouching slightly.

"So, here's what I'm gathering." Smith curbed the impulse to point at his mate. "Your father-in-law's a religious zealot. You've known this for years. You also know he's on a mission to save souls, particularly mine, for some bloody reason. You watch him harangue me until I reject him, then he runs crying to Anne's mum, lamenting my refusal of his 'spiritual guidance.' Then, you come here, having done zilch to help or mediate, trying to coerce an apology from me for what I considered a fair and warranted response to his antics."

"Mate, you told him to bugger off, along with his God and righteousness, or some such phrasing." Leighton slumped back.

Bec checked the lounge to ensure the girls were still watching TV, out of earshot. She returned to the table.

"That's nothing you wouldn't have done in my shoes last night." Smith retorted, taking a careful sip from his coffee. "Knowing you, Bill, you probably would've tossed him over the fence."

A smirk tugged at Leighton's mouth.

Bec, choosing her words carefully, said, "This just seems so unlike you, Steve. I've never seen you lose patience, or respond to someone so... vulnerable."

"Vulnerable?!" Smith felt anger surge, standing abruptly. As he exited the kitchen, he declared the conversation over.

An hour later, Smith re-entered the house from the backyard, having watered the vegetable patch contrary to his instructions for late-afternoon watering.

Bec approached him for a comforting hug, which he accepted. "I'm sorry," he whispered, "For how this escalated."

Bec tightened her embrace. "It's ok. Let's have some lunch."

The girls were quiet, likely at their mother's instruction, but Julie couldn't contain herself. "Are you ok, Daddy?"

"I am, thank you, Julie, Sally." He smiled warmly at both, thanking Bec for the sandwich she placed on his plate. As she withdrew her hand, he took it in his, returning her smile. It was a pleasant lunch, interrupted only by a call Bec took in the other room. Her brief responses indicated it was Anne Leighton, but Smith asked no questions when she returned.

Wednesday evening, while driving home from work, Smith received a call from Leighton. He briefly considered ignoring it.

"How you going?" Smith forced cheerfulness into his voice.

"Good, yeah, good, mate."

"What's happening?"

"Not much. Same shit, different day."

"Yep. Same here."

A pause followed, then they both started speaking, halting after stumbling over each other's words.

"You go."

"No, you. Go on, mate."

Leighton broke the silence. "Look, I've been pondering what you said." There was a pause.

"About what exactly? As I recall, I unloaded quite a bit." Smith attempted a jest more than a confession.

"About my inaction. About me not standing up to Dick."

Smith felt a surge of relief. He didn't want this issue to spiral out of control. There were wives, parents, in-laws, turf wars, and bruised egos involved.

"OK," Smith responded, choosing his words carefully. "Go on, mate."

"Well, I had a chat with Anne."

"Ah, bugger. How'd that go?"

"OK, I think. She understood your perspective, to an extent."

"Really?" Smith fought to keep his surprise in check.

"Yeah, to a degree, anyway. She didn't approve of your... umm, not attack..."

"I know what you mean."

"Alright... well, she thought it was unnecessary, but she was unaware of her dad's behaviour. I think she was quite taken aback."

"She didn't know?" Smith sought clarity.

"Well, she knew he can be overbearing but had no idea he was becoming a pain in the arse."

"Were those her words or yours?"

"Mine."

Smith invited Leighton to proceed.

"Well, not much else to say, mate. She's stuck in the middle."

"Yeah, I get that." Smith still wasn't ready to give in.

An extended pause.

"So, what now?" Smith needed to know where he stood.

"Dunno."

"OK." To Smith it felt like pulling teeth. "Is this the end of it?"

After a brief pause, Smith muttered an obscenity under his breath at a cyclist blocking his path.

"I don't think so. Anne's mum still believes you should apologise."

"Ah, bugger, you're joking." Smith felt like a sacrificial lamb. "Apologise to Dick?"

"Yeah, mate." Leighton's voice dripped with despondency.

"Nup. Not going to happen." Smith matched his despondency.

"Yeah, OK."

"OK." Smith swung into the supermarket carpark. "Better go, mate. Need to grab some milk."

"OK, see ya."

"Yeah, see ya."

But I Didn't Help Him

The whole regrettable matter was swept to the back of Smith's mind for the subsequent week. He felt oddly isolated in his thoughts but avoided spiralling into self-reproach.

Bec had met with Anne Leighton at their favourite coffee shop, and relations seemed to normalise between them. There was no word from Bill Leighton, which wasn't uncommon. A month without contact wasn't unheard of. However, it was one night, a week or so later, just before bedtime, when his wife, sitting on the bed, gently patted the spot beside her, beckoning her husband to sit.

Smith obliged, then turned to Bec and smiled. "What's on your mind, love?"

Bec shuffled a bit on the bed, smoothing her dressing gown over her knees. "Steve, I want to bring up something Bill mentioned. It's about your school days, a topic I don't usually have a right to discuss."

Intrigued, Smith joked, "Well, now, you've caught my interest." Seeing her obvious discomfort, he softened his demeanour. "Alright, I'll stop with the jokes. What is it?"

Bec looked at him squarely. "Bill told me about Dave Morrison from your school days."

Smith's smile persisted, albeit with a forced edge. "Did he now?"

Bec brushed a lock of hair off her forehead, only for it to fall back into place.

"He did. He told me what happened to Dave at school."

Smith's posture stiffened as he processed this. "What about him?"

"Bill told me about the incident that befell Dave in school."

Smith sat upright. "OK, I think I see where this is going." He had already connected the dots. Dave Morrison had been a friend to both Bill Leighton and himself during the initial years of their time at the private high school they attending in Brisbane.

The three friends grew apart in the later years of school, mostly because Bill's sporting prowess in rugby and rowing didn't align with Dave's interests in music, chess, and drama club. Smith, however, had always made an effort to maintain contact with Morrison, who was a gentle, kind soul.

Years after leaving school, Morrison fell into alcoholism and drug addiction, eventually leading to his tragic suicide. It was then revealed he'd been molested by a school History master, who doubled as a guidance counsellor and thus had his own office. Several other boys in the same year level also suffered the same fate. The incident only clicked in retrospect, piecing together odd behaviours they'd noticed back at school. The guidance counsellor was later charged but took his own life before the trial.

"OK, go on," Smith urged. He didn't wish to contribute to the discussion but didn't want to leave Bec hanging as he understood she was trying to help.

"Well, I... We... Wondered if there was any lingering trauma from those school days that might have triggered your reaction to Anne's dad."

Smith almost dismissed the conversation as ludicrous. "Bec, how is that even relevant? How did you and Bill leap from a childhood trauma to me blowing a fuse with Anne's father?

That's bonkers." Smith grinned, rising from the bed. "Excuse me, nature calls."

Upon his return from the bathroom, Bec was still perched on the bed. "What's your take on this?" Bec leaned back on her propped hands.

"I think Anne's dad is a sanctimonious jerk, and that's the whole story. It's got nothing to do with my school or some unfortunate boy who fell prey to a paedophile." Smith fell silent for a moment. "How did Bill even come up with that notion?"

Bec made a nonchalant shrug. "Bill's known you for a lot of years, Steve. A lot longer than I've known you. Maybe he sees something." It was her turn to pee and she asked Smith to wait for her. Smith shook his head in a final dismissal of the idea.

Over the cistern sound, Bec spoke quietly. "That was a severe reaction to someone, Steve. I've never seen you do anything like that."

Smith slumped his shoulders involuntarily. "So you and Bill make the connection between some school time predator and Anne's dad who is..." Smith glanced at his wife. "...who is only a religiously energised senior man..." Smith took a breath and released it through his next sentence. "...and somehow you've concluded that I must have been touched up." Smith leaned back on his hands again. "Can you see how any independent observer might think you guys are nuts?"

Bec Smith did her best to ignore the volley. "When Bill mentioned this boy back at school and what happened to him, well, I wondered, too."

"Nothing happened to him." Smith emphasised the second word, almost yelling it. He looked at his wife with a frustrated expression.

"No, I..." Bec was cut off open-mouthed.

"That fuckwit back at school didn't 'happen' to Dave. That piece of shit preyed on him. He molested a child from a position of trust. He targeted and raped kids, Bec. He had the protection and trust of the school and parents and yet he ambushed and molested kids in his charge. And, might I add, over a long time."

"And you couldn't do anything." Bec leaned away from her husband a tiny bit.

Smith half gulped, half sighed, looking at her with a sense of injustice. She spoke about it as if she understood. He felt a wave of sadness envelop him and a sob begin to form.

"Didn't," Smith managed to say.

"You couldn't, Steve. You were a child," Bec Smith reassured her husband.

Avoiding his wife's gaze, lest she see the moistness in his eyes, Smith recalled the young face of Dave Morrison from grade nine. They sat in silence, with no further attempt from Bec to justify Smith's recent behaviour. That is, until the girls came in.

The next day, Bill Leighton paid them another visit. Smith was working from home on technical proposals when Leighton arrived unannounced. Bec had already filled him in on their bedroom conversation.

"G'day, mate." Leighton looked dishevelled.

"G'day, Bill." Smith scratched his unshaven face.

"Why don't you fellas head out back and I'll bring you a cuppa," suggested Bec, heading for the kitchen.

Following Smith's lead, they settled in the outdoor area next to the back stairs.

"Business OK?" Leighton's voice squeaked, prompting smiles from both men. "Sorry, voice's shot after we beat the 'Boks last night." Smith regretted missing the rugby on TV, having worked late and then held a technical teleconference with the US east coast.

"Yep, all good. Busy. Heading to Mount Isa next week."

"What for?"

"Commissioning some equipment in a new lab at the mine. Providing some training on it."

"OK." Leighton knew better than to ask about the equipment, lest Smith deliver a technical explanation that grew increasingly vague as he realised Leighton didn't understand. He was about to comment on the Pug when he got to the point. "Look, mate, I hope you didn't mind me talking to Bec about… about Dave."

Smith refused to meet his gaze. "No. I understand why you did." He looked up as Bec set down coffees and biscuits. "That was quick, love."

"Kettle was already boiled," Bec replied, walking away.

"She's a good one," Leighton said, meeting Smith's gaze for the first time since they'd sat down.

"Decided to keep her," Smith replied with the faintest hint of a smile. They let the silence linger for a while.

Smith looked at his friend. "Mate, I'm not sure what to say to you," he started, raising his hand to stop Leighton's response. "We were both at school, both Dave's mates. Well, in the early years, anyway. We both didn't see what was happening."

"Maybe we should have."

"How?" Smith was direct. "How did we know that sicko was a predator? We'd just graduated from 'stranger-danger' in primary school. How were we to know that someone like him could be in a high school, in a position like that?"

Leighton straightened up. "He was our mate. We knew what was happening."

"No, we didn't," Smith protested.

"Sure, we did."

"How did we?" Smith stared at his friend, searching for answers.

"We should have picked up on the signals."

"What signals?" Smith was always to the point. "Something you saw might make sense to you now in hindsight, but not back then." The haunting memory of Dave Morrison being ushered into the guidance counsellor's office during ninth grade replayed over and over in his mind. The scene continued to torment him, even after Price's predatory actions were exposed and the police got involved. The image of an adult hand closing the door behind the unfortunate kid persisted. He had briefly questioned Morrison's presence there at the time but dismissed it. If that memory were a videotape, he'd have worn it thin with replays by now.

Smith glanced around the garden for his dog, then surrendered to the search.

"Suppose so," he mumbled.

"Come on mate, we were only fourteen then."

"Thirteen," corrected the other.

"Whatever!"

"Yeah, I know."

"I just wish I could go back. I'd tear that bloke apart," Leighton was growing upset.

Smith eyed him sceptically. "You're joking, right? You didn't even like Dave."

Bill jerked his head up and glared at Smith. "Who says?"

"Says me. You were on your way to becoming a rock star in the school's first fifteen, and the first eight. Kids like Morrison were beneath you by then."

Bill Leighton's jaw clenched so tight he could crack a walnut. A wave of sadness seeped through his anger, making him draw a sharp breath. He looked down.

Smith noticed the softening in Bill's demeanour but remained on guard for any potential threat. "Look, I shouldn't..."

"There are things I've had to grapple with from those school years, too." Bill's body language shifted, opening up as he glanced around, collecting his thoughts. "One of them is how awful I was to Morrison." He gave Smith a sorrowful look. "I always wanted to apologise to him, but thought it was just typical schoolyard stuff that he'd forget. Never knew Price was going after him, too."

Smith didn't question his sincerity. "You weren't really awful. You just stopped connecting with him."

"Yeah, maybe." He looked down again, seething, "What I'd give for five minutes with that rotten Price."

"Me too, mate."

"Yeah."

Leighton took a deep breath, shaking off the memories. "Anyway, I just thought what happened with Dave..."

"Nope." Smith watched as Sally darted out to retrieve a Barbie part from the yard, then scamper back inside the house. She seemed to have an internal radar for locating lost Barbie bits in the backyard. "Not really. I mean, I was already peeved at Anne's dad, but Dave wasn't on my mind."

"What about you?" Leighton nibbled on a biscuit.

"What about me??"

"What if Price had targeted you instead of Dave?"

"But he didn't."

"But he could have."

Smith shook his head as if trying to dislodge such a ludicrous comment from his mind. "No, but he didn't!" He was raising his voice.

Leighton was about to respond, but Smith cut him off. "What's your point?"

"I mean, it could've been you."

"Or you!" Smith pointed at his friend.

"Yes, or me!" Leighton sat back, satisfied that he'd made his point.

Smith shook his head again. "Look mate, I know this whole thing is a mess, but it has nothing to do with Anne's father." He slouched back in his seat. "Alright?"

Leighton gave Smith a sheepish look. "Alright." He too, sank back in his seat. "Can't be that then."

"Huh?" He stared at Leighton, puzzled. The thought crossed his mind that Leighton was searching for some deep-rooted childhood trauma to explain Smith's behaviour at the barbecue. Checking that no children were within earshot, Smith rose from his chair and towered over his mate. Anger surged within him. "What... you're fishing for some juicy headline for your family chat group?" Smith circled the chairs, struggling to keep his balance. "Nearly molested mate loses it on well-meaning father-in-law?" He barely stifled a growl. "Psychological issues detected."

Leighton watched Smith's movements cautiously as the man loomed over him. He didn't like the vibe. "Back off, Steve," he warned, purposely turning his gaze away.

Bec Smith chose that moment to descend the back stairs, a move timed to perfection. She'd been eavesdropping on the men's conversation from a distance and saw an urgent need to intervene. Her sudden appearance caught both men off guard. Smith recoiled from Leighton, unable to muster a calming greeting for his wife as his anger still simmered.

"What's going on, boys?" She divided her attention between the two men. The silence lingered. "Boys?"

"Bill was just leaving." Smith's words grated through clenched teeth.

"I was," Leighton affirmed. He rose, offering a smile to Bec and a brief glance to Smith as he moved past him. "I'll see myself out."

Bec watched him take the path towards the kitchen, then slid into the vacant seat. They sat in tense silence for what seemed like an eternity. "You okay?"

Smith met her gaze across the table, hands flat against the warm, dark wood. "Yep."

"I won't ask what happened, but it didn't look good."

"It wasn't good." Smith felt the family pug nosing around his feet and gave the dog a little shove, only to feel a lick in response. He ignored it. "Bill tried to spin my supposed emotional baggage from a school memory as a justification for my actions at the barbecue."

"He told Anne that?" Bec looked confused.

"No, no," Smith clarified, struggling to keep his patience in check. "Just now."

"He said that?"

"No, but that's what he was implying."

"How do you know?"

Smith sighed, losing the last of his patience. "I wasn't born yesterday, darling."

"Okay." Bec wanted to exit the conversation as quickly as possible. "Look, sorry. I didn't want to interrupt you guys. I just..."

"Yes, you did, Bec." Smith's smile was weary but genuine. "I'm glad you did." He nudged the pug with his foot, a bit more forcefully this time. "I was quite angry."

Bec Smith returned his smile. She extended her hand across the table and he placed his in hers. "I'm glad you're both okay." She rose, smoothing her skirt with a couple of deliberate sweeps of her hand. "Please reach out to Bill as soon as you can to clear the air." She didn't wait for a response, calling the dog to follow her up the stairs.

Smith watched her go, her words echoing in his mind but not quite sinking in. He replayed the haunting memory of the adult hand closing the guidance counsellor's office door behind Dave Morrison. He felt drained, indecisive about whether to stand or remain seated. The day concluded with a late afternoon movie, a promise he had made to the girls. Smith dozed off with Sally nestled against him. Bec let him be.

✧

What? Another Mate's Weekend?

The call from his old schoolmate was a surprise. It had been years since he'd seen Gordon Miles. Gordon was a quirky bloke who could make light of any situation or person. He'd been married young and had two kids whom Smith barely knew. That was okay, though. When it came to school mates, kids and wives took a back seat for a while.

"How've you been?"

"Good, Gordon. You?" Smith almost cracked a smile, anticipating the inevitable wisecrack.

"Stellar, mate. All's well. The kids are fine, and the missus hasn't bumped me off yet."

"That's great, Gor..."

"Bought myself a boat, thinking of going over to Moreton."

Smith was immediately on guard. At school and in the subsequent years, Gordon was a notorious buffoon on the water. If he wasn't ramming into you in canoes, he was pushing you overboard while on a screaming reach on a Hobie.

"How big?"

"You asked me that in twelfth grade, and I told you to bugger off."

"Your boat, you bloody drongo," Smith retorted, dryly.

"Forty-five."

"Nice." Smith's response was somewhat obligatory.

"Rig?" Smith delved into the sail configuration immediately; there was no chance this was a motorboat. They were sailors.

"Masthead sloop. Quite slippery, too. Massive assy."

"Nice." After a brief pause, he asked, "When?"

"In two months. We can make a four-day weekend out of it."

"Bloody hell." Smith was low on leave and wondered if he could take the time off. Plus, he had to deal with the fallout from the burnt-balls weekend when the girls lost three days from their week in Bali and were spouting threats that included "never again" and "can't trust you" sort of language. He pondered if it was worth the effort.

"Bloody hell, what?" Gordon's response echoed the "I have no problem managing my freedoms, what's your excuse?" sentiment, showcasing his impatience with blokes who didn't seem to have complete control over their lives. Smith saw it coming.

"It's just I've..."

"Come on, mate, it's just a couple of days. Sort it out, fella. Didn't buy this boat to sail 'round the cans with the missus."

Smith managed to persuade himself this wasn't a big deal. "Sure, mate. Put me down as a starter."

"Beauty." Gordon half-shouted something to someone with a swift turn of his head. "I'll get back to you in a week or so. Let me know when you get your leave."

Leave. Right. Smith thought that was precisely the term for it. While he enjoyed his mates' company, he hated this part of the discussion with Bec — negotiating time away without her. But for the understandable fallout from the Mount Barney weekend, she had no issue with him taking off for a "mates' weekend." Her only condition was, "Just come back smiling," which left him with a sense of foreboding, perhaps unwarranted, that the cost of his freedom would be servitude for double the time.

"Catch you later, mate."

"Yep." And just like that, Gordon was gone.

Not five minutes later, he received a text from Gordon stating that he'd asked "Lates" (Bill Leighton) but was told there was no way he could go. Smith felt a pang of guilt at being a part of Bill's predicament. The fallout from Leighton's scalded balls episode was severe. He reminded himself to call Bill and catch up. The scolding that Leighton received from Anne after she realised he wasn't seriously injured was intense. She and Bec drove to Beaudesert to see him in the hospital. Their shortened Bali trip was disruptive and expensive. Smith tried to argue that they should stick with their plans and he would see to Bill, but they wouldn't have it; it was an impractical proposal, anyway. The girls needed to make the hospital visit to give them a piece of their minds. Their delayed Bali trip was, he thought, pure righteousness.

For days after their Beaudesert trip, Smith was dismissed by Bec's iconic wave of her arm when she wanted him to know she had no intention of hearing his side. To make matters worse, when Anne walked into the hospital ward, Bill burst into tears. Smith could do nothing but give him a pathetic look. Anne took a moment to register that her husband was not seriously injured and then folded her arms, assuming the most admonishing posture she could. Smith suppressed a wave of anger at her drama. Unfortunately, his face must have betrayed his displeasure enough that Bec moved to stand next to him, looking down at him like a headmistress scolding a misbehaving pupil. Eventually, Anne approached her husband, hugged him, and expressed relief that he wasn't more seriously injured. As she gently extricated herself from his embrace, she shot Smith a death glare, which he received while preparing for a rebuttal, only to be stopped by a firm hand on his shoulder from his wife.

All of this was discussed on the drive back to Brisbane as Anne took over his motel room in Beaudesert for another day and the Smiths headed home.

"Oh, for heaven's sake, Bec. It was a burn. Just a burn."

"That wasn't a burn. It was a scalding, and a serious one at that."

Smith glanced at a row of leafless poplars lining the fence as he pulled up behind a semi on the Toowoomba stretch.

"My point is, it could have been his arm, and nobody would have known."

"That's not the point at all." Bec had turned slightly towards him, hinting to Smith this was going to escalate. "The point is that you felt the need to lie to escape."

"It wasn't a…"

"Yes, it was. Not a little white lie. A big, black one. And you know it."

Smith overtook the semi and settled to just over the speed limit. The blast from the semi's displaced air made the roof rack-mounted fishing rod's tips wave about, catching Bec's attention.

"What's that?" Bec was pointing up at the rods. "You even brought your fishing rods to a bushwalk."

Smith's jaw tightened, but he didn't respond. He traced another line of trees along a fence line, this time native pines. He didn't know what to say. As expected, Bec had, in this and earlier exchanges since their arrival in Beaudesert, turned it into a trust issue. Over dinner at the motel, while Anne was talking to her kids before they went to bed, Bec had laid into him, stating this was evidence that he couldn't be trusted. Smith recalled his own words to his mate before the trip: "… mate, are we going down to Sydney to hang out in girly bars?"

"No. But…"

"Are you having an affair with that blonde in your office? The tall one?"

"No…"

That was Smith's perspective on trust. It was about where he agreed not to put his dick or with which lady he would not share his emotions and feelings, although he thought all this hoo-ha about emotional affairs was a crock. On the Richter scale of trust, they were 8's. For what he was copping such disdain from Bec didn't amount to a 1.

"Look, Bec, you're taking this too far. Making it mean too much. Like…"

"Making it mean what?" Bec interrupted. She had crossed her arms, resulting in her right boob being lifted out of alignment because of her angle to the seat. "I don't have to make it mean anything. You're the ones that seem not to be able to be trusted."

There it was, Smith thought. A break in the clouds. Bec had said "ones."

"Like it wasn't just me, Bec. Bill had a say in this."

Bec's jaw dropped. "Don't even think about it, Steve." She adjusted her top subtly and swivelled a tad more in his direction. "You know that Bill was already in hot water about the floor."

"And how is that relevant?" Smith was intrigued by her train of thought, but dared not show it.

"He wouldn't dare spin such an intricate web of deceit, that's how."

"Oh, for heaven's sake, Bec! Just because he's under the thumb, don't pin that on me." The words were out before he could reel them back. They hung in the air, circulating within the car. Bec had fallen silent — a dangerous sign.

Bec pivoted another few degrees towards him. "So, if a husband is faithful and thoughtful, he's under the thumb? Is that it?" Bec's gaze felt like a drill burrowing into his temple. He had no choice but to break eye contact with the road. He looked at her, noticing a trace of hurt on her face, her eyes starting to well up.

"Of course not, Bec." Smith glanced back at the road, then to her. He signalled and swung into a conveniently situated rest area. Though it lacked shade, a barrage of sunflowers shielded it from the highway. These flora were offspring of seeds dropped by trucks en route to export silos. After coasting past two unhitched dog trailers, he pulled up towards the exit. He shifted the car into neutral and killed the engine. Bec had turned back towards the front; her arms, no longer folded. They both sat in silence, staring straight ahead.

"I'm sorry, Bec. I didn't mean to upset you," Smith uttered, returning the indicator lever to its neutral position and letting his hand rest in his lap.

"How have you upset me, Steve?"

Smith knew better than to look at her. He almost raised a hand to touch his face but forced it back down. He knew she would inevitably ask this after his apology. The truth was, he had no idea how he'd hurt her. He didn't even know whether she was hurt, upset, or if those two emotions were part of the same feminine continuum. He had no other option but honesty.

"I don't know how," he confessed, feeling like he'd been abandoned in a desert, left with nothing but his pitiful words for sustenance. "Could you tell me?" His question was genuine and because of this, she tolerated it.

"Steve, you scare me. I'm scared because I can't understand why you do the things you do."

Smith thought it was perhaps not a rhetorical question and started to respond, but halted.

"Like, why you feel the need to lie to get what you want. As if you don't trust me. Or us. As if we don't have a future built on trust." Then, she broke down, sobbing uncontrollably.

Smith was taken aback. He couldn't comprehend how things had spiralled to this level of distress. Whatever it was, it was severe. In his mind, he flipped through the metaphorical *Handbook for Every Man with an Upset Wife*. He'd heard that joke years ago and thought it a suitable distraction from the daunting, miserable predicament he and the woman he loved were currently in.

Smith unfastened his seatbelt, opened his door, and walked around the car to the passenger side. He swung open the door. His wife didn't look up as he leaned in, slipping an arm behind her warm back and pulling her close. She hugged him back, sobbing against his shoulder, her tear-stained cheek pressing into his. Without a word, they held each other for what seemed like minutes until the ache in Smith's back forced him to straighten up. He gently extricated himself from their embrace, settled onto his haunches with his legs astride the running board, and took her hand. She glanced at him, mascara streaking her cheeks.

"I'm sorry, Bec. The last thing I wanted was to hurt you." As he spoke, Smith's mind was already churning, evaluating the potential consequences of his next statement. "I promise I'll be honest with you from now on."

Bec Smith studied him. "About everything?"

"Yes. Everything."

A ghost of a smile flickered across Bec's face as she turned her gaze forward. It was Smith's cue to get back on the road. Once they were cruising down the highway again, Bec called her friend Jill, thanking her for watching the kids and confirming they were on their way home.

As they navigated the western suburbs of Brisbane, Smith's thoughts were consumed with plotting a weekend sailing trip to Moreton Island with his mate Gordon. He felt a wave of resignation at the idea; he knew he had about as much chance of getting Bec's approval as a snowflake surviving in hell. He was devoid of tactics and certainly lacked brownie points. Yet, he was adamant about maintaining a positive outlook.

That's when the idea struck him, exciting and repulsive in equal measure. He could invite Allen, their next-door neighbour, to accompany him and Gordon. Throughout the remainder of the drive, Smith grappled with self-loathing. He questioned if he was sick or if his judgement had been skewed by Bec's reprimands. But his yearning to join Gordon prevailed. Gordon had extended several invitations in the past that Smith had been unable to accept. The more he declined, the more he feared Gordon would stop asking.

By the time they reached home, Smith had oscillated between discarding and embracing the idea of bringing Allen along half a dozen times. There were countless factors to consider. How would Gordon react if he introduced an absolute dill to the mix? Could he somehow encourage Allen to tone down his boorish behaviour? It seemed ridiculous, but he was desperate. A week of contemplation later, he resigned himself to the fact that he had no other choice. The decision was finalised after the girls had rescheduled their Bali trip, during which he expressed unreserved support, surprising neither Bill Leighton nor Bec.

After a concocted Daddy-story put the girls to bed, he flicked off their lights and saw Bec's silhouette in the doorway. She offered a soft smile as he passed, trailing him into their bedroom and shutting the door behind them.

"I'll miss the day they outgrow Daddy-stories," Smith mused, sprawling out on their bed.

"It won't be for a while. You're quite good at them." Bec laid down beside him, propping her head on her hand, her hair cascading to form a curtain over her pillow. "Maybe you could tell me a Daddy-story?"

Smith turned to her, mirroring her pose, a grin tugging at his lips. "Sure."

"But make it X-rated." Bec's voice dipped into a seductive whisper. "Could you do that?"

Smith's eyebrows almost shot off his forehead and he felt himself getting hard. "Absolutely." He saw she wasn't joking as her head-propping hand was deployed to undo her top button. "You're serious?" It wasn't an unwarranted question. Bec's reaction to his romantic novel writing attempt still stung. He was about to raise exactly that when he thought better of it and wondered if, in that tirade, Bec was just a little curious...

His wife nodded slowly. "Go on then." She kicked off her shoes. One ricocheted off the cupboard, causing such a racket that they both held their breath, awaiting a potential outcry from one of the girls. When none came, they exhaled in relief. "If I'm impressed, you get a button undone. If not, I do one up."

Smith was tempted to pounce on his wife then and there. "Perhaps you could unbutton a few more to give me some leeway." It was only then that he noticed she wasn't wearing a blouse but a button-down dress, from the neckline down to its hem near her knees.

Bec undid another button, revealing the upper edge of her black bra. "That's all you get." She grinned wickedly. "Now, get on with it, Daddy." Her voice had dropped another half octave, venturing into sultry territory.

Smith was no stranger to the art of impromptu storytelling, a skill honed from business presentations and last-minute bedtime tales for the girls. However, he intended this to be his tour de force. He locked eyes with his wife, aiming to gauge his success at stoking her desire. He took a deep breath and shifted his hips slightly, accommodating his growing anticipation.

"Once upon a time, there was a king and a queen who lived in a grand castle by a lake. The king inadvertently insulted a witch, who cast a spell on his queen. With a screeching parting cry, the witch announced that the queen would need to experience an orgasm with a different man every day, or she would die."

Bec's eyebrows shot up. "Every day?" She stifled a chuckle.

"Shhh." Smith offered a mild frown.

"Sorry." Her whispered apology was coupled with a mischievously contrite face.

"So, the king dispatched messengers to gather two hundred young men for an evaluation as potential suitors for the queen, intending to set up a rotation."

Smith gestured towards his wife's dress. "Maybe a button now?"

"Get on with it." She flashed him a smile. "I'll let you know when you've earned it."

In the queen's quarters, her maid noticed her prolonged silence. "Are you alright, my queen? I hope you're not distressed?"

"Distressed? No, no, no. I'm fantasising about all the...adventures I'm going to have, and the guaranteed pleasure each day. How could that be distressing?"

Smith needed to readjust his hips again to create a bit more space.

"My Queen." With that, the chambermaid took her leave.

Late in the afternoon, the first suitor was ushered into the queen's chambers, with the door shut and bolted behind him. The queen lay naked on her bed, her maid trying her best to mask her disapproval with the presence of this commoner.

Bec slowly undid another button, causing her husband to involuntarily bite his lip. "There you go, cowboy."

Smith smiled, sighed, and resumed his storytelling.

"It became obvious that the suitor was scared witless. Despite reassurances, he was convinced he would be executed, regardless of the queen's satisfaction. His fear rendered him incapable of arousal. Yet this contingency was anticipated. Two young, unclothed women were summoned from the dressing chamber, and they promptly attended to the man. Before long, he was as erect and huffing like a prized stallion. One of the women then moved towards the queen and began kissing her tenderly, a gesture that was enthusiastically reciprocated. The other woman led the suitor by his now erect member to the queen's bed. The queen, grateful for the man's thorough cleansing prior to entering her chamber, did her best to maintain eye contact. Emboldened, the suitor began to thrust with all the fervour of a man fighting for his life. A mere minute into the act, the chambermaid intervened and yanked him away from the queen, recognising that he was on the brink of climax before the queen could.

The man was nudged aside, making room on the expansive bed. The two women then focused their attentions on the queen, one suckling at a nipple, the other with her face buried into the queen's receptive folds, her tongue moving skilfully. The queen began to moan and, moments later, threw her arms above her head, uttering a deep grunt as her orgasm rippled through her."

Bec undid two buttons, exposing her bra beneath her dress.

Smith, encouraged by his progress, continued. "The woman attending to the queen's nipple remained where she was, while the chambermaid and the other woman guided the man back to the queen. He re-entered her with such force that she let out a sharp cry. This momentarily startled the man, but her attendants ensured he kept up his vigorous efforts. Each woman grabbed one of the queen's legs, pulling them apart to grant him deeper access. She shuddered and screamed out her pleasure for so long that the chambermaid had to smack the suitor's back, pausing him momentarily to ensure the queen could breathe. Fortuitously, the queen reached her climax without the man doing so, so he was ushered into the adjacent chamber followed by the two women. They attended to his needs, and..."

"Hold on...damn..."

"What?"

"Stop talking!"

Smith hadn't noticed that his wife had slipped her hand beneath her dress and was rhythmically pleasuring herself.

"For goodness sake, just take me!" Bec was shimmying out of her panties, aided by Smith who tossed them across the room. With her dress still half-buttoned, he entered her forcefully and made love to his wife with a fiery urgency. It wasn't long before she climaxed with a muffled shriek, writhing beneath him. Smith grunted as he followed suit, their shared climax leaving them both trembling in the aftermath. They held each other, their bodies still reeling from the experience, until their ardour subsided and the remnants of their lovemaking, damp on their heated skin, cooled in the evening air.

$$\diamond$$

Something's Wrong Here

About a month after his standoff with Bill Leighton concerning his father-in-law, Smith sat in bed, reading with his wife, when he suddenly put down his book and stared blankly across the room.

"Everything alright?" Bec asked, noticing his demeanour.

"Maybe. Maybe not."

Bec set her magazine on the bedside table and turned to face her husband. "What's going on?"

Smith placed his hands carefully in his lap. Bec caught sight of this unusual stillness; her husband was a notorious fidgeter when it came to personal inquiries. "I'm not sure, Bec. This whole situation with Anne's dad has become a bloody mess."

Silent and immobile, Bec hoped he would elaborate. Smith acknowledging his behaviour as "my reaction" marked an intriguing shift.

Smith pivoted towards her. "I just can't shake off this thought about a boy from school."

"Perhaps we shouldn't have brought it up," she suggested.

Smith shook his head. "No. It was already on my mind."

"What do you mean?" Bec was taken aback that Steve had been pondering it yet had never confided in her. "What's been on your mind?"

"This boy."

"What about him?" Bec's tone was as soft as she could manage.

Smith remained motionless. "Maybe not him. Maybe...me?"

"What are you getting at, Steve?"

Smith lifted his hands, then let them fall again, an apparent act of resignation. "I've been considering my role in it all."

A hint of alarm rippled through Bec, but she concealed it, aiming to keep the conversation flowing without steering it. Her next question was the only logical one, yet it filled her with dread. "How were you involved?"

Smith drew in a shaky breath, his hands returning to his lap. "I watched it happen." A tear trickled down his cheek, which his wife tenderly wiped away.

Bec's mind raced with possible follow-up questions, anxiety building about what she might uncover. "What did you see?"

Smith seemed to come back to his senses then. He rubbed his eyes and sat up straighter. "No, no, not that. I didn't mean that." He finally noticed the worry etched on his wife's face. "I'm talking about what I saw at school." Realising his words were causing confusion, he clarified, "I saw Dave enter the predator's office, and I saw Price close the door behind him. Saw it more than once."

Bec's heart sank, then quickly soared with relief. She had been bracing for a revelation that her husband was an undisclosed victim of that predator. "But do you believe your younger self would have understood what you saw? Or what was happening?"

Smith slouched awkwardly and faced his wife again. "That's the thing, Bec. I think I did."

His confession left Bec speechless. She struggled to find the right response, not wanting to trivialise his feelings or ineptly guide him to a more positive outlook. She knew nothing about childhood trauma related to horrific events like institutional rape. The situation was concerning. After a moment, she composed herself.

"Steve, perhaps it would help to talk to someone about this." Immediately, she regretted using the word "help." "What I mean is..."

"I've been thinking the same thing," he interrupted.

They looked at each other, void of expression; she in relief and him in resignation. They hugged and kissed and exchanged goodnights. Smith's last thought before falling asleep was that same vision, processed in yet another attempt to find more memory fragments to splice to it, so he could release or perhaps, incriminate, himself for his boyhood inaction on those days back at school.

Getting Help

It took Smith about a week to seek out a psychologist for consultation. Bec had suggested he begin with a visit to a GP, but Smith was adamant about jumping straight into professional help. Meanwhile, he grappled with waves of doubt. The first round of discussions with Bec took place once again at bedtime. Smith was almost convinced he didn't need any external assistance. He saw the situation as a string of unfortunate circumstances and a momentary bout of irritability. But when he mentioned it, he could tell his wife was treading lightly with her responses. It wasn't long before the conversation took a personal turn.

"So, what exactly makes you think I need help?" Smith endeavoured not to sound too defensive.

Bec was prepared for this. She studied him through the reflection in her dressing table mirror. "I don't think there's anything wrong with you, Steve." She smiled reassuringly. "Nothing like that." She ceased brushing her hair and turned to face him. "But the mind is a tricky thing, and your reaction that day..."

"You mean to that irksome old codger."

Bec chose not to take the bait. "Sure, that could've been part of it, but there were other things that worried me." She tilted her head to brush the other side of her hair more forcefully.

"Like what?" Emotion began to creep into Smith's voice.

She paused, laying her brush down, and turned back to her reflection. "Well, for starters, your attitude towards Bill was concerning."

A flash of annoyance sparked in Smith. "He butted in where he wasn't welcome." Smith moved towards the bathroom, halted, and spun back to face his wife. "And drawing a line from an incident at school decades ago to my current state of mind was just... cheap. He had no right..."

"But he did, Steve." Bec pivoted to face him. "He cares about you and wants the best for you." She smiled. "Just like me."

Smith was about to retort, but Bec interjected. "Bill said some other things as well."

"Like what?"

"Bill mentioned he thought you were much closer to that boy than he was. He remembered instances where you defended him from teasers." She studied his face as she spoke.

"So, I was closer. So what?"

Bec straightened her dressing gown over her knees. She felt like abandoning the discussion, but persevered. "He also brought up what happened when you found out about the abuse, and that this boy was one of the victims." She paused there.

Smith was taken aback. His mate had divulged a lot to his wife. "And...?"

"He said you were incredibly upset. So upset that he wondered if you too had been a victim of abuse. Bill wondered if something had happened to you that you'd never revealed." Her hands folded in her lap, the silk dressing gown slipping off her knee. "He was genuinely concerned."

"He never mentioned any of this to me."

"No, he told me that as well."

Smith remembered his inner turmoil over whether to attend Dave Morrison's funeral. In the end, it was a private service. He attempted to meet with Morrison's parents but quickly realised he had nothing to say to them. After all, he had been out of school for a decade when Morrison ended his life, and Smith hadn't seen him in that time.

"That sounds like a strong reaction for someone you weren't particularly close to," she observed, noticing Smith's second toe tucked under — the peculiar habit he shared with his brother, something she noticed when they last gathered a few Christmases back. It made her smile.

"Just think it would be good for you to look at what's there Steve." She tried to avoid looking at his bare feet again. "What can it hurt?" Bec smiled at him. "You never know what you may find."

Smith thought the whole thing was absurd; the result of a nosy mate and a concerned wife. The thought of sitting in front of a psych of some sort answering questions about himself gave him the heebie-jeebies. While he didn't think it justified all this fuss, he did think there was something going on. His reaction to Dick Walsh was way out of character and he was thinking about his school days a lot of late. He agreed.

"OK, Bec. I'll go."

Bec took his hand and kissed the back of it, then hugged him. "I'm so lucky that I have a man who's prepared to look at himself...has the courage to look at himself." It was a line she had prepared.

Smith stood up, smiled and went into the bathroom. "Need a shower."

$$\diamondsuit$$

Collar Yourself!

"Easy mate! Happy to help!" Steve Smith stood back from the computer desk and felt he'd been able to help his neighbour. He was next door with Jack Keating who had become exasperated with his computer not doing what he needed. Jack and Lorraine were the retired couple next door; their grown up kids lived in Melbourne and Cairns. "Make sure you back up all those files and photos you have," Smith reminded him. He suggested getting some memory sticks.

"Where would I buy them?" Smith's neighbour seemed challenged with every facet of computers.

"Any electronics store. I will send you a text with exactly what to ask for."

"Maybe send it to Lorraine now. She's still shopping. I'll find out if she's near one."

Smith watched while his neighbour opened up an app on his phone and could see that his wife was still in the shopping centre.

"How are you doing that?"

"This tracking app." Keating showed him. "Kids got us onto it." He showed Smith how it's used and sure enough, there was Lorraine Keating's 'dot' locating her deep within the largest local shopping centre, about five km away.

"Wow. How much is it?"

"It's free. Best thing out. We can see where the other is and if Lorraine needs help with something I can go straight to her."

He waved the phone. "Like just now; if I see she's nowhere near a shop, I won't bother her. Or if I see she's driving, I won't call her 'cause I don't want to distract her." Keating told Smith how it's set up. It seemed no challenge at all.

Smith was impressed. "Oh I'm onto that mate. That's a great tool."

That night he excitedly raised the issue with his wife. The possibilities for improved communication, coordination and safety for Bec and the family were animating to him.

"A what?" Bec Smith was rubbing moisturiser into each finger.

"A locator app. Jack and Lorraine next door use it."

"What does it do?" She was not clear what Smith was talking about.

"One app is on your phone and one on mine. We can see where each other is on a map in the app."

"So you can see where I am just by looking at your phone?"

"Exactly." Smith was happy she'd caught on.

Bec Smith turned to him from her chair. She looked at him without expression. "Like a tracking collar, in case your dog runs away?"

"What?" Smith didn't like the sound of that.

"An app that tracks your wife? That what it is?"

"No. Well, yeah. But you can see where I am too." Smith sensed the discussion was going off the rails.

Bec Smith looked hard at her husband again. "Are you nuts?" She slowly stood, her tube of moisturiser still uncapped. "You want to track your wife, do you?" She lifted her hands to her hips. "Why not just put a microchip in me? Like Smokey's?"

Smith was horrified. "No. No. You don't get it. This can be a safety thing. I told you...Jack and Lorraine use it."

"They're close to moving into a retirement home. Jack has had two heart attacks and Lorraine has had a stroke. Kind of a different situation, don't you think?" She walked towards their ensuite bathroom. "Their doctor probably put them onto it." She stopped, turned and walked a few steps back towards her husband. "So you really want to put a tracking collar on me?"

"No! Look there are good things you can do with..." He was walking toward her, holding his phone up.

Bec Smith raised her hand to stop him talking. "Let's dump that idea right now, huh Steve? And I'll forget you even suggested it." With that, she turned and walked into the bathroom, energetically closing the door.

Smith slumped onto their bed. "Holy crap!" he muttered to himself. He shook his head and wondered how the idea got so badly twisted, so quickly. That was the most absurd exchange he'd had with his wife. "Put a microchip in her? Seriously?" Smith could not understand how the pragmatic appeal of such a tool was missed. She'd totally "played the man" on this one.

Things remained frosty between them until they went to bed. The matter wasn't raised again.

It was during the following weekend that he saw his neighbour watering their garden. They exchanged waves and Jack walked to the fence. "G'day Steve. How'd that app go? Give it a burl?"

"Don't ask." Smith rolled his eyes.

"No good huh?" Jack was keen to reciprocate for the help his neighbour had given him. "I can get one of the kids..."

"No, no mate it's not that. Loading the app is fine. Bec freaked at the idea of a tracker."

"No kidding?" He looked worried. "Strewth." The two blokes looked at each other for a while, Keating pensively rubbing his beard.

"I know. Didn't expect it." Smith withheld the microchip remark.

Keating didn't want to intrude; he did his best to extricate himself from the discussion. He was sorry he'd maybe contributed to conflict between his neighbour and his wife. Smith also didn't want to continue talking. They went about their affairs with a wave.

His wife's rejection of an idea that Smith thought had merit really irked him through the week ahead. That her response was bellicose was confounding. What could have created such distrust? He wanted to confront what was behind her response. He decided to come home from work to try to discuss it over lunch the next day.

"Lovely!" Bec Smith welcomed the idea of lunch together. She smiled, giving him a hug before he left for work. "I'll make a salad and we've got that new corned meat."

"Great, Bec. See you at twelve-thirty or so."

Smith's morning was light, including two teleconferences, both technical, which allowed him to work his budget spreadsheet in parallel. He texted his wife that he was about to leave work.

Bec Smith had put on a light blue dress and made herself up for her husband. She looked and smelled great and he enjoyed their hug. She was pleased that Smith had made the effort to come home for lunch.

The girls were at school and pre-school, so they were alone but for their pug. They settled into a lovely lunch, sitting beside each other, talking, smiling and touching.

"Had Stacey over for morning coffee. We had a laugh about your 'wife tracker'." She giggled. Smith stiffened. Bec looked at him. "You really are a silly sausage." She smiled, planting a long kiss on his cheek. She reached over to pick up the salad. "Never a dull moment with you, Steve," she chortled. Smith forced a smile.

Despite his wife's dig, opening a discussion about trust seemed a ridiculous notion now. He did his best to put the matter out of his mind and just enjoy being with his wife.

After lunch they had a hug and Bec suggestively reminded him that the kids weren't there and she'd just put new sheets on the bed. Smith wasn't in the mood and feigned busyness. After a warm hug and kiss, he took off back to work. Not only did his wife think he was an idiot, now his neighbour did too. And Stacey probably shared it with her drongo husband. He was not happy and he remained so through the day.

Smith couldn't let go of it. During the drive home from work, he wondered how he could show the value of this app idea in real time. He considered covertly installing the app on Bec's phone and showing her just how valuable it could be. He was confident the app could be put onto her phone without her finding it. Time and time again he'd mused what a dog's breakfast her phone was; apps spread over so many screens, gaps everywhere, it drove him nuts, but every offer he'd made to tidy it up was met with fierce rebuke.

Then there was Bec's repeated use of the "silent" function, which disabled the audible ring and message notifications. She would forget to restore the sound after a meeting, for instance, and not hear that her phone was ringing, sometimes for the rest of the day. It also drove Smith nuts and more than once he'd asked why she had a phone if she can't know someone's ringing her. He pleaded with her to switch the phone off instead of putting it on "silent." Her response was bewildering.

Smith knew his wife's phone password because he'd had to reinstall apps when she'd mistakenly dumped them or couldn't find them. Did he dare? That night he could not get over his dismay with Bec's lack of trust of him, exemplified by her response to the app idea. He did his best to dismiss it.

The next night, while Bec was helping the girls with their homework, in the dining room, Smith found her phone, installed the app and disabled all its notifications. He entered the code provided by his app and linked the two phones. He relocated the app icon on her phone to the fifth or sixth screen, inside a cluster of shopping discount apps. He put her phone back on charge and joined the family downstairs. He wondered if he had just done something ludicrous. However, he was confident that time would deliver an opportunity for the app to be of assistance to his wife and family. He told himself that, once he'd proven the app functioned correctly, he'd not look at it until an emergency warranted it.

Nothing happened for well over a month. He had kept to the promise he made himself to not look at the app.

During dinner on a Thursday night, Bec Smith sheepishly admitted she'd lost her phone and needed to buy a new one.

Smith looked up from his soup. "Really?" His mind raced. Her phone was almost $1000 and barely a year old. "Have you called it?"

"Yes but..."

"Oh no. Let me guess." He looked back into his soup and then at her. "You left it on silent."

Bec Smith smiled guiltily.

"Was it on vibrate? Sometimes that's enough noise..."

His wife didn't look up but shook her head. "No I hate that. Freaks me out when it goes off."

It was apparent Bec was feeling awful about it. Smith had no intention of making her feel worse but did not want to fork out for a new phone.

"When did you last have it?"

"At the shops, after I took the girls over to Anne's this morning. I think I lost it in the shopping centre."

"Or had it stolen."

"Yes. Or stolen."

"Sure it's not at Anne and Bill's place?"

"Yes. I went back there and we turned the place upside down."

Smith looked at his daughters, who were curiously silent. "Do you girls remember where Mummy's phone is?" The kids both looked at their Mum.

"Steve I've asked them and they don't know."

"OK." It was then he remembered the passwords that his wife had stored in code in the "Notes" app on her phone. They weren't the entire password; some detail was omitted but a half smart thief could work some of them out. Months ago, she dismissed his concern, so he dropped it.

"So I'll go to the same store tomorrow and see if I can get another phone." Smith didn't respond.

He stood. "Excuse me, need to go to the little boys room." The girls snickered. Bec Smith watched with a smile as her husband walked out. "Beautiful soup, thanks darling."

Once in the toilet, Smith took his phone from his pocket and launched the locator app. Within seconds, and with great relief, he could see that her phone was at the Leighton's place, toward the front of their house. She had 48% battery left according to the app. He shut down the app and returned to the dinner table after washing his hands.

"I'm sure we'll find it darling. I wouldn't worry."

"Don't know how. I'm worried about the banking apps." She expediently didn't mention the abbreviated passwords, which must have been worrying her, Smith thought.

"I'm sure it will be fine Bec."

She looked at her husband. Atop her concern for the threat to their wealth and security was his reaction to her losing her phone. "Why wasn't he losing his shit?" she asked herself. After he'd helped with the washing up, she gave him a long hug and a passionate kiss on the neck.

"How lovely, darling. What did I do to deserve that?"

"I'm just grateful you didn't get upset with me over the phone."

"Of course, darling. Could have happened to me," Smith offered generously.

"Just, well, thank you."

They separated but stayed holding each other. "I'm sure we'll get it back sooner or later." Smith smiled.

A half hour later, while Bec Smith was supervising bath time, he grabbed his phone and went out to the back yard after disabling the sensor light. He called Bill Leighton.

"G'day Steve."

"Hey mate." Smith went straight to business. "Listen I need you to find Bec's phone."

"Yeah Annie told me. Where do you want me to look?"

"It's at your place."

"No mate. They looked for it."

"No, it's at your place."

"Didn't I just say it wasn't?"

"Bill, listen to me for a sec." Smith paused and collected his thoughts. "It's at your place. I know for sure. I can tell you…"

"Mate what the fuck are you up to?" Leighton interrupted, a little annoyed.

Smith realised "full disclosure" was the only way he was going to get any cooperation out of his mate. He gave Leighton the low-down on the app situation, interrupted by his mate bursting into laughter.

"Let me see if I have this right, mate. Bec told you not to put a tracking app on her phone but you did anyway?" He let loose a nervous chuckle. "Are you right in the head, bloke?"

Smith had no patience for Leighton's musings. "You going to help me or not?"

Bill Leighton thought about that question. He was a junior partner in a tax accountancy firm. He gave personal and company tax advice to A-listers and billion dollar companies on a daily basis. He had no doubt about answering their most difficult questions in sometimes stressful and confronting meetings. But, he had grave doubts about answering the question just put to him. The last time he did something dodgy with Steve Smith, he ended up in hospital with scalded nuts and a very upset wife. Leighton was, of course, going to help his mate, although he thought Smith deserved some table-turned brinksmanship. "Am I going to help you out? Hmmm. Now why would I have any hesitation in saying yes to that?"

"What the fuck mate?" Smith was incredulous.

"OK. What do I have to do?"

Smith let out a sigh of relief. "OK. Bec's phone is on silent so you won't be able to locate it by ringing it. So it..."

"Why is it on silent?" Leighton interrupted.

"Mate, take a breath." Smith continued. "The phone's somewhere near the front of your house. I'm guessing in the lounge room or maybe outside on the porch. Go have a look. But if you find it, don't say anything to Anne."

"Why not?" Leighton was suddenly feeling quite wary.

"Because you're going to delete the tracker app before you tell Anne you found it."

"Whoa mate. Not sure I like that. I mean...fucking with Bec's phone..."

"You're not. You're just deleting that app."

"Maaaaate...?"

Smith was feeling tense. "What?"

"Just go fess-up and tell Bec how you found her phone."

Smith knew that was coming. A pang of guilt hit him. Perhaps Leighton was right. Best to fess-up now and at least Bec will get her phone back.

"Steve..?" Bec was on the back landing squinting into the dark. "That you?"

"Yeah darl, just on the phone." Bugger. Who makes night calls from a darkened back yard? "Be up in a sec Bec."

His wife wondered what her husband was up to. She walked back into the house.

"That Bec?" Leighton was getting concerned.

"Yep. Hold on."

An idea struck Smith. He held the phone by his side and gave it some thought. "Mate you there?"

"Yep."

"Shut off all the lights down that end of the house and then call Bec's phone. When you call it, her screen should illuminate or flash and you might be able to see it."

"When?"

"Now."

"Now?"

"Yes now. What's the problem?"

"The kids are in the lounge room doing their homework."

"Shit." Smith was becoming exasperated. He was running out of puff and with only 32% battery left on Bec's phone, he had to do something. The thought of Bec unnecessarily buying a new phone in the morning made him grind his teeth.

Smith heard the screen door squeak open. "Steve? You OK?" It was Bec again.

"Yeah darl."

"What are you doing?"

"Hold on Bec."

Smith realised he had to come clean with his wife and then go get her phone. There was nothing else to do.

"Mate you there?" Smith returned to his phone conversation.

"Yep."

"OK. I'm going to go tell Bec about the tracking app."

There was a silence. "Orrite fella." Leighton felt like he was saying good luck to his polar explorer mate before turning back to base camp. He hung up.

Steve Smith shoved his phone into his pocket and walked up the back stairs under his wife's gaze. He stepped onto the back landing, taking her hand. "I know where your phone is."

Bec Smith became excited. "Where is it?"

"At Bill and Anne's place."

"They found it?"

"No. But it's there."

She was confused. "Steve I told you we turned the place upside down."

"Bec, it's there."

"How are you so sure?"

Smith took out his phone. He launched the tracking app. There, over the top of the Leighton's house, clearly seen, was a dot with a "B" next to it.

"What's that?"

"It's the tracking app. That's why I know where your phone is."

Bec Smith took a breath. "How does your phone know where my phone is?"

"Here it comes," Smith agonised under his breath. "I put that tracking app on your phone, Bec."

His wife gasped, taking her hand back, covering her mouth. "You did what?" Her brow came down. "How? When?"

"About a month ago." Smith could barely look at her.

She glared at Smith for an agonisingly long period. He didn't dare flinch.

"Give me your phone."

He gave it to his wife. "It's the app next to the bank icon. You just…"

Bec Smith turned away slowly and with a grunt, threw his phone like it was a hunting boomerang. It arced over the fence and splashed into the Allens' pool. Without looking at her husband, she walked inside and went up to their bedroom.

Smith was left to marvel how his wife could throw that far.

The next day, Bec Smith found her phone behind a pot plant in the corner of the Leighton's lounge room. Stacey Allen found an iPhone at the bottom of their pool during her morning swim.

The Smiths now both use the tracker app as do the Leightons. Bec Smith changed her phone password.

Tell Me More, Mr. Smith

The second meeting with the psychologist kicked off smoothly. Smith was in high spirits, surprisingly having found some enjoyment in their initial chat, though a hint of frustration managed to sneak in. The psychologist, a pleasant woman whom he guessed to be in her mid-forties, exuded respectfulness in her questions and expressions. Despite his nerves, Smith held back, answering briefly only when prompted.

During his retelling of the incident, he realised he was purposefully withholding conclusions or explanations. He found it rather peculiar and slightly bothersome that Brenda, as the psychologist introduced herself, didn't probe too much into what he'd shared. Sure, she asked a few questions, but they were mostly clarifications. By the end of their first meeting, Smith thought he'd given her ample material for at least some observations, if not deductions. But no insights were forthcoming.

Smith was also wary about his issue's seeming insignificance compared to stories flooding the media about child abuse victims. He wasn't an abuse survivor and had no intention of entering that discussion. As the second session kicked off, Smith found himself questioning his presence there. He figured an honest start would be to share this thought.

Brenda, however, steered the conversation in an unexpected direction. While she didn't dismiss his self-declaration as a "non-abuse survivor," she remained relentless in her inquiries about his school experiences.

"Why do you think you're not deserving of this conversation, Steve?" Brenda positioned her hands in her lap. "There are no labels such as 'abuse survivor' or 'non-abuse survivor' in this setting." She scratched her face delicately with a pencil-thin finger before returning her hand to her lap.

"Well, Brenda," he started, realising he was quite fond of her name. "On the trauma scale, I'd reckon I wouldn't even register, while an actual abuse survivor might be a solid six or seven out of ten, at least." As the words left his mouth, he realised how absurd it was to quantify suffering in this context. Her serene, impassive face threw him off. He almost wished she would burst into laughter, mocking him. At least that he could handle.

Halfway through the session, Smith decided he needed to assert himself more. He expressed his belief that his sadness stemmed from guilt over not helping his school friend. Yet, it seemed Brenda wasn't entirely convinced. He voiced this feeling to her as well. By the end of their chat, he felt disoriented. He was dealing with a straightforward issue and began to wonder why he didn't just drop it and move on. Perhaps Dick Walsh got what he deserved, and Bill was just being a wuss for not confronting him first. But that wasn't a thought he could share with Bec. Instead, he opted to share more general observations and feelings, interspersed with silent introspection — all in a bid to reassure her about his mental state.

As he'd anticipated, Bec was interested but didn't probe too deeply into his therapy experience. He stuck to his "script," and she seemed content. Smith had requested that their therapy sessions remain a secret between them. With a chuckling, "of course, Steve!" she agreed.

The third session didn't go as well. He found himself circling back to the insignificance of his "issue," downplaying it against the hardships a real "abuse survivor" might be experiencing.

Finally, the psychologist shook her head and dropped her hands from her lap.

"OK, I want you to drop that and not raise it again."

Smith felt she was admonishing in tone. "OK, sure."

"So I'm going to summarise what I think I've heard from you Steve, in two and a bit sessions. Let me play it back and see if you're OK with it."

"OK."

Brenda locked her gaze with his, unblinking. "You had a dispute with someone who you felt was after you. His actions made you uncomfortable. You thought there was a religious undertone to it. You were particularly displeased since it echoed previous encounters. To the spectators, and this man's wife, your fervent rebuttal looked like an attack."

She had her notebook open but wasn't referring to it. Smith spotted a scar on her left ankle and quickly redirected his gaze back to her face.

"We good so far?"

"Yes."

"Righto. So, your friend and wife — out of concern for you — brought up the historical abuse of a childhood mate and wondered if this might be a reason for your reaction to this man's advances."

Smith stiffened. "Well, not 'advances'. I wouldn't phrase it as 'advances'."

Brenda switched her pen to her other hand with a smile. "What would you call it?"

Smith was not a fan of this turn of events. *Are we playing word games already?* He tried to show his irritation, but wasn't sure he was successful. *Why is she hung up on a word?* He let out a sigh, crossed his legs, and slumped a bit in his chair. His mind drew a blank.

"I don't know. Don't have a word for it."

"Alright. Let's leave it at that."

"Attack." Smith blurted it out.

Brenda looked up from her notes. "Attack? Is that what it felt like, Steve?"

Smith could feel his frustration growing. "I suppose so."

"Alright. That's a potent word." Brenda offered a half-smile as if to soften her comment. "How did this man's actions come across as an attack?"

Smith uncrossed his legs, remembering past sales training advice about body language and openness in discussions.

"I hadn't invited his attention. I showed zero interest in what he was peddling previously. It was like he singled me out as if I were an easy target, I suppose."

Brenda swiftly scribbled some notes. "Did you feel like you had to defend yourself?" She studied him closely.

"I suppose so, yes."

"And if you hadn't defended yourself, what do you think would have happened?"

Smith sat up and leaned forward, his hands coming together under his chin. "I'm not sure." For the first time, he felt a genuine connection with this medical professional.

"Did you feel vulnerable?"

"Not vulnerable, no."

"How would you describe it?"

"Angry."

"Okay. Angry." Brenda flashed a quick smile, as if they'd just accomplished something. "Why do you think you felt angry?"

"It felt invasive. He was imposing his will on me as if I needed it." Smith settled comfortably back into his chair. "And I didn't appreciate it."

"Did you consider leaving?" Brenda reached behind her to grab something while asking. "You know, just walking away?"

"Why should I?"

"I'm not suggesting you should have, Steve. That wasn't my question."

Smith considered her question reasonable. "I had done so before when he started on me."

"That day?"

"That day and at a previous family event at my mate's place." Smith elaborated. "This bloke is the father of our close friends. Father and father-in-law."

"Tell me about him."

"What do you want to know?" Smith would have preferred not to.

"Perhaps what you find disagreeable about him."

Smith's gaze drifted past Brenda to a photo on her desk. It was of a woman about Brenda's age. She was attractive. He wondered if she was Brenda's...

"Steve?" He was jolted back to the present.

"Oh, right. Sorry."

"What did you find disagreeable about him?"

"His presumption that I would just stand there and take his tirade."

"How would you describe the power balance between the two of you?"

Smith was becoming impatient again. "That's a strange question. Not sure this has anything to do with power."

Smith's gaze flickered from the photo on Brenda's desk back to her. She had subtly shifted in her seat. He was itching to make his escape. "I'm not convinced this is going to be fruitful, Brenda. It feels like you've already drawn your own conclusions about me and are steering the conversation in that direction." Smith was rather chuffed with his eloquence.

She swivelled her chair again and picked up a red pen, passing it to the other hand that was clutching her notes. "We're not here to jump to conclusions about you." She raised her hand to cut off Smith's incoming rebuttal. "We're here because something happened that elicited a reaction you find concerning."

"Well, it's more like my wife found it concerning."

Brenda swapped hands holding her notes and gifted him with a smile. "To me, Steve, you come off as a mature, independent thinker." She forced another smile. "I have a hunch this has more to do with your own concerns than your wife's."

Smith found that remark oddly judgmental. His eyes strayed to the photo on her desk, lingered for a moment, then returned to her. Mulling over her words, he finally conceded, "Yes, alright, it is a concern to me."

Brenda's face remained impassive. "Okay, Steve. It seems like you're downplaying the need for professional help, like your feelings aren't serious enough to warrant attention." Smith froze, feeling exposed.

"Childhood trauma can surface in a myriad of ways and at different stages of one's life."

"I wouldn't exactly call it trauma."

"Sure, I can." Brenda's smile widened, genuine and compassionate. "You hold on to a memory that, in your own words, haunts you. This memory might stem from your past inability to help a vulnerable friend who was violated — maybe even more severely. This is not a judgment of your past self, or your present self. Don't get hung up on semantics. I'm not here to label the emotions that were provoked that night with your friend's father-in-law. However, I am convinced you were triggered. What I want to know now is how you felt towards that man when he was, to borrow your words, 'at you.'"

Smith frowned, then forced himself to relax. "I told you I felt attacked."

"I think that describes more what happened." She emphasised the last two words, a slight frown creasing her brow. "I want to know how you felt." She stressed the final word.

Trying to suppress his irritation, Smith pressed his lips together. "I'm not sure I felt anything."

"Steve, please lower your hands beside your chair."

Smith complied.

Brenda offered a thankful smile. "At the very moment before you 'lost it' at him, what were you feeling?"

Smith let his mind drift back to the incident. He fell silent for a while. "Alone." His own answer startled him, but it also brought a sense of relief.

Brenda remained expressionless. "Alone. Why 'alone,' Steve?"

For a brief moment, Smith was back in high school, watching an adult hand close the door. Brenda's question brought him back to the present.

"He cornered me away from everyone else at the barbie. No one could hear what he was saying. No one could see I was being verbally assaulted. No one knew what he was trying to coerce me into."

Brenda smiled again. "Alone is a good description, but it's more an assessment of your situation. Sure, you could argue it's a feeling, but I need you to dig deeper. What did you feel then?"

Smith was stumped. He wasn't sure there was anything else. But then it hit him. For a moment, he was back there. "I was scared."

Once again, Brenda smiled. No validation, no gratitude, no recognition—just a smile. "Steve, what do you think you were frightened of?"

Suddenly, Smith felt unstable and ravenous, as if his blood sugar level had taken a sudden nosedive. He caught Brenda's gaze, pressed his lips together, then let his eyes drop to the floor by her feet. Realising he'd been scrutinising the tops of her feet peeking over her shoes, he awkwardly averted his eyes. Brenda had him pegged.

"Stay with it, Steve." Her voice was soothing and warm.

Taking a deep breath, Smith nodded in acknowledgment and allowed himself to relax in his seat. "I was afraid I might do something I didn't want to."

This time, Brenda's smile vanished. She straightened in her seat, shifted the pen to her other hand, and took a deep breath.

"May I propose a thought?"

"Go ahead."

"Perhaps you felt alone, vulnerable, and uncertain of this man's intentions. There were others nearby, yet none were privy to your predicament. You wanted to escape, but that seemed impossible." Her gaze didn't waver. "In the field of psychology, we often discuss the concept of 'the lizard brain'. Have you heard of that?"

"No." Smith refrained from guessing.

"It's our most basic instinct that has kept us safe since birth. It acts in the most primal way, identifying poten- tial threats and making decisions to ensure our survival." Brenda's eyes bore into Smith, but he resisted the urge to deflect. "Understand, it acts based on previous experiences, whether correctly or incorrectly interpreting signals from our environment and interactions. It will issue commands to you, and you will have no choice but to follow them." Brenda turned slightly, placing her notes on the desk. "My sugges- tion is that your lizard brain detected something it didn't like. Its responses are limited — 'fight or flight' are the most well-known, among others. My belief is that when Mr. Walsh 'came at you,' as you put it, your lizard brain commanded you to 'fight.' You didn't clock him one —" Brenda caught her Aussie slang with a chuckle, "— but you certainly let him have it verbally. That reaction was likely a mix of primal and intellectual responses." She finished with a smile, her hands settling in her lap.

"Guess that makes sense, since he had come at me before." Smith shrugged, nodding at the same time.

Brenda smiled again. "I'd venture to guess that the sense of threat you experienced on a primal level first originated in your childhood." She glanced at her notes but didn't seem to be reading them. "There's another possibility I'd like you to consider." Her eyes returned to his. "Perhaps you knew something was amiss with what you witnessed back at school. You couldn't put your finger on it, but something was off. Maybe you identified this teacher as a potential threat to yourself."

Smith subtly tilted his head, shrugged, and squinted. "I was never near him—the teacher, I mean. I wasn't involved in any way."

"I understand. But perhaps you feared something wasn't right, and if it could happen to that boy, it could happen to you."

Smith sank deeper into his chair. A chilling sensation began to creep over him; he shook his head in denial. His legs felt like leaden pipes, and his lips were pressed tightly together.

"What's happening now, Steve?" Brenda's tone was tranquil yet assertive, and she pointed towards his chest.

Smith opened his mouth to talk but he could not make any sound. His mind took him back to the History class with that man, seemingly and repeatedly giving him more attention than he was due as a class member. The times when that teacher would stand next to him while in-class exercises were being completed with his crotch closer to his ear than he'd think necessary.

"Oh my God." Smith listened to himself almost as a third person.

"What are you feeling, Steve?"

Smith looked at her, his eyes watering. He drew a quick, deep breath. "I don't know."

"Give me a word."

"Fear." Smith almost whispered it. "Fear." Smith looked at her, more directly than he had in any session to date. He put his face in his hands and spoke through them. "I wanted him to leave me alone."

It was then when Smith realised what was going on. He did have a sense that David Morrison was somehow in trouble. Smith had seen his face in class and he seemed upset. That was the class after lunch. Smith and his friend were going to end up in that room together. He knew it. He didn't want it because he had seen the upset in David's face. But he knew he was a "nice boy" like David was. Smith heard his psychologist talking but was not listening. He felt empty. It was one of the worst feelings he'd had.

The session wound up and once Brenda was satisfied that he was OK, he left. He left his phone turned off and drove home, all the while thinking of his now-departed friend and how he might have been a victim. There were a lot of things that he knew now that he didn't know anything about, back then. He didn't know what to make of it. Smith wondered if his reaction to Anne Leighton's father was rooted in this part of his life's story. He wasn't sure. He wasn't sure he would ever be.

Whatever it Takes

Several days later, Smith found himself ready to undertake his "mission impossible." It was time to venture into sailing with Gordon. Like any seasoned strategist facing high-stakes, he'd honed his game plan and felt confident he could pull it off. The "Jim Allen factor" wasn't fully accounted for, but Smith remained convinced that involving him was a strategic necessity.

After another bedtime story session with the girls, he found his wife, Bec, in the kitchen mending one of his socks.

"Aw, thanks, Bec!"

Lifting her head, Bec gifted him a smile before returning to her task.

"Been thinking..."

"Yes...?" Her voice was soft and melodic.

"About your suggestion that I spend time with Jim..."

"Jim who?" Bec didn't bother to look up.

"Jim. Next door Jim."

Bec lifted her gaze, her face painted with confusion. "Jim Allen?"

"Yes, Jim."

His wife regarded him with a quizzical expression. "Ye-esss...?" Her response was cautious, even curious.

"Well, I've been pondering on a potential activity I could invite him to join me in." Hearing his own words, Smith's confidence wavered.

"What's that?"

He took a breath, ready to make his pitch, but Bec cut him off.

"No, forget *what*. Why?" She'd stopped mending the sock, placing it on her lap and turning her full attention to him.

"Why?" He hadn't anticipated this line of questioning so early on.

"Yes. Why?"

Smith collected himself. "Just been thinking they're our neighbours, and perhaps I could be friendlier."

Bec regarded him sceptically, maintaining a tight-lipped expression. "Hmm?"

"Don't you think?" Steve felt his plan teetering on the brink of failure.

"I do."

"Something's come up, and I thought it might be a good opportunity to involve one of my old mates, and Jim."

"Which old mate?" Her face remained unreadable.

"Gordon."

"Gordon? You haven't seen him in years."

"Yes, because we've both been busy being dads." He felt this was a solid counterpoint.

Bec held his gaze. "What's Jim got to do with it?"

Steve found himself floundering. Had he messed up? Could he have circumvented involving Jim? *Stick to the plan*, he reassured himself.

"Like I said, Bec, it might be a good activity to involve Jim in."

Bec, who'd been completely still throughout their discussion, rose and walked over to the kitchen counter. "Coffee?"

"Decaf. Thanks."

"Have you asked him?"

"Who? Jim?"

"No, Gordon."

"Gordon invited me."

Bec swivelled to face him. "Why would you invite Jim Allen? He doesn't even know Gordon."

Holy crap, Smith thought. His plan was derailing. "As I mentioned, it's an opportunity to spend time with Jim."

"Have you asked Jim?"

Before he could answer, Bec continued. "And have you asked Gordon? About Jim coming?"

"Haven't asked either. Wanted to talk to you about it first."

"How do you know..." Bec paused and turned to her husband again. "What's the activity?"

"The what?" He didn't need her to clarify, but he needed a few extra seconds.

"What are you planning with Gordon?" Bec's patience was wearing thin.

Here we go, he thought. "Gordon has a boat and plans to sail to Moreton Island for four days. In three weeks."

Bec rested her hands on the counter, shaking her head. After holding the pose for a few seconds, she turned to face him, crossing her arms and breaking into a smile.

"I think that's a fantastic idea. I'm sure Jim would be thrilled. I'll mention it to Stacey tomorrow."

"I can tell Jim."

"I'll tell Stacey." It wasn't a suggestion—it was a declaration.

Smith returned her smile, their gaze locked. He had roughly three seconds to back out, to reveal the plot, but he let the moment slip.

"OK, thanks, darling," Smith chuckled, walking away, his mind churning over how to break the news to his mate. Crikey, he hadn't even confirmed there was room on the boat. Gordon hadn't mentioned inviting anyone else, but... Oh, bugger.

Back in his office the next day, Smith called his old mate to discuss the matter.

"Sure, mate. There's room." Gordon didn't seem fazed by the odd prospect of bringing an unknown aboard for the weekend. Smith felt a pang of guilt; clearly, Gordon trusted him to bring along a decent bloke. You know, not a total galah; someone who knows how to sail and won't turn green at the first wave. He envisioned Jim Allen and slumped in his chair. He pondered whether he could've pulled this off without involving Allen but dismissed the thought as hypothetical.

Around 10 a.m., Bec sent a text confirming that Jim was keen to go. Well, that settles it, he thought.

After a gruelling day, Smith arrived home just before sunset. Jim Allen was standing in his driveway, arms crossed, chatting with Bec. He ignored Smith until he'd stepped out of the car.

"Moreton Island, huh? Looking forward to it." Without another word, Allen walked past him, arms still crossed, heading towards his own house.

Smith watched him go, then turned to his wife. At a loss for words, he just raised his eyebrows. Bec, arms also crossed, returned the gesture, pursed her lips, and walked towards their front steps. "You're a strange one, Steve Smith," she muttered, her tone indifferent.

Smith stood in his driveway, laptop bag in hand. It was still possible that Allen would immerse himself in the yachting experience and be altogether affable on the bay. It was all he could hope for. He took a deep breath then followed his wife into the house.

A few days later, he called Jim Allen to discuss what to bring. Allen was "yeah, yeah, yeah" all the way through. Smith asked if he got seasick, secretly hoping Allen would admit to severe nausea so he could justify dropping him from the crew. He didn't. Or at least, he claimed not to. By the end of the conversation, Allen mentioned a trolling rod, but Smith assured him it wasn't needed as there would already be two on the boat.

"Got one anyway," was Allen's retort, to which Smith grunted, ending their chat.

The weeks flew by with minimal discussion about the upcoming sail to Moreton Island. With a day to go, Smith checked in with Allen, surprised that his wife hadn't been bombarding him with reminders; he suspected their wives were conferring.

Stacey Allen had offered to drop them off at the Manly marina on the shores of Moreton Bay. On the morning of their departure, a brisk southeast wind blew at fifteen knots. Smith met Gordon in the car park, their firm handshake morphing into a backslapping hug. It was great to see him. He introduced Jim and Stacey Allen, and Gordon flashed Smith a wink and a head tilt as she opened the boot of their Mercedes SUV. Inside was a mammoth overhead reel on a short, powerful game rod, poking through the dropped back seat. It looked brand new.

"What the hell are you going to do with that?" Gordon beat Smith to the punch. "Going for a world record marlin?"

"Mackeral," Allen retorted dismissively. He turned to Stacey and planted a long, passionate kiss on her lips, making sure the other blokes witnessed every second of it. Gordon squinted while Smith merely shrugged.

Once Stacey had left, they carried the gear out to the boat where Gordon showed Allen to his bunk. With the yacht featuring a centre cockpit layout, Gordon claimed the aft cabin while Smith had the bow bunk. The quarter berth was left for Allen. He just stared at it.

"That?"

Gordon exchanged glances with Smith, then turned to Allen. "Sure, it's a full berth."

Allen remained silent and dropped his gear onto the bunk. Gordon and Smith busied themselves prepping the boat to leave. The vessel was packed with food and booze; they'd agreed to split all costs. Gordon had spent most of the day at the boat and they were ready to set sail. After starting the engine, he and Smith began untying the spring lines. By the time they returned to the stern, Allen was busy setting up his oversized trolling rig. Gordon shot Smith a "what the hell" look, but Smith tried to play it cool. Once Gordon was out of earshot, he approached Allen.

"Jim, don't you think we should get the boat ready before fiddling with your fishing gear?"

Allen shot up and glared at him, startling Smith so much he stepped back. "Yes, sure Steve." He left his gear scattered on the deck. "What needs to be done?"

Smith pointed at the fishing tackle. "All of this needs to be stowed before we depart." Without waiting for a response, he turned to join Gordon, who was adjusting the jib sheet track block positions. Gordon leaned in, lowering his voice.

"Who is this bloke?"

Smith glanced at him, already weary from the thought of Allen on board. "He's my neighbour."

Gordon studied him, a myriad of comments left unsaid. When they returned to the stern, Allen had finished rigging his lure and the rod was in the rod holder.

Gordon approached him. "Sorry, mate. No lures on rods unless they're in the water."

Allen looked puzzled. "What?"

"You've got to remove the lure until you're actually using it." Gordon tried his best to explain, while Smith decided to keep a safe distance from the conversation.

"Why?"

"People can get tossed around on a yacht and end up with a lure hook lodged in them. Especially with treble hooks." He gestured at the lure beside the gigantic rod.

Allen scoffed. "It's going in the water as soon as we cast off." His tone was defiant, and Smith began questioning the enormous mistake he'd made. He'd never spent so much time listening to Jim Allen and didn't like what he was seeing or hearing.

Gordon stood quietly for a moment. He wasn't one to back down, and Smith could see he was weighing whether to escalate the situation before they even left the marina. He glanced at Smith, then back at the boat. "Alright, let's go." He headed for the helm. "Jim, release the aft line when I say; Steve, you handle the forward line. Springs are already off."

"Right!" Smith made his way towards the bow.

Smith had to crane his neck to keep an eye on Allen through the dodger and past the mast. Allen went to the stern and seemed to be more interested in his rod's position than the task at hand. To Smith's disbelief, Allen relocated the rod from the starboard side transom holder to the port side holder, right next to the aft line cleat. Smith was puzzled, wondering if Allen had perceived some obstacle to his planned fishing on the starboard side.

"Let go all!" Gordon commanded, dropping the engine into reverse and spinning the wheel in preparation to depart. But Allen was still fumbling to secure his monstrous rod in the transom holder. Unseen by Gordon, Smith chose to hold onto the bow line for the time being.

"Aft line still on!" Smith hollered loud and clear, prompting Gordon to whip his head aft. Smith still hadn't released the forward line, compensating for the wind pushing against the bow.

Finally securing his rod, Allen bent down leisurely and lifted the aft line from the stern cleat.

"No! Leave the aft line on!" Gordon yelled, instructing Allen not to unmoor it. The chance had passed; Allen's delay had misaligned the boat, making it unsuitable to back out. Still clutching the aft line, which was pulling him to the rail, Allen turned towards Gordon, ready to deliver a snarky retort.

As he swivelled, he lost his balance, flinging his arm out to steady himself. His arm collided with the aerial on the solar panel frame, and in a reflex, he pulled back sharply, driving one of the treble hooks on his lure into his upper side forearm. A shriek of pain echoed as his body weight hung from the hook. His face contorted in agony and shock. He let go of the aft line.

"Oh shit," Smith muttered, watching the spectacle unfold in slow motion. He knew he had to grab that aft line quickly, or Gordon's boat would drift into the neighbouring cruiser. Disregarding Allen's yelps of pain, he sprinted the length of the boat, grabbing the boathook en route and shoved past Allen, threading the boathook through the mooring line loop just before it floated out of reach. The strain of holding the boat echoed in his grunt.

Gordon was flabbergasted. He couldn't fathom how they hadn't even dropped lines before someone injured themselves. Allen's cries of pain reverberated like a gunshot. Passers-by from neighbouring boats peeked out from their covers or stepped onto their decks to investigate the commotion. Once the boat was secure, Smith turned to Allen, whose howls were still echoing.

"Jim. Cut it out. You're OK, mate."

Allen stared at his arm, the hook tip and barb hidden well beneath his skin. "How am I OK?" he shrieked. Smith was concerned he might faint or go into shock.

"Gordon, fetch some pliers." Gordon, who had remained at the helm, glanced forward to see the bow line still secure, then darted below deck, reappearing with a pair of large cutting pliers. He carried them aft, where Allen had ceased his wails but was now swearing at them at the top of his voice.

"Jim. Cut it out." He turned to Gordon. "Help steady him in case he topples over." The lure hook embedded in Allen's arm had come loose from the runner. Gordon steadied Allen from behind, enduring another round of needless wailing.

Smith snipped off the lure from its trace and unhooked the other treble hook from the rod runner. The lure fell to be hanging out of Allen's arm with the second treble hook swinging free, which they needed to be cautious about should Allen flail his arm. It gave Smith the first good look at it. The hook was through into his arm but not deeply. It had punctured his skin parallel to his musculature.

He looked at Gordon in an apologetic way. Gordon just shrugged.

"Alright, let's get him seated." They carefully lowered Allen onto the deck. Nearby onlookers began offering unsolicited advice. A lady pushed through the crowd, announcing her intention to call an ambulance.

"No. No need." Smith spoke firmly, managing to dissuade the lady.

"Why the bloody hell not?" Allen retorted, visibly upset. "I've got a bloody hook in my arm." His voice was shaky and high-pitched.

"I can get it out," Smith assured, his tone still firm. "No worries."

That's when Allen fainted, slumping into Gordon's arms.

"For Pete's sake," Gordon grumbled, growing impatient.

"Hand me the pliers," Smith motioned to Gordon. "I can remove it while he's out cold."

"You'll do no such thing," the lady who'd wanted to call the ambulance retorted, moving closer to the scene.

Gordon lowered Allen onto the deck and they positioned him beside the folded cockpit table. "The lady's got a point, you know. This bludger might accuse you of assault."

It was the first time Gordon expressed his opinion of Allen. What a debacle. *I'm the bludger*, Smith thought.

After regaining consciousness, Allen sat up, sipping water provided by Smith who'd fetched it from the saloon. Smith had called Bec to ask Stacey to come to the marina and take him to the hospital, considering Allen was irritable and panicking.

For a good twenty minutes, they sat in silence. The ambulance lady had provided some ice wrapped in a towel, which Smith pressed onto the wound. Allen barely glanced at the two men, while Smith and his mate exchanged uncomfortable looks. They had secured the hook in Allen's arm with Elastoplast, lure still attached, after reassuring him it was necessary. They hadn't even tried to remove the hook from the lure. Gordon had to escort Allen to the marina gate as it required a swipe card for access.

Once Allen was gone with Stacey, Bec bombarded Smith with questions over the phone.

"Where did you come back from?"

"We never left."

"What? This happened in the marina?"

"Yep."

"How?"

"He just slipped or tripped and fell onto the lure."

"Bloody hell, Steve. Seriously?"

"Hold on, Bec. Gordon warned him to remove the lure from the rod for this very reason. Jim ignored the advice and made a fool of himself in the process."

"Bloody hell, Steve." Bec Smith was about to argue that her husband was responsible for his guest, but she held her tongue.

"I know. It's not serious. I could have removed it, but he wouldn't let me."

Bec knew he was capable. She'd seen Smith remove a triple hook from a kid's arm years ago on the Gold Coast after a wayward cast by another kid. "Did you try?"

"Couldn't get near him. He was shrieking like a banshee and then he fainted."

"He fainted?"

"Yep."

"Bloody hell, Steve."

"I know, Bec. I know."

"So, what are you going to do?"

"What do you mean?"

"Are you going to Moreton? You may as well."

Smith hadn't considered this, as Gordon was sitting patiently. "Hang on, I'll ask Gordon. Call you back."

Gordon was up for it. Smith called his wife back.

"Maybe if you call Stacey and ask if she's alright with it."

Bec agreed it was a reasonable request. "Sure. I'll call you back."

Around ten minutes later, Bec called back. "Stacey's fine with it."

"Great, thanks Bec." Smith thought he heard a chuckle but wasn't sure if it wasn't a sob. "Bec? Are you alright?"

"I probably shouldn't tell you this." Bec Smith took a breath and sighed. "Stacey called him a big sook."

Smith didn't know whether to laugh or cry. He remembered Stacey was on the land before her parents were killed. She probably copped worse than this even as a teenager. He decided to say nothing.

"Jesus, Steve. You and your mates."

"OK, Bec, we're off. See you in a few days." Gordon, over-hearing the affirmative outcome, gave the thumbs up.

"Love you." Smith really did.

"Love you, too."

Kids, Backyards, and Snakes

Sunday mornings: full of kids, breakfast spreads, and newspapers that remain untouched. The final hour of *Australia All Over* blared from Smith's ancient red and silver radio, situated next to the barbecue. The radio was a relic, easily forty years old, and just as vital to Sunday mornings as bacon. Sally had a friend over, filling in as a playmate for Julie, who was allowed to watch cartoons on the bedroom TV, lounging in her parents' bed. Smith swapped out a gas bottle and stowed the old one at the foot of the back stairs, watching Smokey enthusiastically mangle a one-legged Barbie stolen from the girls. He made no move to intervene. The girls thudded down the back stairs, passed him and the dog, who promptly dropped the Barbie and slunk away, sensing mischief. They beelined for the mango tree by the back fence, housing a half-constructed treehouse some kid-heights off the ground. They assisted each other up to the first branch while Smokey resumed her assault on the doll with an almost feline pounce.

Smith ambled over to Smokey. "Feasting on your prey, are we?" A light tap on her hindquarters drew a subdued growl, prompting Smith to chuckle. "Calm down, silly. I'm not going to fight you for it."

Bec appeared on the back patio, Julie bouncing energetically on her back. Smith grinned and waved. She descended the stairs and approached him, hugging and kissing him, her nose bumping his cheek due to Julie's acrobatics. "Beautiful day."

"Yes, splendid. As only October in Brisbane can deliver." Smith cherished this woman. She smelled divine, and their tender moments from the previous night were fresh in his mind. He surreptitiously slid a hand to her breast, confident the kids were oblivious.

"Hey, you, quit it," Bec chided with a smile. "Julie, go play with the girls." She tried to dislodge Julie from her back.

"No. I'm a koala." Julie clung tighter, burying her face in Bec's neck.

"Daddy, can you please get this koala off me?"

Smith beamed. He revelled in his role in the family, adored being a father. He cherished the gentleness he so easily gave to his daughters. He enjoyed their playful games, reading stories, and building blanket cubbies. He was even unbothered by the messy realities of parenting — being vomited, pooed, and wee'd on — all of which had happened. It was all part of the journey of parenthood, and he was wholeheartedly invested.

"Is this koala ticklish, Mummy?" Smith plastered on a mischievous dad expression, raising his arms in slow, zombie-like fashion.

Julie squealed in delight and protested as Smith advanced towards her with wriggling fingers. "No! Don't tickle." It was Sally who clung to Smith's leg.

"Oh no, I've got another koala on my leg." Smith swung his leg, child and all, continuing his zombie walk towards Bec. Just as he was about to tickle Julie, his other leg was encased in child as Chrissy, Sally's friend, decided to join the fun. The problem was, it was the leg Smith was about to step on, causing him to stumble towards Sally. Moments later, they all collapsed onto the grass, parents and children tickling and giggling. After a few minutes, the younger girls scampered off to the mango tree. Smith and his wife brushed themselves off, only to hear a scream from near the back fence. They whipped around to see Sally rolling on the grass clutching her hand. She had let out a panic cry and was preparing to emit the second wail once her body decided it was time to breathe again.

Out on the rear veranda, Smith peered at Sally's hand nestled in a tea towel filled with ice. "Looks like she might've busted a digit."

A distressed wail escaped Sally and she burst into tears anew.

With no words needed, Bec scolded Smith, her head shaking and eyes rolling in exasperation.

Her pinkie was darkening and swollen at the knuckle. "I'll fetch the car and we'll head to 'Hotel-Oscar-Sierra-Papa' to confirm," Smith said. Their phonetic alphabet code stood for "hospital," a secret code that wasn't so secret after Bill had decoded it before Julie, earning himself a good dose of sass from his wife and a "you thick-headed dill" from Smith.

A new hospital was just a few suburbs away, nestled inside a sprawling university and health campus, picturesquely surrounded by bushland. Julie sat in the coveted front seat while Bec and Sally huddled in the back. After dropping Chrissy at her house, Sally could exhibit her injury, now resting on an ice pad, to her folks. The veteran parents lavished a suitable amount of sympathy upon her.

Smith pulled up at the emergency entrance, leading to a sprawling waiting area, curiously unpopulated save for one man who was called away as he approached the girls. A hospital employee emerged to gather some information, an unexpected kindness considering she usually worked behind a protective glass window.

"The doctor will be with you shortly," she assured them, a comforting smile on her face as she gently ruffled the patient's hair before walking away.

"I'm scared, Mummy." Sally's whimpering began anew. They'd withheld paracetamol due to uncertainty over upcoming medical procedures, which likely meant she was in pain.

Fifteen minutes ticked by. "Can't believe it's this quiet." Bec sounded more intrigued than impatient.

"I reckon... Sunday..." Smith's thought was interrupted by a long, harsh squeal of tyres at the entrance. He and Julie turned to the sound just as an ear-piercing shriek reached them even before the automatic doors swung open. A man scrambled from his blue 4WD, making a beeline for the entrance with an urgency that bordered on violence.

As the doors fully retracted, they witnessed the chilling sight of him carrying a limp child, her arm bandaged from hand to shoulder. The woman in the car released another heart-rending scream, drawing Smith's attention to two more children in the back seat. The man, presumably the father, sprinted towards them, his own desperate cry echoing through the premises.

"Help! I need help!" His plea resonated through the entire hospital, marking his distress. He paid no heed to Smith and his family. He tried to kick open the secure doors leading to the emergency medical area, but they held firm. He yelled again, prompting the earlier administrator, a doctor, and an orderly to appear at the now open doors.

Smith turned to see the mother and her two children rush in from the entrance. The children, a girl and boy around Sally's age, were visibly distraught and crying. Their mother's expression was a cocktail of horror and despair, a face Bec later admitted she would never forget.

"Snake bite. Brown. Roughly an hour ago. She's unconscious," the father shot out, maintaining control over his words and emotions to ensure his message was crystal clear.

"Did you clean the..." The doctor's question was cut off as the doors swung shut. The mother crumpled to the floor, her face buried in her hands as she wept. Her children, visibly distressed, stood frozen, tears trickling down their faces. Bec sprung into action, aiding the mother to her feet.

"You head in. We'll look after your kids." There was an instant connection between the women, silently conveying the profound trust and responsibility entailed in such an offer. Invigorated, the mother reassured her children before turning towards the emergency room. The door was pulled open slightly for her. She disappeared inside, leaving a tangible void behind her. Smith gathered Sally and Julie close, while Bec knelt on the pristine hospital floor, wrapping the other children in a comforting embrace.

It was then that they heard the mother's screams from behind the closed doors, followed by the father's cries. The heart-wrenching wails of distress seemed to cut through the air, with the father's particularly gut-wrenching. Smith suspected they were witnessing their daughter's life teetering on the edge. Bec and Smith exchanged a glance before focusing their attention back on the children.

"What happened, Daddy?" Julie's eyes brimmed with tears.

"The little girl was bitten by a snake, Julie."

"Is she going...?"

"Shhh. No more now." Smith cut her off before the inevitable question could be asked, holding his girls tightly. Bec shifted a little, continuing to envelop the other children in her arms.

Around forty-five minutes passed before the door to the emergency room opened again, revealing an orderly. His expression suggested a shift in fortune, and not for the worse.

Smith transferred the girls from his lap to the adjacent seats, an action they accepted without their usual resistance. He met the orderly halfway, listening attentively.

"Tell her we're fine. Stay with her child. We'll look after the kids."

The orderly nodded, gave a small wave to Bec and the children, then turned back towards the doors, ensuring they closed gently behind him.

Bec had relocated to the seats, the two children now perched on her lap. Their crying had ceased, but as Smith approached, they looked up anxiously. He sat down beside Bec and gestured for Julie and Sally to join him. He then addressed the other children.

"Your sister is going to be okay. The doctor has given her medicine, and your mum and dad will stay with her for a bit longer. We'll get you something to drink and keep you company until your mum or Dad comes out. Is that okay?"

Stunned by the recent events, the children didn't respond. With the hospital shop not yet open, Smith located a vending machine in the next wing, acquiring drinks and an assortment of muesli and chocolate bars. They quietly enjoyed the impromptu feast, sitting in near-silence for another hour until the door finally opened again, and the father stepped out. His appearance was one of exhaustion, his eyes red-rimmed from tears. Smith approached him, extending a hand.

"Steve Smith."

"Jack Grainger."

Smith gestured towards his family as they walked towards them. "My wife, Rebecca. And Sally and Julie." Grainger offered them a weary smile, and Julie reciprocated with a shy wave.

Grainger's children had already launched themselves from Bec's lap, rushing into their father's waiting arms. He knelt to meet them, scooping them up, one in each arm. They embraced him silently, their faces hidden in the crook of his neck. His size was imposing, but his gentle demeanour was palpable.

"I can't thank you enough," he turned towards Bec, peering around Smith. Bec responded with a reassuring smile.

"How is she?" Smith typically deferred to Bec for such conversations.

"She's recovering now. But we lost her for a while." A suppressed sob cracked his voice, the final word stumbling upwards involuntarily. He paused, gathering himself. "I guess you might have figured that," he said, referencing the commotion they'd heard from the emergency room.

"Sure, mate," Smith responded modestly.

They stood in silence for a moment, both of the Smiths aware it could have easily been one of their own children in that room.

"What happened?" Smith finally asked.

"Sam..." He trailed off, turning his head as if someone had called his name from inside the emergency room. "We live out on a small property in Brown Plains. Samantha went out to get some eggs and came back with a snake bite. Thank God, I saw it."

"Brown, huh?" Smith had encountered his fair share of snakes.

"Yep." He seemed to relax slightly. "Big bugger. I saw the bite, and then luckily found the snake. I thought she was done for." He drew a deep breath, working to control his emotions.

"You drove her here? No ambulance?"

"Didn't wait. Just bolted here." For the first time, he allowed a small smile. "I reckon I've collected quite a few fines from those red-light cameras. And I've dented the other side of the car," he chuckled, adding, "Used to drive rally."

"Mate, good on you."

Smith glanced at Bec. "She going to be OK?" It was the only question that truly mattered.

Three more people had wandered into the waiting room, the last person taking a moment to study the Grainger's car.

"We think so. Anyway, I better head back in." He took a step away, then pivoted back. "By the way, I'm sorry you got pushed back in line. One of your kids unwell?"

"It's Sally's finger. We thought she'd broken it." Smith raised his voice, "How's your finger, Sally?"

Sally raised her hand and beamed. Smith felt a pang of pride at her maturity and understanding of priorities.

Grainger ambled over to Sally, crouching down to her level. "May I see?", he asked gently. Sally glanced at Bec who smiled back, offering an unspoken reassurance. Sally carefully laid her hand in his, the bruising around her smallest knuckle quite noticeable. "I see you've hurt it," he looked up at Sally who appeared a touch bewildered. "Thank you for being so brave, so my little girl could go in first." Sally grinned back at him, holding his gaze.

Smith was moved by the gentle nature of this burly man. Bec stifled a sob, a tear streaking down her cheek. Grainger rose and strode past Smith, lightly touching his arm as he went. He paused and turned back.

"Mate, could you park my car for me? I completely forgot about it. If it'll start, that is." Grainger grinned. "Keys are still in it."

Smith nodded, motioning towards the emergency room, silently urging him to return to his family.

Not long after he'd parked the Grainger's car, two police officers entered, and Smith had a hunch about their visit. He gestured them over. The officers seemed a bit taken aback by the summons. Smith stood as they neared, passing Julie to the seat next to him. He caught Bec's eye, noticing a hint of apprehension about his next move.

"You fellows here about that four-wheel drive?" Smith recalled Grainger's admission about his aggressive driving over traffic islands and hitting signs en route to the hospital. He figured he could be of some assistance.

"What is your name, please, Sir?" The police looked a little more impatient.

"Steve Smith. Is it about the four-wheel drive car that came here?"

"Not sure what you mean, Sir. What is this about a four-wheel drive?"

"Oh. Sorry. I think I have my wires crossed. Sorry, officers." Smith expected them to be on their way but they stood there.

"Do you have something to tell us, Sir?"

Smith began to think he had made an error. He looked at Bec who had that all too familiar "what the hell are you doing" look.

"No. Sorry. I don't. I was mistaken." This time Smith stood back and found his seat, lifting Julie onto his lap as a curious form of protection.

The police looked at Bec who smiled and then back at Smith and walked off.

"Are you mad? You don't even know these people, and you want to talk to the police on their behalf?" Bec's voice was a sharp whisper, trying to avoid drawing the kids' attention. "Honestly, Steve, you do some strange things."

Smith was growing annoyed with this public reproach. "Alright, alright, point taken."

When the hospital administrator finally beckoned Bec and Sally into the emergency room, they looked around but couldn't spot the Graingers. Sally's finger wasn't broken, and the doctor advised against strapping it. They returned to the waiting room just as the Graingers, minus one daughter, emerged from another hallway. They sunk into the chairs across from the Smiths.

"Big morning," Smith yawned, having barely slept the night before.

"Indeed."

"My wife, Bronwyn. These are Rebecca and Steve Smith."

Pleasantries were exchanged with nods and smiles.

"Sally and...?"

"Julie." Julie offered her own name with a grin.

"I guess you've already met Bradley and Melissa."

"Yes. They seem pretty worn out, I think," Bec turned to their mother with a curious look.

"They said she'll be fine. The antivenom must've done the job. So fortunate I got a look at the snake." They continued to chat for another ten minutes, ending with a round of handshakes and a lingering hug between the mothers. After exchanging contact details, the Graingers then made their way back to the emergency room after buzzing for access.

A month later, the Smiths received a card and a letter from each of the Grainger children they'd cared for that day. Featured prominently in the attached family photo was the youngest Grainger, Samantha, smiling widely despite the absence of her two front teeth, very much alive and well.

Too Close to Losing It All

Steve Smith was jarred from his thoughts by a knock at his office door. The endless budget spreadsheeting was threatening to scramble his brain. His relief, however, was short-lived as he saw who the visitor was. Barb Chisolm, the national HR manager visiting from Melbourne, entered the room and shut the door behind her without a word. Making herself comfortable in a chair across his desk, she placed her hands in her lap, maintaining a disconcerting silence. Smith had worked with Barb when she was based in Brisbane. He respected her candour, effectiveness, and worldliness. As silence persisted, Smith could hazard a guess why she was there, but he knew better than to jump the gun.

Smith had inherited his office when Jason Walker relocated to the Singapore branch. Jason's childless marriage had recently collapsed, and he had jumped at the international assignment. Smith, who had just been promoted to sales manager for Queensland, was then asked to fill in as the acting national sales manager during Jason's two-year absence. This meant increased travel, more responsibilities, and a significant uptick in workload — not to mention this corner office where Barb now sat. A recent reorganisation put the sales managers from each state and several customer service and logistics personnel under Smith's leadership. His wife, Bec, was supportive and understanding of the additional demands on his time. His salary had been duly increased, albeit not to the national sales manager level. Smith was still green when it came to leadership, but he believed his candour and supportive nature would serve him well.

After an unnerving moment of silence, Barb finally spoke. "Anything we need to discuss, Steve?"

"Regarding what, Barb?" Smith retorted, feigning ignorance.

Barb paused, studying the placement of her hands before meeting his gaze again. "Look, Steve, we've worked together for some time. I'd like to think I have a good sense for these things." She glanced around the room, seemingly gathering her thoughts. "If you're facing any troubles or difficulties, don't hesitate to call on me for help."

Smith was about to deflect, but decided against it. He wanted this conversation to end, and was relieved when Barb stood to leave. She paused at the door, appearing ready to add something else but changed her mind.

"Thanks, Barb. I appreciate it," Smith managed to say.

Barb offered a smile and an eyebrow raise, her pursed lips conveying what Smith took as a silent reprimand. She exited the room, leaving Smith alone once again with his thoughts.

Smith cradled his head in his hands, gradually sliding them up until they were in his hair. He was shocked at how he'd nearly bungled things. He'd been irresponsible, naive, and downright foolish. Reflecting on the events from a couple of months prior, he couldn't believe how innocently it all began.

It was a Monday. Veronica, his colleague, started with her usual cheery greeting. "How are you this morning?"

"OK, thanks," Smith replied.

"Just OK?"

Smith internally shook his head. "What's up?"

"Just concerned about you. You seem stressed all the time lately."

Smith barely registered her comment; he was preoccupied with another impending problem. "I'm fine, thanks," he replied dismissively.

"OK. Hey, can we go over the quotes for the electrical parts inventory holding? They're all in now."

"Sure."

"Today?"

"Sure."

"OK, I'll be over in thirty. Bye."

Smith didn't respond, simply replacing the phone in its cradle. He wanted to call Bec, his wife, and tell her he'd be home for lunch, but he quickly decided against that as well. He was juggling so much; he couldn't afford to drop a single ball. So much felt out of his control back then.

Shaking his head again, he replayed the near disaster. He hadn't seen it coming. He thought he was simply skirting the edges of a working relationship, fully in control and enjoying the frisson that Veronica brought. But it wasn't just a frisson. That was a ridiculous understatement. He didn't want Veronica reporting to him for valid business reasons. They'd been working together for months. She was competent and pleasingly skilled at logistics. But she remained one of the most stunning and desirable women he'd ever met.

Smith had never mentioned to Bec that Veronica Jacobs was now under his supervision. He didn't want to stir up any worry, especially considering Bec's previous comments about his reaction to Veronica during their first meeting.

Smith wasn't certain when everything started to spin out of control. He either missed the warning signs or chose to ignore them. Veronica had invited him for a drink after work, which filled him with a sense of anticipation. She was married, so what's the harm? He had met her husband once, a tall, strapping man with a French accent. Smith and Veronica had gone to the local pub together, shared a polite exchange of ideas over two drinks, and waved to each other as they drove out of the car park.

"No problem," Smith had thought on his drive home. He wasn't sure why Veronica had invited him for a drink, but he didn't dwell on it. He had noticed her slightly revealing yellow top and forced his eyes away, at least when she was looking. He didn't mention to Bec that he'd had a drink with Veronica. It seemed like no big deal at the time. The visual would be tucked away for private fantasies, and nothing they'd discussed could be seen as improper or suggestive if Veronica ever brought it up in the future.

Although it seemed to foster a more harmonious working relationship between them, Smith couldn't shake off the troubling incidents that had followed. One such day, Veronica had strolled into his office after he'd just given a service technician the boot. It was an unpopular move, considering the man's seniority, but after several warnings regarding his conduct and performance on customer sites, Smith had no choice but to let him go. He'd walked the technician to the door, exchanged handshakes, and offered some empathetic remarks. Upon returning to his office, Smith sat in quiet contemplation, filled with regret over the unavoidable decision.

That's when Veronica, appearing more stunning than ever in one of her tightest tops and shortest skirts, slipped into his office, shutting the door behind her.

"Veronica, I..." Smith began, but she interjected.

"That must've been hard to do." Moving behind his chair, she added, "God, you must be so tense." Her hands rested on Smith's shoulders, lingering there as if gauging his reaction.

Smith was taken aback. Since his marriage, no other woman had dared to touch him so casually. Veronica began massaging his shoulders, the unexpected intimacy causing him to stammer,

"Jesus..." Guilt surged among the many emotions flooding him, but he remained silent. The massage lasted maybe thirty seconds before Veronica abruptly stopped.

Walking past his desk, she turned towards him, her expression mischievous, and said, "I think I'd better stop there, huh?" And then, she was gone.

Left alone, Smith was both flustered and aroused. The end of the workday found him hastily packing his computer for home. Veronica had already left her office.

Smith climbed into his Audi, phoned home, and had a cheerful conversation with Bec about a BBQ dinner. No sooner had he hung up and taken the first turn out of the office, when his phone rang again. He answered without checking, assuming it was his boss in Melbourne wanting an update on their mining tender.

"Steve Smith."

"It's Veronica."

Caught off guard, Smith replied, "Hi. What's up?"

"I thought you might be!" A chuckle barely audible on the other end.

Smith wasn't sure he'd heard her right. "What's that, Veronica?"

"Come on, Steve. I know you were getting hard while I was massaging your shoulders."

Smith was shocked and horrified, yet a trace of amusement stirred within him. This was an entirely new side to Veronica. Speechless, he could only gape at the audacity of her comment.

"You don't have to say anything, Steve. Your body told me everything and I can see how you look at me. Any time you want to fuck me, I'm yours. See ya." And then she hung up.

Nearly rear-ending a stopped bus, Smith hastily swerved into a side street and shifted his car into neutral. He was flushed and rattled. "What the fuck," he mumbled, repeating it to himself five times over. A barrage of thoughts assaulted him: *Who would say such a thing? How the hell do I face her on Monday? Did I somehow encourage this? She's married. Why would she say that to me?*

Smith drove home in a state of confusion, annoyance, and a hint of guilt, battling the nagging thoughts about Veronica. He needed to clear his head before he got home. If Bec could pick up on the slightest hint of the Veronica the horse incident, she'd be suspicious about Veronica Jacobs' more than explicit proposition in a heartbeat. Smith contemplated calling Veronica and tackling the issue head-on, but immediately dismissed the idea. An after-hours call logged to her would only stir more trouble. *Leave it be, just clear your mind*, he chided himself, echoing the now familiar refrain, *What the fuck?*

His weekend was a cocktail of family obligations and lingering worries about Monday. How was he supposed to handle this with Veronica? Should he go straight to HR? Sunday morning greeted him with an unwanted reminder: a vivid, sensual dream about him and Veronica at a hotel.

After Sunday breakfast, Smith decided to confide in his friend, Bill Leighton. At least, he'd have a sounding board for his predicament. He called Bill on his way to the store.

"G'day mate," Bill answered cheerfully.

"Bill, how're you going?"

"Orrite. What's up?"

"Just heading to the shop for Bec."

"Yeah, me, too. Good hubbies, hey."

"Listen, I need your take on something." Smith recounted the Friday incident in as much detail as possible.

"Shit, mate. That's dangerous ground. What have you told her?"

"Nothing. This happened late Friday arvo."

"Mate, you need to go to your HR people ASAP."

"You reckon?"

"Bloody oath. Are you familiar with your HR team?"

Smith parked his car at the store and turned off the engine, leaving the phone connected. "The one in Brisbane just started. The national manager, I know well."

"I'd be contacting her. But tread carefully. Some shit always sticks."

"What does that mean?"

"Come on, what do you think it means?"

Fear started creeping in. "Just spell it out for me. You seem to know more about this than I do."

"She could spin any story she wants, like you making a move on her. All she needs is a hint that you're going official, and she might. She doesn't report to you, does she?"

"Yes, she does."

"Damn, mate, you need to get in touch with your HR folks right away."

"Jesus. How do you know so much about this?"

"Listen, while you've been gallivanting across the country for work, I've been cooped up in an office my whole life. I've seen men hung out to dry. Not just one. At least one case was absolute crap, concocted by a woman who was passed up for a promotion."

"No kidding?"

"No kidding, mate. It's true. She slapped him with sexual harassment charges. Poor bloke lost his job, and then his wife left him. Devious bitch. I knew she was trouble."

"Did you warn him?"

"No, but I'm warning you." Smith heard Bill's car door open. "Gotta go. Catch up later, mate."

"See ya." Smith sat in his car, mulling over his predicament. After completing his shopping, he drove home, wrestling with a new worry — had he written anything in an email that could be used against him if Veronica decided to make a scene? He didn't think he had, but come early Monday morning, he tiptoed out of bed without waking Bec, opened his laptop on the kitchen table, and started scanning through emails linked to Veronica, on the lookout for any potentially damaging language. Suddenly, a company email linked chat box popped up — it was Veronica. Smith nearly jumped out of his skin in alarm.

Her text appeared. "You're up late."

He didn't answer it.

Another text box popped up. "OK, look I just wanted to say that we shouldn't have done that on Friday."

Smith looked at the message, again in horror. The "we" had him sitting back in his chair in alarm. He slammed his computer shut and stepped back from it, catching his leg on the chair leg, causing him to step back to slam his back against the fridge. Two glass vases toppled, rolled off the fridge top and smashed onto the kitchen floor. It seemed only seconds before the hall light went on and Bec was coming down towards him with fright in her squinting eyes. She saw her husband standing there.

"Bec! Stay there! Broken glass!"

Bec Smith halted abruptly, glancing over her shoulder to make sure the kids were not about to run past her. The kitchen clock was within her sight.

"Jesus, Steve, it's past 2 am."

"I know. Let me just clean this up. Please, go back to bed, Bec." Smith had to convince her he was okay.

"Alright." Bec didn't seem entirely convinced. "I'll shut the hall door to keep the kids out." As she started walking back to their bedroom, she turned around, "What broke?"

"Two vases."

"Oh, shit." With that, she continued on her way.

Smith waited until the hall door was closed and carefully navigated his way through the glass shards towards the closet housing the broom and vacuum. Being barefoot was a risk, but his calloused feet offered some protection.

After cleaning up the mess — without using the noisy, state-of-the-art vacuum cleaner Bec had bought recently — he stood over his closed laptop, contemplating his next move concerning Veronica. Bill's warning, "some shit always sticks," had him on edge. He tucked his laptop back into his work bag and limped back to bed, almost certain a piece of glass had lodged itself in his foot.

He slept poorly that night, dreamless and restless. His alarm sounded off all too soon, and he needed Bec to extract the glass from his foot before he headed to work. Such procedures always concluded with Bec's plea for him to wear shoes, at the very least, thongs. The splinter-removal ritual was a well-rehearsed act in their household: Smith lying prone on the couch, his feet hanging over one end, while their daughters sat on him, tasked with "keeping Daddy still."

"Assume the position," Bec motioned towards the sofa.

"Girls! Daddy's got a splinter!" The declaration was followed by two excited shrieks as the girls raced to claim their spots atop their dad. Smith barely had time to protect his head — an essential precaution learned after Julie once kneed him in the ear during the scramble for positions.

Bec always had to remind the girls to stay still, especially Julie, who was perpetually intrigued by the sight of her mum probing their dad's feet.

"Steve, your feet are like leather," Bec remarked, a common complaint during these operations. Smith savoured the attention, finding an odd sense of enjoyment even in the mild discomfort of the needle. His thoughts momentarily drifted to the absurd situation he was in with Veronica Jacobs, the potential threat it posed to his family causing a shudder. He remained uncertain about his next steps, save for one thing: he had to go to the office, and Veronica would be there.

With the glass shard finally out and on his way to work, his phone rang. This time he checked the caller ID before answering. Much to his dread, it was Veronica. Smith braced himself.

"Hi, Veronica."

There was an awkward pause.

"Hello?"

"Hello, Steve. This is Veronica."

"Yes, hi Veronica." Smith was unsure about where the conversation was headed.

Another pause ensued.

"Hello."

"Yes, I'm here."

Growing alarmed by the call, Smith prodded, "What's up, Veronica?" No sooner had he uttered the words than he regretted it, half-expecting some innuendo from her. It didn't come.

"Steve, I want to apologise."

Smith was tempted to ask "for what?" but he refrained. He remembered Negotiation-101: he who speaks first, loses. "Go on," he urged, striving to keep the conversation as formal as possible.

"I shouldn't have said what I did to you."

Smith felt thankful that they were talking but he was on high alert. She could be sitting in front of her HR rep or her friend as witness and on speaker phone.

Smith pulled over into a parking bay so he could better concentrate.

"I agree with you." He wanted to keep the ball in her court, ensuring he spoke as little as possible. He bit his tongue, a trick he used during negotiations to stay silent through uncomfortable pauses.

"OK, I see you're upset with me."

Smith needed to stay quiet, but he felt compelled to say something. The compulsion won. "Yes, I am."

"Oh, thank God. I can't stand the silent treatment." Her candidness made it hard for him to keep his composure. He didn't want this conversation, but he wanted one at work even less.

"What do you want, Veronica?"

"Just to be friends."

Smith was taken aback by her crafty approach. After what she'd said to him at work on Friday, he couldn't trust her. He recognised her intelligence, but also suspected some underlying cunning, though he had little evidence of it. He needed to decline her plea for friendship but feared she might react poorly. The warning, "some shit always sticks," echoed in his mind again. He had to end this conversation without leaving room for a follow-up discussion at work.

"I'll see you at work." His tone was quiet, non-confrontational.

Another pause.

"OK."

Then, she hung up.

Smith felt no relief at the end of the call. The situation was far from resolved and would stay that way until he was certain she wouldn't approach him again. He pondered what could have prompted her audacious proposition on Friday. Had he sent her signals, maybe complimented her work in a way she might've misconstrued? Classic him, blaming himself instead of seeing her proposition for what it was — an absurd and inappropriate suggestion in a workplace.

He pulled out of the parking lot, resuming his commute while contemplating whether he should take the matter to HR. She had apologised, after all, and he still had to work with her. He decided to jot down an account of what Veronica had said, including the when and where, in his meeting record book. He needed a witness, someone to confirm that he wrote the entry at a certain date, without them necessarily knowing the contents. He'd ask Vanessa in the lab to do it.

Upon arriving, Smith made his way to his office, keeping his gaze firmly on the floor. He entered, shut the door, settled at his desk, plugged his laptop into its dock, and logged in. He was still forty minutes away from his first teleconference on the mining project. Unprepared, he started working through his notes. The last thing he wanted was a knock at the door. He lifted his head with an intentionally annoyed expression, only to see Veronica through the glass pane. She gestured towards a coffee in her hand. He smiled resignedly and gestured her in.

"I'm guessing you didn't have time for a coffee, so here you go." She walked in and closed the door behind her, placing the coffee on the credenza to the left, then moving to be in front of him across his desk

Smith gave a grateful smile but couldn't ignore her unbuttoned blouse and the absence of a bra. She backed away from the desk, intentionally causing her breasts to sway. She then leaned against the bare wall directly in front of him, provocatively pushing out her chest. He could see the darkness of her nipples. He was unable to talk. So much was going through his mind; as much fear as arousal. One clear thought stayed for a microsecond longer than the rest. She was one of the most stunning, sexy, naturally beautiful women he'd ever seen. She quickly unbuttoned her blouse, progressively freeing her breasts. Then she pulled her blouse free of her skirt and walked backwards to sit onto Smith's desk, leaning backwards until her hair curtained across his keyboard.

"Hey stop..." Smith could barely speak.

"They're real, you know." Veronica was laid out across his desk, one hand cupping her breast and the other reaching out for him. Smith was flabbergasted to see her smiling. He should've stood up by now, but he felt like he was frozen in place. He tried to stand again, to no avail. The phrase "what the fuck" echoed in his mind, like an error message on a malfunctioning DVD player's LED screen. Suddenly, the door swung open, and Vanessa Rountree leaned into the office, snapping a photo with her smartphone. Then another. As she retreated, Smith heard an apologetic "Sorry, Steve" before the door shut. He felt overwhelmed, ready to explode in anger and eject this woman from his office, toplessness and all. But Veronica had already stood up and was buttoning her blouse, her back to him. She walked over to the wall unit where Smith's jacket was lying, put it on, and zipped it up. Aghast, Smith watched her slow, deliberate movements. She pulled out a chair and sat down, placing her hands in her lap, lifting her head to look directly at him.

"So, here's what happens now, Steve."

Smith felt like he was in limbo. This woman should've been tossed out of his office by now, yet she was still there. Instead, Vanessa now had a photo that could potentially end his career and his marriage.

She took a breath, stopped, and then took another breath. "I should never have done what I did to you on Friday. It was unfair and inappropriate. I want to sincerely apologise for what I said and did."

Smith attempted to interject, but she raised her hand to silence him.

"That picture will be kept as insurance to prevent you from going to HR. I'll destroy it in five years or so. I promise you, nothing like what happened on Friday will ever happen again."

A flicker of hope that she was being sincere crossed Smith's mind. Despite his current state of shock, he remained on guard.

Veronica pushed a strand of hair behind her ear, which promptly fell back onto her face. She let it be. "My marriage is over and I've been using drugs to cope. I really need this job now because my ex-husband gambled away all our money." Tears welled in her eyes. "I'm so sorry."

Smith remained silent and vigilant, though utterly stunned.

Veronica stood up, nodded at Smith, and exited, quietly shutting the door behind her.

Smith stared blankly at the wall in front of him, utterly shell-shocked. In just a few days, he'd gone from contentment to agitation to disaster. He felt cornered, forced to go along with what she'd said. It could've been a blackmail attempt, but he had his doubts. He glanced at the time on his computer, trying to snap back to reality. The office phone rang. It was Vanessa from the lab.

"Hello?"

"It's Vanessa. I know you must think what I did was horrible, but Veronica and I are friends. She's been left in a terrible situation by her jerk of a husband. She couldn't risk you going to HR, even though you would've been completely justified. I can't believe she did what she did to you."

Smith stayed on high alert. "Ah ha."

"I promise you that photo will never see the light of day. It's just insurance. I've already deleted it from my phone... It's on a flash drive now." A pause. "I'm really sorry, Steve. Without realising it, I think you played a part in what happened."

Smith felt his hackles rising in defence. "No way. I never..."

"Hold on, I didn't mean that," she interrupted. "I gave your novel to her to read. You know...the one with the dirty chapter three? I know I shouldn't have. Maybe that and the coke she's been using... It's my fault."

She sneezed away from the phone. "Sorry, Steve. We both know you're a decent man. Really sorry you went through this."

Smith gathered his thoughts and decided to give her no acknowledgement. "Gotta go. Got a teleconference." He hung up without hearing any more.

He'd continue to not say anything to Barb Chisolm. He was not sure what she had picked up with her "radar" and while that concerned him, he needed to get this whole sorry thing out of his mind. He had some concern that someone saw something that day but he doubted either Vanessa or Veronica would have said anything. He'd been working well with Veronica for months since the incident. Not once had she made mention of anything to do with that day or time. Even years later, Smith would shudder at the very thought of it.

The Last Laugh

The commotion kicked off just past 1 a.m. Smith leapt from his bed, disoriented and groggy, wondering which dog was howling so hysterically. He initially thought a dog may have been hit by a car, but upon opening the front door, he realised the ruckus was coming from the backyard — either his own or a neighbour's. Making his way to the back door, he noticed his wife Bec and daughter Julie were already up, carefully descending the stairs. Then, he saw the doggy door was ajar — odd, as it was supposed to be locked shut.

The yelping ceased, replaced by the persistent barking of several neighbourhood dogs, obviously riled up by the chaos. Smith flicked on the floodlight illuminating most of the backyard. There, in the middle, stood their pug, Smokey. Her nappy was not only off but shredded into pieces, strewn across the yard. She simply stood there. Smith wondered if she was staring at someone or something near the house. He heard Bec coaxing Julie back to bed, assuring her everything was okay. As Smith cautiously made his way into the backyard, Bec began whispering inquiries.

"Don't know, Bec. Can't see anything but Smokey," he replied, his voice as quiet as possible as he navigated the back stairs. Approaching the pug, she growled. He halted. "Smokey? You okay, girl?" It seemed his voice broke some kind of spell, as she then slowly ambled past him towards the house. She didn't appear injured. The Christmas tinsel the girls had wrapped around her collar was still intact. Next, he turned his attention to the torn nappy. "What the hell?" he thought to himself. "How did she do that?"

Bec was petting Smokey on the landing when Smith returned. "She's shaking, Steve." Bec looked up at her husband, concern etched on her face. "Maybe she's been attacked." They both examined her for puncture wounds.

Smith took a step back as he pieced together the scenario. "No, she's been..."

Bec looked up again. "What?"

Smith shook his head, scanning the area to ensure the kids weren't in the kitchen or on the landing. "I bet she's been mounted by another dog."

Bec stood up in surprise. She gazed at her husband for a few seconds. "What other dog?"

Smith gave her a "how should I know" look. "Maybe that one?" he suggested, as a dog a few houses away resumed its barking.

The two humans exchanged a prolonged look.

"The doggy door was open," Smith blurted, not intending to assign blame.

"I locked it last night," Bec defended.

Smith shivered. "I'm getting cold, Bec. Let's call it a night."

"OK." Bec turned Smokey towards the house, and the pug started walking slowly towards the stairs.

"Hold on. Don't let her in," Smith called out louder than he intended.

"Why?"

"Well, if she's just been romanced by some randy mutt, we don't want dog 'mess' tracked all over the house."

"Jesus, Steve." Bec halted Smokey at the door.

"I'm serious."

"What am I supposed to do?"

"Hand her over." Smith motioned for the dog.

"And what are you going to do?"

"Give her a hose-down."

"Don't you dare!" Bec was aghast.

"Damn it, Bec, just give her to me. I'm not going to hurt her." He gestured impatiently.

Reluctantly, she passed the dog to her husband. "You're crazy. Don't get her wet."

Smith lifted the pug, who offered no resistance. He walked over to the hose at the corner of the house. That's when he felt a slimy substance on his arm and noticed the mess the pug had left behind on him.

"Bloody hell. Bugger me," Smith groaned, revulsed. "Bec, come over here."

She stepped down from the landing and saw what had her husband in a tizzy.

"Oh my god."

"Turn on the hose and aim at her backside while I hold her," Smith commanded, his sense of disgust escalating.

Bec adjusted the hose to a gentle stream and began to rinse Smokey's rear. "Turn her around... oh, no."

"What?"

"I think you're right. She's swollen and a bit bloody down there."

"Just rinse her off," Smith demanded, his patience wearing thin. It was late, it was cold, and he was involved in the ridiculous process of cleaning their violated dog with a garden hose at nearly 2 a.m.

"OK, it's fine now." Bec had carefully cleaned Smokey's underside. The pug was now shivering uncontrollably. "Sorry, Smokey," she soothed, patting her.

Smith set Smokey down, expecting her to shake off the water, but she just stood there, dejected, staring into the backyard.

The night wrapped up with Smith shutting off all the lights and Smokey sequestered in the laundry room, dry and warm on her rug. Both Smith and Bec took showers before sliding back into bed. They shared a goodnight kiss and clicked off their bedside lamps.

Early Thursday morning, their daughters burst into the bedroom. Neither Smith nor his wife felt inclined to move.

"Go back to bed," Smith beat his wife to the command.

"Is Smokey alright?" Julie asked.

"Where's Smokey? We can't find her," Sally chimed in.

"Go back to bed, girls. Smokey is fine. She's..."

Their mum's explanation was cut off by the intrusive blare of the alarm clock.

"Oh, crap." Smith felt like he'd been hit by a bus.

Half an hour later, they were all gathered in the laundry room, looking at Smokey, who was gazing back at them. She seemed fine and attempted to walk out of the laundry room. The nappy Bec had put on her the previous night was still in place.

A couple of days later, during an early breakfast, Smith lifted his gaze from his eggs and turned to his wife. "Is the dog next door neutered?"

"Which dog? The Allens' kelpie?"

"Yeah." Smith wiped his mouth with a napkin. His wife gestured towards her face, indicating he'd missed a spot. He wiped his mouth again.

Bec backed up to the kitchen counter, bracing herself with both hands. She could sense what was coming. "Let's not go there, Steve, okay?"

Smith flashed a grin at his wife. "It was just a question."

"With you and Jim, nothing is ever 'just a question'," Bec retorted before heading out of the kitchen to wrangle the girls for breakfast.

Smokey's incident dropped from the family's primary concerns, and life resumed its normal rhythm. About three weeks later, the pug began to vomit and pant heavily. She'd even growled at the girls, which was a first. Bec took her to the vet.

"Hi, love," Smith answered his mobile, seeing his wife's caller ID as Veronica Jacobs exited his office, their inventory meeting concluded.

"She's pregnant."

"Who's pregnant?" The question slipped out before Smith could think.

"Smokey."

"What?" The late-night dog washing incident from a few weeks ago flashed through his mind. "How do you know?"

"The vet said so."

"How does he know?"

"She."

"What?"

"She. The vet is a 'she'."

Smith shook his head, trying to free himself from the irrelevant correction. He swallowed what he was about to say to his wife, taking a breath and aiming for a constructive approach, discarding the thoughts scrolling through his mind about their lack of diligence in managing a dog in heat.

"What now?"

"No idea, Steve. I guess we're going to be parents again."

"Parents to what? Who knows if an alien octopus didn't come down from space and inseminate our dog?" Smith was becoming exasperated that this ridiculous matter was consuming his time at work.

Bec Smith uttered a brusque goodbye and ended the call. Pursuing the conversation was futile when her husband was in such a state.

That evening, with the girls assisting Bec in washing up, Smith found himself on his phone, googling dog gestation periods. He remained mum in front of the girls. As they took their showers, he broached the subject again.

"I'm going to chat with Allen next door."

"About what?" She already knew.

"Their dog. Mating with ours."

"Don't be ridiculous, and don't you dare."

"I bet it was that kelpie."

Bec Smith slung a tea towel over her shoulder and placed her hands purposefully on the opposite side of the table, lifting her chin to meet his gaze. As the tea towel slid off, she didn't flinch. "I'll say this once, Steve. You are not to go next door and talk to Jim Allen about their dog, our dog or any dog." She held his gaze. "Promise me."

Smith grinned. The girls burst into the kitchen, each clutching a rag doll. They instantly sensed the tension and stood there, glancing between their parents. "Alright, this is getting silly," Smith declared, rising from his seat. "Who wants a Daddy story?" The girls squealed with delight at the prospect of a premature evening tale. He trailed after his girls, stealing a glance at his still-seething wife.

"Steve...!" Bec called out a warning, but he'd already disappeared.

A few days later on a Saturday morning, while Bec and the girls were out shopping, Smith spotted Jim Allen in his front yard. Smokey had started to "show" and remained grouchy, but the vomiting had ceased. Smith found himself within earshot, and Allen saw him.

Smith couldn't help himself. "Your dog got our dog pregnant." He didn't want to holler too loudly and wondered if Allen heard him. Evidently, he had.

Jim Allen dropped the handful of letters he'd retrieved from his ornate mailbox. He stood there, slack-jawed, then trudged back towards his house, leaving the letters scattered on the ground. He seemed distressed, repeatedly casting upset glances in Smith's direction. Smith chalked it up to their strained history. Allen had never forgiven him for the hook-in-the-arm incident and they rarely spoke, although Stacey and Bec remained close friends. Smith found Allen's reaction odd. "Bugger it," he mumbled to himself.

Later that afternoon, Smith saw Stacey and Bec talking. He was about to fling open the back door when he heard Stacey sobbing. Then she and Bec leaned towards each other, sharing a comforting embrace over the fence. The angle of the insect screen didn't afford a clear view, but it was evident that Stacey was upset. Deciding to leave them be, he retreated to his office to print out notes for a meeting scheduled for the upcoming week.

Smith was facing away from the office door when he heard it close. It was Bec, and she looked visibly upset.

"Are you OK, Bec?" Smith was concerned.

Bec shook her head. As he dropped the papers he was reading and began to walk towards her, she raised her hand, causing him to halt mid-stride. Suddenly, he was worried.

"What's going on?" Smith was switching to crisis management mode.

Bec gestured him to the seat at his desk and pulled up another chair for herself. Smith sat down, his concern deepening that something was indeed awry.

Bec continued to shake her head. She rested her hands in her lap and raised her eyes to meet his. "How could you?" She held back a sob. "How could you say such a thing?"

Smith was taken aback by the raw emotion and accusations from his wife. Clearly, terse responses wouldn't suffice this time. He leaned back in his chair, not slouching but giving the impression he wouldn't be confrontational. He took a deep breath. "I'm not sure I understand what you mean, Bec," he said, as calmly as possible.

Bec simply stared at him.

"Please, Bec. I genuinely don't know what you mean." Smith was concerned; it had been a while since he'd seen his wife this upset.

She shook her head again. "How could you be so hurtful, Steve?" Bec shrugged, seemingly attempting to comprehend something.

"Look, Bec, I really don't know what you're referring to," Smith cautiously replied.

"The Allens. You laughed at them, Steve. About them not getting pregnant."

"What?" Smith quickly scanned his recent interactions with Allen. He'd barely acknowledged Allen's existence, let alone... Then it hit him.

"That thing?" He remembered shouting out to Allen on Saturday morning. He wanted to laugh but knew better.

"So you admit it!" Bec pushed her legs out as if to distance herself from him.

"Why not? It probably was their dog, Bec."

"What are you on about, Steve? I'm talking about what you said to Jim."

"So am I." Smith felt as though he was venturing into surreal territory.

For the first time, Bec's expression shifted from horror and disgust to a blend of confusion and repulsion. "What did you say to Jim?"

Smith was about to confess when he caught himself; his training in communication and negotiation kicked in. "What does he think I said?"

Bec's expression hardened into annoyance. "Don't play word games with me, Steve." She halted and took a breath. For the first time, she considered the possibility of a misunderstanding. "You made a joke about them not being able to conceive."

"Who?"

"The Allens."

"What?" Smith was utterly perplexed.

"The Allens. I thought you must have heard."

"Heard what, Bec?" Smith was now more curious than irate.

"The Allens have been trying to get pregnant." Bec searched her husband's face for any reaction. His eyebrows shot up in surprise.

"Blimey." Smith realised what had transpired. "Oh, bloody hell, Bec. I understand now."

Bec remained silent, not even blinking.

Smith sighed. He was going to face the music now, having explicitly been told by his wife not to approach Jim Allen. Time to fess up. Smith leaned forward, resting his elbows on his knees. "Alright. On Saturday, I shouted out to Jim that his dog had impregnated ours." Smith paused, hoping for any acknowledgement from his wife. None came. "I guess I used the word "pregnant" when I shouted to him." Smith fidgeted nervously. "And I guess he misinterpreted me and thought I was making a joke about them."

Bec folded her arms. "What else did you say to him?"

"Nothing. Nothing, Bec."

"Are you sure?"

Smith wasn't thrilled by the inquisition, but he played along. "Absolutely."

Bec unfolded her arms. She straightened her skirt and brushed some lint off it. "They were told on Friday that they had failed to conceive again." She observed her husband. "This is their third IVF attempt." Her voice wavered slightly, and her eyes started to glisten. "Then you fling that awful joke at Jim."

"Dammit." Smith felt like a complete buffoon. He could see how Allen might have misinterpreted him or latched onto the most hurtful interpretation. "Bloody hell, Bec."

They sat there, staring at each other. Then came the inevitable.

"I asked you not to speak to Jim." It wasn't a question.

"You're right." Smith refrained from making any excuses. "I'm sorry." He nervously rubbed his chin. "Why didn't you tell me they were trying?"

Bec's anger finally broke loose. "It's none of your bloody business!" A tiny speck of spit shot from her mouth, narrowly missing the printer. "Bloody hell, Steve! That information was entrusted to me as Stacey's friend, in confidence!" She inhaled sharply, realising her volume was rising. "If you could manage your damned pride and weren't such a bloody tosser, Jim might have confided in you!" Her voice was back to its previous level.

Smith was relieved to see her anger. He deserved it.

There was a knock on the door. Bec asked the intruder to give them a moment alone.

"What now?" Smith had shifted into damage control mode.

Bec pondered for a moment. "I think we should both go see them. Explain what happened."

"Alright. When?"

"Today. Tonight."

"Alright."

Bec arranged with the Allens for a visit that night. Julie was tasked with babysitting Sally since they'd only be next door and wouldn't be long. No further discussions were had between Smith and Bec. The plan was simple: explain the misunderstanding and apologise. They had no idea how it would be received.

Both Stacey and Jim were clearly upset, but nobody had heard from or spoken to Jim.

The ring of their elaborate doorbell set their Kelpie off. "What's the dog's name again?" Smith had forgotten and didn't particularly care.

"Bull."

"Of course, it is." Smith's joke was met with a glare from his wife that could have melted steel. They were welcomed into the Allens' home, a mansion compared to their humble abode. Within fifteen minutes, they had offered sincere apologies and explained the misunderstanding, which the Allens graciously accepted. Smith was moved by the couple's commitment to starting a family, something he'd taken for granted with his own children. He kept his comments to a minimum during the visit, only expressing his regret for causing them distress and admitting that he'd learned a valuable lesson. They said their goodbyes with a firm handshake from Jim and a warm hug from Stacey. It was only then that Smith noticed the kelpie's anatomy. He tried and failed to subtly point it out to Bec, eventually giving up, knowing that any deviation from his apologetic stance could result in his immediate divorce.

The Smiths returned home in silence. As they reached their gate, Smith was about to ask Bec if she had noticed the kelpie's testicles. He thought better of it. "Sorry. Nothing", was all he could muster.

A week later on Saturday morning, Jim Allen approached Smith by the fence. He was holding his mobile phone, saying he wanted to show Smith something. Smith was pleased to see Allen being friendly and hoped for an improvement in their relationship. That hope was dashed faster than Smith could blink.

"Have a look at these beauties." Allen held up his large iPhone, displaying a website proudly titled "Pug-Kelpie Cross," featuring some peculiar looking dogs. They somewhat resembled kelpies, but with squashed snouts and odd facial markings. "Say hello to the grandkids." Then a huge grin spread across Allen's face.

The penny dropped. Smith looked at Allen incredulously. "What the...?"

Allen took back his phone with a jerk. "Yep. I guess you can say we're going to be 'prick relations.'" He burst out laughing.

Smith could not believe what he was hearing. He turned to see if Bec was within earshot but Allen had managed the exchange perfectly, without witness. "You bastard..." He let it go without control. "How did...?"

"How did Bull get over? He can jump your piece of shit fence. Really gave it to your little mutt." Then he burst out laughing again, walking away. He turned, walking backwards, again laughing. "I guess Bull had the heart for a pity fuck." Then he was gone.

Steve Smith stood there for what felt like minutes. Nothing came through his mind. He slowly turned toward the house. Smokey was standing behind him. He looked at her, still blank.

Then he kneeled, taking time to give his beloved dog a nice pat. "Good girl, Smokey."